A TAPESTRY OF MURDERS

The Man of Law's Tale of mystery and murder
as he goes on pilgrimage
from London to Canterbury

A TAPESTRY OF MURDERS

The Man of Law's Tale of mystery and murder
as he goes on pilgrimage
from London to Canterbury

P. C. Doherty

HEADLINE

First published in 1994
by HEADLINE BOOK PUBLISHING

10 9 8 7 6 5 4 3 2 1

British Library Cataloguing in Publication Data

Doherty, P. C.
Tapestry of Murders
I. Title
823.914 [F]

ISBN 0-7472-0967-7

Typeset by Avon Dataset Ltd., Bidford-on-Avon

Printed and bound in Great Britain by
Mackays of Chatham PLC, Chatham, Kent

HEADLINE BOOK PUBLISHING
A division of Hodder Headline PLC
338 Euston Road
London NW1 3BH

To Peter Randall (also a clerk);
Education Officer, in grateful thanks
for all his assistance and the many
good laughs we've shared over
the last twelve years.

Historical Foreword

In 1308 Edward II married Isabella, daughter of Philip IV of France. Edward II proved to be an incompetent king and alienated his nobility both by his disastrous war policy and his love of rustic pursuits such as digging ditches and thatching roofs.

In 1322 Roger Mortimer, Earl of March, led a rebellion against Edward and his favourites the de Spencer lords. Mortimer was first imprisoned and then fled abroad. In 1325 Edward's wife Isabella managed to flee to France and joined Mortimer in exile. In 1326 Isabella and Mortimer returned to England.

The Prologue

The rain had fallen all night as clouds, grey and sullen, swept across the fresh green Kentish countryside. The downpour had been so insistent that the pilgrims were confined to a large three-storeyed timber and plaster tavern near the Dominican friary in Dartford. Naturally they were growing restless. Since leaving the Tabard in Southwark they had enjoyed the cool spring breezes, the clear birdsong and the peace of the countryside. It was the morning of the year and blossom hung white and pink on the boughs of trees. Even the poorest labourer sang as he tended his narrow strip of land, looking forward to a rich harvest under a strengthening sun.

Harry the taverner, sitting in the inglenook of the tavern's great fire hearth, anxiously stared around the assembly of pilgrims. By Satan's cock, he thought, a motley crew and so ill to please! Take the knight, with his steel-coloured hair and weather-beaten face. His sharp, hooded eyes constantly watched the monk. Harry rubbed his thick lower lip. There was real hostility between these two. The knight and monk apparently knew each other and, whenever the monk came within a yard's distance of him, Sir Godfrey's hand would fall to the ivory-hilted dagger stuck in his belt. The knight's young son, the fresh-faced squire, was equally watchful.

'Do you think it's anything to do with the knight's tale?' Harry had asked the saintly, but poor, parson.

'God be my witness, sir!' The fellow replied. 'What would a monk know about ancient Thebes? About the glorious King Theseus or cousins such as Arcite and Palemon and their rivalry over the fair Emily?'

'No, no, I don't mean that,' Harry growled, turning his back so the others couldn't eavesdrop. 'I mean the other tale the knight told – about the Strigoi, the blood-drinkers, the Shape-shifters who plagued the town of Oxford?'

The poor parson simply crossed himself and walked away. Nevertheless, Harry continued to speculate. The monk, with his brown-berry, glistening face, balding pate and shrewd, merry eyes, seemed an affable fellow; he was a good horseman, skilled in hunting, or so they said. Harry glanced across the tavern to where the monk sat deep in conversation with the snow-bearded franklin. Never once had he seen the monk bless himself or say a prayer or make any reference to the Monseigneur, his noble Saviour, Jesus Christ.

Harry turned away, hawked and spat into the white ash of the fire. Other tensions lurked amongst the pilgrims. Across the taproom, in a far corner, the red-faced, bearded miller had awakened and was fiddling for his bagpipes.

'Oh, go back to sleep, you drunken sot!' Harry murmured.

Next to the miller, the cook, his ulcerated leg showing beneath his cloak, was having a violent disagreement with the sour-faced reeve. The pretty but prim-faced prioress kept heaving deep sighs and, with her handsome chantry priest in tow, moved around the taproom from one group of pilgrims to another, as if she found everyone beneath her notice. Harry studied the prioress scornfully; her gown was of the finest material and her shoes, soft-leather buskins, were decorated with imitation pearls. She toyed with that brooch around her neck with its silly phrase *Amor vincit omnia* and stroked her lapdog, which she fed on the finest bread soaked in milk.

'A fine lot,' Harry murmured, rubbing his face in his hands.

'Sir? Are you well?'

Harry looked up.

'As fine as can be, Master Chaucer.'

Harry's eyes became guarded. He liked the fellow but was wary of him – he had heard the man of law remark how influential Chaucer was at court. A diplomat, a poet, a controller of the customs, Chaucer looked merry enough with his sparkling eyes, smiling mouth, rubicund face and neatly clipped moustache and beard. Sharp as a pin, Harry thought. A man of quick eye and ready wit, Chaucer had a penchant for marking people's foibles with a gentle mockery.

Chaucer sat down on a stool next to the taverner.

'Not as good an inn as your Tabard,' he murmured diplomatically.

Harry's broad face broke into a grin. 'I thank you, sir. And it's true!'

His critical gaze swept the taproom.

'The rushes are clean and the tables are scrubbed, but the pies are stale and too heavily spiced.' He wrinkled his nose and tapped Chaucer's knee playfully. 'Thank God spring is upon us! Soon it will be succulent capon, fresh lamb and pork crisp to the touch, eh?'

'But not until we've been to Canterbury.'

'Aye,' Harry breathed, staring down at the white ash in the hearth. 'I want to go there, climb the steps to the Lady Chapel

3

on my knees and pay homage to the blissful martyr's bones.'

'Why?' Chaucer asked.

Harry grinned but shook his head. 'Master Chaucer, you know better than that. It's my secret!'

'So many secrets,' the poet whispered, stretching out his legs. 'Have you observed, Harry, how many of our pilgrims know each other?'

'Aye, Master Chaucer, I have also noticed how you know many of them.'

Now it was the turn of the courtier poet to smile enigmatically. He pointed to the tavern window, now streaming with raindrops.

'If it goes on much longer, we'll need a ship to take us to Canterbury.'

'If it goes on any longer,' Harry quipped, 'we'll never reach the blessed shrine!' He gestured towards his fellow pilgrims. 'They'll be at each other's throats before nightfall.'

'So, what about your wager, Harry?'

The taverner pursed his lips. 'You think now is the time?'

Chaucer shivered and looked around the darkened taproom, where the rushlights and candles flickered.

'Aye, now is the time,' Chaucer said. 'But not for one of your pleasant tales. For something terrifying – a dark tale of blood and passion.'

'It's the good wife of Bath's turn next,' Harry said, staring across to where the broad-faced, merry-eyed five-times widow was regaling a bored manciple with stories of her pilgrimages to St James Compostella and to Cologne in Germany.

'Let's begin,' Chaucer murmured.

Harry needed no second bidding. Getting to his feet, he clapped his hands until he had silence.

'Fellow pilgrims, merry souls all.' He beamed. 'We journey

4

to Canterbury to pay homage to the blessed martyr's bones.'
He pointed to the window. 'Unless we drown first!'

The pilgrims laughed politely but watched attentively. They
regarded Harry as their leader and all tacitly agreed it was time
they relieved their boredom.

'What about a tale?' Harry asked. He jabbed a stubby finger
at the smoke-blackened rafters. 'Remember, each of us is to
tell two such stories – a merry one during the day to entertain
and ease our passage. The other at night, dark and sinister, to
chill the blood?'

'But we were only supposed to tell such a story at night,' the
pardoner objected in his high-pitched voice, his bony fingers
clawing at his dyed yellow hair.

'Well, we might as well be in bed now,' the wife of Bath
quipped.

'We?' the shipman murmured.

'That was not an invitation to you.' The wife of Bath sniffed,
shifting her large rump on the stool and flouncing out her
petticoats above her laced leather boots.

'She's like a drawbridge,' the summoner murmured, his red,
greasy face breaking into a smirk. He scratched his bulbous,
wart-covered nose.

'Who's a drawbridge?' the wife of Bath snapped.

'Some women are,' the summoner retorted. 'They go down
for any man.'

The wife of Bath stared at him, pop-eyed. Then, with a
screech of rage, she flung herself at him, her broad-brimmed
hat slipping to the back of her head as she pummelled the
laughing summoner with her fists.

Harry the taverner had to intervene. He seized her by her
meaty arms, pulled her off the raucous, drunken summoner

and sat her gently back on the stool.

'Just ignore him, mistress,' he advised.

He paused, caught by the clear gaze of the woman's ice-blue eyes. Harry blinked. He had always considered the wife of Bath as an over-dressed frump with her costly, purple-embroidered shawl, snow-white wimple and great black hat. A sow in silk he had once concluded: her face was broad, her cheeks ruby red but now, close up, he saw her blue eyes brimming with tears at the muffled sniggering of some of the pilgrims and, suddenly, she seemed innocent and childlike.

Harry grasped her podgy, beringed fingers. 'In your youth,' he whispered, 'you must have been a beautiful woman.'

The wife of Bath sighed; her eyes became guarded and shrewd. 'In my youth,' she declared for all to hear, 'I was a fair fortress. Men sought to storm it but few were allowed within my gates. But once they were' – her hand went to her lips in a gesture of mock innocence – 'what a paradise they found.' She glared at the summoner. 'As for you, pig-turd, you wouldn't know a lady if you saw one!'

'The important word,' the summoner snapped, 'is "if"!'

Harry walked over to the man and brought a heavy boot down on his toes, pressing hard enough to make him wince with pain.

'Shut up!' the taverner hissed. 'And, whilst I'm at it, keep your hands away from the franklin's belt!'

This dispute would have continued further if the miller, now snoring in the corner, cradling his bagpipes as he would a baby, hadn't given a loud fart and fallen off his stool. The ensuing merriment caused by the miller's fuddled awakening, followed by more braying noises from his rear end, convulsed the pilgrims either with outright laughter or polite giggles until even the grey-faced knight smiled wryly.

Harry, pleased at the break in tension, clapped his hands again.

'Remember our wager!' he bawled. 'Each pilgrim tells two tales. There's a prize for each kind. The day is dark and we sit in this tavern and squabble. So, let's have a tale of foul deeds and night-black hearts.'

'And who will tell the tale?' the ploughman asked. 'We can't sit here quarrelling all the time!'

'I will sing you a dark song.' The man of law spoke up from where he sat quietly in the corner.

All the pilgrims looked at him. The man of law got to his feet, hitching about his shoulders his costly, striped gown fringed with lambswool, his thumbs tucked into the leather belt round his slim waist. Harry studied him. A quiet fellow, he judged. When the lawyer spoke his tone was often cynical and, when asked about the law, he could quote it freely from the first statutes of King Henry III to the most recent Acts of Parliament. Harry pursed his lips.

'It's best if I do,' the lawyer continued, his dark, sardonic face relieved by a smile. 'Otherwise we'll sit debating until the Second Coming!'

Harry caught the sombre-eyed lawyer's gaze and realized that the man of law kept glancing at the prioress, who was sitting primly, feeding costly milk sops to her lapdog. A strange group, the landlord mused. The prioress, Dame Eglantine, looked up, blushed and bowed her head as if she was embarrassed by the man of law's declaration. Others, too, became slightly agitated, their quick movements not missed by the sharp-eyed Harry. The manciple half-rose to his feet, his jaw slack with surprise, until he remembered himself and sat down. The summoner put his heavy tankard down, looking now as drunk as he pretended to be.

'The man of law is right.' The knight spoke up. 'Let us have his tale now.'

There was a general murmur of approbation and Harry waved the man of law to a heavy, carved chair at the head of the taproom table.

'Be our guest, master lawyer. Tell us a tale of dark deeds and murderous hearts.'

The man of law smiled thinly. Hitching his belt round his waist, he took his seat and the goblet of wine Harry placed in front of him.

'Oh, I will,' he declared. 'I'll tell you a tale of treacherous intrigue, the subtlety of princes and the lust for power. I'll tell of bloody deeds carried out in the dark of night, though not far from the eye of God!'

The Man of Law's Prologue

In a chamber high in Castle Rising, which towered so forbiddingly above the flat Norfolk countryside, Isabella the dowager queen, mother of the puissant Edward III, was preparing to die, or so the rumour had it along the corridors and galleries of that stark, rambling castle. The life thread of the old queen was about to be cut: dying of the pestilence, everyone kept away from her. The old queen, her once-famous blonde hair now a dirty grey, lay back against the bolsters and stared at her beloved squire, Vallence. In so many ways the young man reminded her of Mortimer, the great love of her life, the Welsh baron who had shared her exile before rushing back to England, like God's own vengeance, to sweep aside her feckless husband Edward II and his powerful henchmen the de Spencer lords.

'All gone,' she breathed, 'like shadows in the sunlight. Vallence, everything is ready?'

The young squire nodded and opened his mouth to speak, but the queen's hand shot out, vigorous for a woman who was supposed to be dying. She pressed her fingers firmly against the young man's lips.

'Enough! Enough!' Isabella whispered. 'Is the coffin ready?'

Vallence nodded. 'A lead casket.' He tried to keep the excitement out of his voice. 'It will be put into an oaken coffin. The king has agreed that you be taken along Mile End Road and buried at Greyfriars.'

Isabella smiled and nodded.

'He is not coming here?' the squire asked anxiously.

'Why should he?' Isabella murmured. 'What do we have in common?' She spat the words out. 'Let him wage his bloody war and turn the fair fields of France into blood-soaked acres! God will have his vengeance and so will I! Vallence, I ask you again, is everything ready?'

The young squire nodded.

'Then leave me. It is time I died.'

Words between the pilgrims

The man of law broke off his tale. The wife of Bath clapped her hands.

'Your story is about Isabella,' she crowed. 'That Jezebel, the She-Wolf of France!'

'An evil woman,' the physician contributed. 'In her youth they say she was beautiful. She married King Edward, the grandfather of our present king, but brought him as low as Hell!'

'Played the two-backed beast she did!' the pardoner screeched, flicking his yellow hair back. 'Edward had a lover, Hugh de Spencer, so Isabella had her paramour, Roger Mortimer.' He stretched his neck like an old hen and stared around the assembled company. 'Oh, yes, I know my history. Isabella met Mortimer in the Tower and they became paramours. They fled to France and returned with an army.'

'I was a boy in London at the time,' the reeve spoke up, eager to share his knowledge. 'The king fled west with de Spencer as the mob rose against him. I was in the markets along Cheapside. They trapped some of de Spencer's ministers in St Paul's graveyard. Tore them from their horses and hacked them to death, leaving their poor corpses gutted and bleeding

11

like slabs of meat on a butcher's stall!'

'I was only a chit of a girl,' the wife of Bath said, 'but I remember the excitement well. They executed de Spencer you know, at Hereford. A kinsman of mine saw him die. They built a special scaffold.' Her voice fell to a whisper. 'Hanged and drawn he was.' She made a chopping movement with her hand. 'His balls cut off like that!'

'And what happened to her husband, the king?' the ploughman asked.

'He was taken to Berkeley Castle,' the wife of Bath answered, 'and thrown into a deep pit with the rotting corpses of animals. He was meant to die there . . .'

'But?'

The wife of Bath adjusted her wimple. She leaned forward, pleased to have everybody's attention.

'One night murderers entered the king's cell. They threw the unfortunate prince to the ground, placed a table on his back and thrust a red-hot poker up into his innards, so the corpse would show no mark. My kinsman,' she added proudly, 'saw his corpse in its coffin before it was buried in Gloucester abbey church.'

'What happened to Isabella?' the ploughman asked.

'For three more years she and Mortimer ruled the kingdom,' the wife of Bath said, 'with her son, our noble Edward, as their puppet. Then Edward asserted himself. One night he arrested Mortimer at Nottingham Castle and sent him to be hanged at Tyburn for the murder of his father.'

'And Isabella?'

'She was banished to Castle Rising until her death.'

The knight spoke up. 'I was a member of the guard of honour at her funeral.' He narrowed his eyes and gazed at the man of law. 'On the day the queen was buried, there was some excitement was there not?'

The man of law was staring across the tavern at the prioress. 'Oh, there was excitement,' he replied at last, shaking himself from his reverie. 'But listen awhile, for the old queen's burial brought about more bloody murders.'

The Man of Law's Tale
PART I

About the middle of a Thursday afternoon, two men, John Waters, a blacksmith, and William Bramwell, a baker, were crossing the desolate waste at the foot of Primrose Hill, going towards the White House tavern near St John's Wood. The day was both dark and cold and they were looking forward to hot spiced food and a jack of ale. They could already see the lights of the tavern faintly in the distance when Bramwell suddenly stopped. He grasped his companion's arm and pointed towards a large reed-filled pond with two black, stark trees above it. Not far from the pond ran a deep ditch shrouded with thickets and brambles and, amongst these, on the rim of the ditch, they glimpsed in the fading light a long, silver-topped cane, a pair of fringed gloves and an empty sword scabbard. Both men hurried across. Bramwell bent over to pick the gloves up and, in doing so, noticed something lying in the ditch.

'Good Lord!' he cried, stepping back. 'There's a dead man here!'

They pulled the brambles back to reveal, lying face down in the bottom of the ditch, the corpse of a tall, lean man clothed in black. Their terror increased when they saw six inches of a sword point protruding from the man's back just under the right shoulder blade. They looked at each other and stared down. The body lay in a crooked position, not flat against the bottom of the ditch but turned slightly towards the left bank. One arm, the left, was doubled back under the head, the other flung out. At first sight it might even seem that the man was only sleeping. Bramwell crouched closer and stared at the white face twisted in the crook of the arm. He fought back the bile which rose in his throat as he glimpsed the bluish, bloated skin and blood-filled eyes.

'Who is it?' Waters whispered.

'I don't know,' Bramwell replied. 'But he's well dressed and he lies on his own sword. Is it suicide or murder?' He peered more closely. Then, 'I think I do know him,' he whispered hoarsely. 'God save us, it's the judge, it's Lord Stephen Berisford!'

In the Locked Heart tavern off Pig Alley near Chick Lane, Wormwood, a professional assassin, sat quietly in a noisome corner of the taproom where the floor was soaked in rat urine. A beggar, filthy-skinned and clothed in rags, came up to the table, fawning and bowing. Wormwood kicked out and the creature scuttled away, losing himself at the end of the long, dark taproom. Surely, Wormwood thought, he was safe here? Surely the Guardian of the Gates would keep his bargain? It was past nine in the evening and the tavern was still thronged with drinkers. The din was horrid. Wormwood stared through the fug. Most of the noise was coming from another, lower, chamber down some stairs at the far end. Wormwood ordered more ale but when it came he sent it back, complaining that it was cloudy, and demanded instead a cup of sack. Then he left his seat and walked the length of the taproom and down the stairs into the dirty, thronged cockpit. A huge crowd was gathered there. Lords, gallants, clerks and apprentices rubbed shoulders with every type of villain, both high- and base-born, the city could muster. They all stood around the sawdust pit shouting wagers and taking bets. In the pit itself two huge cocks, their black silk plumage dusty and blood-stained, fought like savage gladiators. They circled and clawed each other until one collapsed in the dust, a pile of blood-soaked feathers, whilst its conqueror, covered in gore, stretched its neck out and crowed in triumph.

Wormwood felt himself shiver and looked around. When, he thought, would the messenger come? A wench, lush and comely, her lustrous hair falling down to her white, bare shoulders, was studying him. The black paint around her eyes contrasted sharply with the ivory paleness of her skin. She smiled at Wormwood and moved her body suggestively, stretching languorously, her eyes never leaving his. Wormwood, the wine warming his belly and firing his blood, grinned back. Why not? He had done what the Guardian wanted. Surely, the labourer was worthy of his wages? Wormwood felt his loins stir. A little pleasure? Why not? He moved across.

'Mistress, can I buy you a drink?'

The assassin secretly commended himself for his courtly manner. He knew how to treat a lady, even if she was a lady of the night. The woman thanked him with her eyes and they moved back to the seat Wormwood had found for himself in a window embrasure.

'You're a Scot. Your accent betrays you.'

The woman's voice was soft and throaty. She sat close to Wormwood. He smelt her cloying perfume and felt the warmth of her thigh against his. Like all men in the presence of a beautiful woman, Wormwood felt he had to talk. Ordering fresh cups of wine, he regaled the girl with stories of his importance and industry, hinted at his wealth and smirked at her comments about Scots being fierce drinkers and great lovers. The hours passed and the tavern began to empty. The woman, as if she would take no refusal, grasped Wormwood by the wrist.

'I have a room here,' she said. 'Warm and comfortable. No need for the coldness of the streets.'

Wormwood needed no further encouragement. He followed the woman up the rickety stairs, admiring the sway of her hips, her well-turned ankles and her high-heeled shoes with gold roses on the insteps. She opened a door at the top of the stairs and Wormwood followed her into the chamber.

'What now?' he murmured.

The woman giggled. Wormwood heard a tinder strike and a long candle flared into light. The woman walked towards Wormwood, the candle bathing her face in a circle of light.

'Here, hold this,' she said.

Wormwood grabbed the candlestick. 'You wanton wench! Come here!'

The woman smiled, her eyes sparkling as she placed one long, beautiful hand on his shoulder. Her blue, cat-like eyes held his and, for a few seconds, the assassin knew something was wrong. The smile went from her face and her eyes became heavy-lidded. He opened his mouth to scream and tried to step back, but too late. The knife, held in the woman's hand, took him deep beneath the heart. He felt the room sway. He wanted to scream at the pain that shot through him.

'The Guardian greets you,' the woman whispered. 'And bids you adieu!'

Words between the pilgrims

The man of law paused to order some food from the tavern kitchens.

'I am hungry,' he explained apologetically, 'and telling a tale makes you aware that, though your head and mouth be full, your stomach is empty.'

'Then fill it merrily!' Harry exclaimed. 'For this is a sombre tale for a man of law.'

'There are deeper shadows yet.'

And the man of law turned away as a servitor, summoned by Harry's bellowing, came in to know his pleasure. He'd hardly closed the door behind him when the pardoner screeched, 'Oh, Lord, save us!'

All eyes turned to him.

'Oh, Lord, save us!' the pardoner repeated. 'I have heard of this evil man.'

'The Guardian of the Gates?' Harry asked.

'Aye, sir, him.'

'Who is he?'

'Oh, you wouldn't know,' the pardoner replied. 'You live in Southwark well beyond the law of the city, but across the river the Guardian of the Gates holds sway. Or, at least, he used to.'

The pardoner narrowed his colourless eyes. 'He comes and goes like the wind! He is never seen but his presence is always felt.'

'What do you mean?' the squire asked.

'There's a legion of rogues and vagabonds in London,' the monk interrupted. 'And, by Satan's balls, they are legion! They have a prince, the king of the beggars, the man who calls himself the Guardian of the Gates for no one can enter London's underworld without his permission.'

'Nonsense!' the reeve from Norfolk snorted.

'Nonsense?' the pardoner yelped.

'It's not nonsense,' the man of law spoke up, tearing his eyes away from Dame Eglantine. He paused as the servant returned with a piece of fish lightly grilled, served between a manchet loaf smeared with butter and covered in a parsley sauce.

The man of law thanked him.

'Now, listen all,' he said between small, neat mouthfuls of food, 'and you'll know the truth about the Guardian of the Gates!'

20

PART II
Chapter 1

Nicholas Chirke woke with a groan.

'Too much red wine!' he muttered. His mouth and throat were still coated with the claret's richness.

He got up, swaying slightly, and looked down at the bed cover, studying its design of negroes riding elephants. The elephants seemed to move across the bed with a life of their own. Nicholas removed his nightshirt and doused his face in the basin of cold water which stood on its wooden rack. He dried himself with a rag and slumped back on to the bed. The red flush of wine still lingering in his blood was deceptive. He was freezing, so he slipped on his robe of black damask and his nightcap edged with gold lace, both presents from his sister. He crossed his arms and looked round the chamber he called his 'private paradise'.

'Store up treasure in heaven,' he muttered to himself, laughing softly. He hoped there was treasure in heaven, to compensate for its paucity here on earth. Nicholas considered himself to be one rung below those poor tawdries who paraded in St Paul's Walk with so little in their purses and so much on their backs. He had very little of anything – two chests (only one of them his own), three stools (one broken), a lavarium, two changes of linen, half a woollen carpet and a faded wall hanging showing David pursuing Bathsheba, a gift from a grateful client who had been unable to pay his fee.

Chirke looked across at his tall box-chest. It contained a silver candelabra and a gold candle snuffer which he knew he should really sell as he only had one candle and that was made of tallow fat. He lay back on the bed and stared at the plaster ceiling. Was he resentful? No, his sister and his brother-in-law, John Gawdy, were generous to a fault. He hated the thought of taking from them and that included the feast John had organized the night before. It was for men from John's guild-ward, but Nicholas had also been invited. He'd spent the previous day loitering around St Paul's trying to attract custom, dreaming of fat fees and intricate cases involving mortmain or writs of *quo warranto*. Of course, nothing had turned up and Chirke had returned through the dank streets as ravenous as a wolf. He had eaten his fair share of pike in hot mince sauce, roasted blackbird and quince tarts, as well as taking generous cupfuls from the large flagon of red wine John had served. Nicholas closed his eyes – here he was, a scholar of Norwich Grammar School, Trinity College Cambridge, and of the Inner Temple, a lawyer at the early age of twenty-eight, living on the generosity of his sister.

Chirke stood up and swallowed his self pity. Today things could change. Sir Amyas Petrie, Member of Parliament and Sheriff of London, had raised his little finger to help his distant kinsman for the second time. It had been Sir Amyas's influence that had won Chirke a coveted place in the Inner Temple, but when Nicholas had tried to thank him Sir Amyas had ignored the letter. Now Sir Amyas, at the dizzying height of his power, had issued another summons for Nicholas, 'his beloved

kinsman', to meet him in his private chambers near Chancery
Lane. Nicholas sighed and rose. The meeting was fixed for
noon. He peered through the horn-glazed window, but a river
mist had rolled in, hiding most of the Poultry and Walbrook
under an icy blanket. Nicholas heard the bells of St Mary le
Bow and the deeper tones of St Paul's and reckoned it must be
ten in the morning. He scrubbed his teeth with a mixture of
honey and vinegar until his fingers hurt and dressed in his best
faded jerkin over a hole-ridden cambric shirt. His breeches and
hose were new, however, being a Twelfth Night present from
John and Catherine. Nicholas remembered the clinging cold of
yesterday and put on three pairs of woollen stockings before
forcing his protesting feet into a pair of tight leather boots. He
combed his jet-black hair and hid the shame of his poor clothing
under his heavy, striped lawyer's gown.

Chirke made sure the rushlight was extinguished and stepped
into the freezing, narrow passageway and went up a flight of
stairs to Scathelocke's garret under the eaves. He pushed the
door open; the small chamber was empty, the coverlet pulled
across the pallet bed. The room, as always, was clean and tidy,
his manservant's possessions neatly arranged on the chamber's
two shelves or put away in the great iron-bound chests
Scathelocke always kept locked. Chirke felt intrigued and
embarrassed. He was snooping because, like any lawyer, he
was curious and Scathelocke was an enigma. Chirke rested
against the doorpost. How long had he known him? A year?
Yes, almost a year. Chirke had been in St Paul's, waiting with
the others, searching for customers. He had seen Scathelocke
walking up and down the Mediterranean, the main aisle of the
cathedral nave. The fellow seemed to be talking to himself so
Chirke drew closer and concluded he was either crazed or

chanting some incantation. The next day Nicholas, flushed with pleasure at securing a case, a lucrative quarrel over an old man's will, had been accosted by Scathelocke as he left the Bishop's Head tavern opposite St Paul's.

'Do you need a servant?' the fellow had asked. 'I am Henry Scathelocke. I have no references but I am honest and able. I can sew, read and I am thrifty.'

'Can you now?' Chirke had replied, the bowls of claret rendering him as joyful as Bacchus. Chirke had studied the man, noting his clean fustian clothes, clear blue eyes and child-like face despite the neatly barbered red beard and moustache.

'Yes, I need a servant,' Nicholas had replied in a gust of drunken generosity. Why not? His brother-in-law needed help around the house and Chirke was sure his fortune had turned for the better. He had been right, or nearly so. Scathelocke was a good servant; he was thrifty in everything except his appetite. But Chirke's luck had not improved. Nevertheless, he could not turn the man away. John and Catherine liked him; Scathelocke was dexterous with his hands and a bulwark against the twins. However, the fellow was a mystery. He had no past, no friends or family. Was he a fugitive? Chirke wondered. His voice was low and well educated and he could speak both French and Spanish. Once, when they were both deep in their cups, he had shown he was equally proficient in Latin and Italian. Where had he received such an education?

'Nicholas!'

He heard his sister call from downstairs. Chirke looked once more around the room. The chamber smelt fresh, with the fragrance of crushed herbs, candle wax and perhaps, something richer. Incense? Was Scathelocke a devil-worshipper? Chirke grinned. He doubted it – Henry had joined him in Father

Thompkins's choir at St Mary le Bow, where his voice, a deep bass, was a good foil to Chirke's tenor. The lawyer shrugged and went downstairs into the stone-flagged kitchen. A fire roared in the hearth and the air was juicy sweet with the fragrance of freshly baked bread. The twins, six years of age and as alike as peas out of a pod, sat round-eyed like two small owls on either side of Scathelocke, who was relating one of his fantastical stories. The manservant, his eyes closed in concentration, solemnly intoned, 'In Ethiopia dragons exist, no, not like the serpents in the Amazon where the men with no heads live. No.' He stopped and raised a hand at the boys' excited cries. 'No, that's another story. These have yellow eyes and purple skins.'

Scathelocke opened his eyes and winked at Nicholas, who nodded back and stared curiously at the slattern rotating the spit, basting a joint of lamb in its own sizzling juices, and seeming impervious to the blasting heat.

'Good morning, Nicholas.'

Catherine swept in through the kitchen door, her face cheery under its mop of black hair. Nicholas embraced her, hugging her in his arms as he had when they were children and she was a princess and he a giant. Catherine, although brown-eyed and dark-skinned when she wanted to be blue-eyed and fair, was always cheerful as a sparrow.

'Nicholas!' she cried breathlessly.

He let her go. 'Forget my own strength,' he mumbled.

She made a face, smoothed her green taffeta dress and scurried round the table, setting places for the meal. Nicholas suddenly swore and hurried back upstairs, ignoring his sister's shriek not to use such language in front of the children – he had no illusions about his nephews, two imps from hell who regarded him as their natural victim. He found the leather belt, purse and wallet he had forgotten where he had thrown them the night before. He grabbed them and hurried back downstairs. Catherine had finished laying the table. She placed two tankards, platters and cunningly devised bottles of German beer, a novelty for each bore the grave, bearded face of a Hanse merchant. Bowls of steaming hot broth were also served. Scathelocke, summoned from his protesting audience, sat down next to Chirke and grabbed his horn spoon. Nicholas looked at his sister, raised his eyes heavenwards at his servant's constant appetite, and followed suit. He broke up the hot manchet loaves and dipped the morsels into the meat-enriched broth. Then he looked up nervously. His sister hadn't moved and she was watching him intently. Chirke's heart sank; he knew what was coming.

'Where's John?' he asked.

Catherine, not to be deflected or diverted, simply gestured with her hands towards the front of the house, where John and his apprentices had set out their stall of cloth and leather goods. Chirke began to eat but Catherine just stood there.

'I had a letter from Robert,' she said.

Nicholas narrowed his eyes. 'I don't want to know,' he muttered. 'I never want to know.'

He glared at Scathelocke's enquiring face and bowed his head. Catherine moved towards him restlessly, like a disturbed mother hen. Why, she wondered, could not Nicholas make peace with his brother? Why couldn't he go back to the old manor house outside Norwich and heal the wounds? But she knew the answers to her own questions. It was all the fault of that bitch Beatrice, with her beautiful face and itching loins, who had been Nicholas's only love until one clear spring morning when he had found her with his brother. Catherine's world had exploded into shouted curses and the clash of steel as the two men she loved most after her husband fought over a woman she hated. Nicholas had left – when? Six years ago, just after the Hilary term had begun – and never returned home since. He looked up at her now, his dark face stubborn, his strange eyes – one blue, one green – narrowed in fury. His lips, normally ever ready to smile, were thin and tight and the laughter wrinkles around his eyes had gone. Catherine hid her concern and anger and smiled at him.

'I'm sure good fortune will come of your meeting with Sir Amyas Petrie,' she said. 'Mother always said he would help.' She lightly brushed her brother's black beard and moustache with the cloth she held in her hand. 'But you should see a barber first.'

Then she turned away and fled from the kitchen before Nicholas could glimpse the scalding tears in her eyes. Her brother popped the last piece of bread into his mouth and finished off the dry, tangy beer.

'We should go,' he murmured.

He called to his sister that they were leaving, but, hearing no reply, took up his cloak and went out. Scathelocke picked up his own cloak, promised the children he would finish the story on his return and quietly followed his master. John Gawdy, busy behind his stalls in front of the house, saw them leave, grinned and shouted, 'Good luck, Nicholas!'

Nicholas smiled back. John Gawdy, with his open, honest face, stocky frame, unruly red hair and light green eyes, was a man with no pretences who lived for his wife, his children and his beloved guild. He was shouting at his apprentices, who scurried backwards and forwards with bales of cloth, leather belts, purses, panniers and jerkins, piling the stalls high, ready for business. Nicholas shook John's hand and mumbled that he may have upset Catherine. John raised his eyebrows and grinned. He was no stranger to the occasional violent clashes between brother and sister and, long ago, he made a decision not to take sides.

'Catherine soon forgets,' he murmured, one eye on an apprentice who was carrying too much. 'But you take care, Nicholas. Tread warily and good fortune may be yours!'

As soon as Nicholas and Scathelocke had turned into the street and up into Cheapside, under the pointed gables of the houses, they felt the cold blast of the icy wind. The ground underfoot, a mixture of dirt, slush and the refuse of chamber pots, was frozen rock-hard. They pulled their mufflers up and held their heads down as they passed Scalding Alley, the Old Jewry and the King's Wardrobe. The noise now grew to a resounding din. All along Cheapside rose the clatter of barter and brawling.

'Fish! Who'll buy my fish?'

'Lily-white vinegar! Lily-white vinegar!'

They walked on, past stalls of rotten fruit and scabrous sausages and pedlars hawking mackerel and rosemary. A tinker banged his drum. 'Do you have brass pots, skillets or frying pans to mend?' he bawled.

Carts rolled by, slipping and cracking on the uneven cobbles. A funeral bell rang from a nearby church, almost drowned by the strident call of a pig-killer's horn. The taverns and cookshops were open and the smell of rich ale, fresh bread and mouldy food camouflaged by tangy spices hung thick in the air. Nicholas felt Scathelocke tense as he always did when they entered some crowded place. Nicholas stopped and took his manservant by the shoulder.

'What is it, Henry? What's wrong?' he asked, as he had

asked before. He scrutinized Scathelocke's pale face. 'Are you sickening? Do you need some physic?'

Scathelocke shook his head.

A bailiff trotted by, dragging a woman convicted as a whore within the city limits. She wore an iron brank over her head and the bailiff pulled the poor woman along as if she was a dog. Nicholas stepped aside. Scathelocke turned his back and Nicholas was sure that he was trying to hide his face, though he failed to conceal the fear in his eyes. Nicholas sighed. Should he have introduced this man into his sister's house?

'Henry,' he whispered. 'What do you fear? Who are you?'

'And you, master,' Henry grated. 'What about you? Who is Robert? Who is Beatrice? Why do you not return to Norwich? Your sister talks about it as often as you do in your cups or sleep!'

Nicholas smiled sourly. 'Some day, Henry.'

'Aye, master. Some day. But let us both keep our secrets. We have business to attend to.'

Nicholas took him by the elbow and they walked up past the forbidding mass of Newgate prison and the stocks already filled with miscreants – a pedlar, a manservant caught in lechery, a couple of pickpockets. Nicholas thought about Scathelock. Was he a lecher? Had he fled from his wife and family? Where did he go at night? To the brothels and bawdy houses of Southwark or Whitefriars? He leaned closer.

'Tonight, Henry, Father Thompkins says he has a new French madrigal which he will allow us to sing in the nave.'

Scathelocke nodded and the conversation turned to the joys of a five-voiced choir and the merits of plainchant. Nicholas and Scathelocke turned into Holborn and across to Chancery Lane, near Staple Inn; the houses here were richer and bounded by gardens, although nothing grew under the freezing blanket of ice. Sir Amyas Petrie's house was the grandest. It stood in its own grounds, framed with massive black timbers – thick, broad oaks, gilded and embossed with intricate devices. Between the timbers the white plaster gleamed like pure snow. Each of its four storeys jutted out slightly over the one on which it rested and all the windows were of mullioned glass with linings of lead. Nicholas lifted the great, brass knocker, in the form of a knight's helmet, and brought it down hard.

A servant ushered them into a panelled hall with thick woollen carpets on the floor and on the walls exquisite murals in which Nicholas recognized the influence of Dutch and German painters. They were led up an oak staircase and into a long gallery where it was so dark that the wax candles in their silver holders had already been lit. The servant tapped on a door at the end of the gallery.

'Come in!' A soft and cultured voice responded. The sheriff's chamber was panelled with oak in the modish ribbed-linen pattern. The polished floor was covered with rugs. Because the windows were small the room was dark, but candles bathed the area around the oak desk in a golden pool of light. Sir Amyas sat behind the desk, one beringed hand silently drumming the desk-top whilst the other shuffled documents about. He looked up and smiled, his swarthy bearded face under its flat cap losing some of its harshness, though the deep-set eyes remained hard as he studied his distant kinsman. He tugged his robe closer about him and leaned across the desk.

'Good day, Nicholas.'

He gestured for Nicholas to sit on the high-backed chair in front of the desk. Scathelocke he ignored, as if the manservant didn't exist. Nicholas made himself comfortable as the sheriff half-turned to glance at the middle-aged man sitting quietly on his right.

'Master Chirke, may I introduce Sir Roger Hobbedon, mayor of this city.'

Nicholas acknowledged the man's smile. At first glance Hobbedon seemed likable enough, though his close-set eyes were narrow and secretive.

'Sir Roger is present this morning only as a witness,' Sir Amyas said. 'You would like some wine?'

Nicholas nodded and the sheriff went over to a small desk and brought back a tall-stemmed Venetian glass. Nothing was offered to Scathelocke, standing silently behind his master.

'Master Chirke,' Sir Amyas began again, 'you are a good lawyer with bleak prospects, yes?'

Nicholas sipped from his glass and stared back. He knew his law: 'In doubt say nothing'.

'And you have a name for honesty.'

'From whom?'

'From de Guysers.'

Nicholas smiled. De Guysers was a poor foreign merchant who had appeared before the justices of Westminster for not obeying city trading regulations. Nicholas had pleaded de Guysers's case, trying to exploit loopholes in the law. He had lost the case but, because he had failed, had not charged a fee. Now he wished he had. At first his honesty had been lauded around St Paul's but he got no more cases and the praise had swiftly turned to mocking laughter.

'I'm told that you never go back to Norwich,' Sir Amyas said abruptly. 'Never revisit the cathedral school. But you remember it, Nicholas, nestling under Blanche Tower?'

Nicholas knew he was being teased. He vividly remembered

the cathedral school, with its stark classroom where Master Timmons with his long, black cane had revealed the mysteries of Latin, Greek, Grammar and Logic. Like all schoolboys, Chirke had spent a lot of his time gazing through the window, open even in the depths of winter, at the great square keep the Bigods had built on a hill dominating the town. He and Beatrice had often walked in its pleasant gardens which sloped down to Mousehole Heath.

'Painful memories?' the sheriff asked slyly. 'But not of Cambridge, surely? I understand you studied there? Medicine under the great Doctor Fabianus, the physician who cut open bodies?'

'The doctor had a licence to do so!' Chirke snapped.

Petrie smiled as if he had won a point and Chirke tensed. The sheriff was teasing out his past like the good lawyer he was, allowing his victim to speak, fearful of the ominous pauses between the simple but abrupt questions. Of course Chirke remembered the white-washed rooms and blood-soaked tables of Cambridge where Doctor Fabianus opened and inspected the corpses of hanged men and women, remembered the dirty white flesh, the flapping skin, the stench of their silver-blue innards and other organs piled high on dirty plates. He could not tolerate it and had decided on law. Sir Amyas Petrie, grinning there like some jester, knew all this.

'After Cambridge I, like you, Sir Amyas, went to Pegasus,' Chirke said, using the slang term for the Inner Temple. 'I studied in the Round Church, inspected the Templar tombs, ran riot in Fleet Street and bought the law books of Richard Popple. I did so because of your influence. I sent you a letter of thanks. I doubt if you recieved it, for I had no reply.'

Sir Amyas merely laughed and snapped his fingers. A fresh

glass of wine was thrust into Chirke's hands but he had drunk enough and placed it on the desk. Petrie should stop playing with him, come to the point. Instead, Sir Amyas asked, 'How is your mother, my kinswoman?'

Nicholas thought of her, slim and petite, her face lined with care. If only she had not taken Robert's side!

'My mother is well.' Nicholas pushed his chair back as if to rise. He felt like snarling at the sheriff and fought to control his temper. 'Sir Amyas, why am I here?'

The sheriff pursed his lips and nodded.

'A frank question should obtain an honest answer. I wish to offer you a post.'

Nicholas remained silent.

'You seem ill pleased. You have an offer of preferment elsewhere?'

'No, Sir Amyas, but not even a loon would buy a horse he's never seen.'

Sir Amyas forced a smile. 'I would like you to be a member of my household.'

Nicholas stared back. 'As what? A servant?'

'No.' Petrie's good humour dulled. 'As a member of my inner chamber, as my cursitor.'

'You mean thief-chaser?'

'No!' Petrie retorted. 'I have no need of bully-boys or riff-raff. I need someone who knows the law as well as the darkness of the human heart, someone who will be helpful in ensuring that justice is done and evil prosecuted.'

Nicholas thought that from what he had seen the law had little to do with justice but perhaps this was not the occasion to say so.

'A cursitor!' Sir Amyas insisted. 'A man who seeks out the

facts – the truth. A lawyer who would ostensibly' – the sheriff emphasized the word – 'help me prepare my brief and produce evidence admissible before the justices. Five shillings a week, the right to dine at my board once a day or draw the same in kind from my stores. New robes at Christmas and Midsummer and all reasonable expenses, provided the list is accurate and acceptable to my steward.'

Nicholas sat back and looked up at the painted ceiling. Should he accept this excellent preferment? He would be no longer a free agent but the sheriff's errand boy. An appentice in finer robes?

'What you do,' Petrie interjected as if reading his thoughts, 'when I do not need you is a matter for yourself.'

Nicholas thought of Catherine's and John's generosity, of how his sister had fretted about what might happen to him, of how she would love to send news back to Norwich that Nicholas was working for no less a person than the city sheriff.

'My manservant?' he asked.

'Your manservant,' Sir Amyas snapped, 'has nothing to do with me!'

Nicholas stared out of the window above the sheriff's head and noticed that it was beginning to rain. Sir Amyas turned in his chair, for the first time bothering to notice Scathelocke, a look of deep distaste on his face. Henry sat tensely, his shoulders bowed. Nicholas was sure the sheriff was going to say something.

'I accept,' he said, louder than he intended.

'Good!' Sir Amyas sighed and sat back in his chair. 'We have an indenture ready for you.' He leaned across the table. 'We also have a task.' He smiled. 'That is the real reason for this meeting. It is important and could be dangerous.'

Sir Amyas cleared his throat and clasped his hands. He sat back in his chair and stared up at the ceiling.

Nicholas looked quickly across at Hobbedon, who sat still as a statue. Nicholas realized suddenly that Hobbedon was really there as Sir Amyas's witness; to guarantee that the sheriff could not later be accused of speaking treason.

His stomach heaved. What was this about, he wondered? What terrible secrets were to be revealed? Sir Amyas didn't need him as a cursitor but to perform some special feat which could not be left to others.

'Now, kinsman, listen well,' Petrie began. 'On August 22nd last, Isabella, mother of our noble lord Edward III, died of the pestilence at Castle Rising in Norfolk.' He glanced quickly at Chirke from under heavily lidded eyes. 'The old queen's life is well known. She opposed her husband, King Edward II.' Petrie paused. 'She fled the kingdom and joined Roger Mortimer in France. They both claimed to be exiles from the English court, driven out by the pernicious influence of Hugh de Spencer, Edward II's favourite.'

Chirke knew the sheriff was choosing his words very carefully – and, in truth, he was dealing with most serious and sensitive matters. Sir Amyas coughed and cleared his throat before continuing.

'Now Edward and Isabella enjoyed a marriage which provided the courts of Europe with platefuls of juicy scandal. Nevertheless, one has to be careful when talking about the parents of our present king still waging his bloody war against France.' Petrie smiled as if he sensed Chirke's thoughts. 'A short lesson in history, eh, kinsman?'

Sir Amyas abruptly leaned forward across the table. His voice dropped to a hoarse whisper so that Chirke wondered if

35

Scathelocke, still standing behind him, could even hear what was being said.

'King Edward II,' Petrie continued, 'was a man who liked the best of both worlds, whether male or female.' He wetted his lips. 'But that was due to the sinister influence of Spencer. Now, in September 1326, the queen and Mortimer landed in Essex, the kingdom rallied to them. Edward and his favourite, Hugh de Spencer, were caught in South Wales. De Spencer suffered the full rigours of law, being executed as a traitor. The king was sent to Berkeley Castle where he later died. The present king, a mere stripling of fourteen summers, was crowned but real power lay with Queen Isabella and her henchman Mortimer. Well, at least until the winter of 1330, when our present lord reasserted himself. He arrested Mortimer and sent him to the gallows. His beloved mother he banished from the court and she went to live in the fortress of Castle Rising.' Petrie twisted his head slightly and looked in mock innocence at Chirke. 'You have my meaning, kinsman?'

Nicholas actually found it hard to keep his face straight. Everyone knew that Edward had been murdered at Berkeley by assassins, sent by Isabella, who had forced a red hot poker up into his bowels. It was common knowledge, too, that Mortimer had been arrested at Nottingham Castle in the queen's own bedchamber. Nicholas looked away and stared into the fire.

'You have no questions, kinsman?'

Nicholas smiled. Sir Amyas gave a small sigh of relief.

'Very good, kinsman,' he said. 'It's best not to bruit abroad the doings of the high and mighty.'

'But how does this concern me?' Nicholas asked.

'I will tell you. But, first, the indenture.'

Chapter 2

Sir Amyas rose and went across to a chest in the corner of the room. He drew from it a roll of white vellum which he laid out on a small table, a writing tray beside it. He then took the inkpot from where it had been warming in the inglenook and beckoned to Nicholas, who walked over and looked down at the document, on which, in an elegant hand, was written: 'An Indenture made this day, the 25th of November, in the thirty-first year of the reign of King Edward III, between Nicholas Chirke, gentleman, and Sir Amyas Petrie.' Chirke smiled sourly. He hid a flicker of resentment at the way Petrie had assumed he would accept the post. He felt like a coney trapped in the hay – whichever way he moved he would be caught. He shrugged. What matter? He took the quill, dipped it into the blue-green ink and signed his name with a flourish. The document incorporated all the terms Petrie had listed – fees, robes, food and stores.

Sir Amyas smiled and pushed the indenture aside. 'Now,' he continued, 'Isabella died on 22nd August last. Because she had fallen sick of the pestilence, her body was brought quickly along Mile End Road and, on 26th August, was interred at Greyfriars in London in the shadow of St Paul's.' Petrie laughed self-consciously. 'The old queen, perhaps aware of the evil she had committed, wanted to be dressed in the robes of the Franciscan order of the Poor Clares and buried in the Franciscan church.' Sir Amyas smiled, 'Which, by coincidence, also housed the mangled remains of her lover Mortimer. The funeral was fairly swift. The requiem mass was sung in the morning and the body interred.' Sir Amyas paused. 'That afternoon the queen's trusted squire, Vallence, attempted to board a Venetian galley which, we think, was sailing for Dieppe.'

'But Vallence was French, surely?' Nicholas interposed.

'Yes. He had entered the queen's household some ten years previously.'

'And his mistress was dead?'

'Yes, I know what you are saying. Why shouldn't Vallence go back to France? But, dearest kinsman, there's more to this than meets the eye.' The sheriff fingered his lips and stared over his shoulder at Scathelocke. 'First, however, I must insist that your manservant leaves. Sir Roger will escort him out.'

Chirke turned and nodded at Scathelocke who, without a second glance, followed the mayor, slipping like a shadow from the room.

The sheriff waited until the door had closed behind them.

'Sir Roger had to wait till you signed that indenture. What I am now going to say only concerns you and me.' The sheriff sipped from his wine goblet. 'Now Vallence had been watched. We believe the old queen entrusted him with a secret – perhaps a document that might cause great scandal for England and for our king personally. Isabella had, during her exile at Castle Rising, on a number of occasions asked to go to France, on the grounds that her kinsmen there requested her presence.' Petrie toyed with a quill on his desk. 'Her son, the king, always refused his permission. Then, on the afternoon of the queen's funeral,

Vallence was stopped on the quayside at Queenshithe by soldiers from the royal household. Instead of surrendering, he drew his sword and dagger. In the ensuing skirmish, he was sorely wounded and taken to the hospital of St Bartholomew's in Smithfield.'

'And the Venetian galley?'

Sir Amyas shrugged. 'Venice is a powerful city. The king draws heavily on its bankers and the Venetians love our English wool. We have no quarrel with Venice or its ships. Anyway, even if we had, the galley, warned by the affray on the quayside, slipped its moorings and sailed down the Thames.'

Chirke nodded and glanced at a tapestry hanging on the wall of the chamber. He tried to curb his feeling of unease. Petrie was drawing him into deep and treacherous waters. Everyone knew about the scandals surrounding Isabella's life and her desire to return to her home country was understandable, though a possible source of embarrassment. Her son, Edward III, was now waging a bloody war against France, claiming the crown of that kingdom by virtue of his mother.

'Kinsman?'

Chirke glanced at Petrie. 'What happened to Vallence?'

'As I said, he was taken to St Bartholomew's, where he was visited and questioned by myself and two leading aldermen of the city, Sir Ambrose Venner and Sir Oswald Cooper. A justice, Lord Stephen Berisford, was also summoned.'

'Ah. The one who recently disappeared? His corpse has been discovered on Primrose Hill.'

'The same. He had to be there because Vallence's affray had taken place in his ward. But listen, I questioned Vallence. He would not confess to being party to any secret but then he recognized Berisford who, by chance, had often sold supplies

39

to the old queen's household. Vallence beckoned him over, grasped his arm and whispered hoarsely, "St Denis! St Denis knows it all!".'

'What did he mean by that?' Chirke interrupted.

'I don't know. Vallence died a few minutes later.' Petrie stared into the fluttering candle flame. 'Some time later,' he continued smoothly, 'King Edward instructed Lord Stephen Berisford to investigate the circumstances surrounding Vallence's death. After all, Vallence had been mortally wounded in Berisford's ward and had been known to him, albeit tenuously.'

'Did Berisford explain why Vallence called him over or babbled about St Denis?'

'Yes, he did. Apparently Berisford sold supplies to Vallence for the Queen Isabella's household. Now and again they would talk about this or that – mere chatter. But he said he could not explain what Vallence meant; he thought he was simply delirious.'

'And the secret Vallence was supposed to be carrying?'

'We don't know whether it was a document or a verbal message. Whatever, at the beginning of November Berisford was commissioned to find out.'

Chirke looked askance. 'Some two months after Vallence's death?'

Sir Amyas smiled lazily. 'We, er, tried other means first. They proved fruitless so we went to Berisford.'

'Now Berisford is murdered!' Nicholas exclaimed. 'He was reported missing for days before his corpse was found in a thicket outside London?'

'Exactly,' Petrie replied. 'Let me explain. Berisford was a strange fellow. He was a coal and wood merchant with a house and yard next to the Thames near Westminster. He lived there with his old clerk, Mawsby.' Petrie stopped and looked at Chirke. 'Did you know Berisford?'

'No, but I had heard of him.'

'Yes, he was well known in legal circles. A tall, solitary man, he always wore a black, broad-brimmed hat and was for ever wiping his mouth with a rag. Still,' Petrie played with his wine goblet. 'A good justice, of Scottish extraction, Berisford was entrusted by the king to investigate this matter. Berisford may have been a melancholic man but he was most assiduous in his investigation. He questioned both Sir Ambrose Venner and Sir Oswald Cooper. However, a few days before his disappearance, last Saturday, the feast of St Luke, he began to prophesy his own death. He was playing at quoits when he abruptly broke off, exclaiming to a companion, "I cannot get along in your company." To another he said, "I am to be hanged." On another occasion his clerk, Mawsby, found him weeping as he ate a bowl of whey and brown bread. Mawsby asked him what was the matter and Berisford replied, "I am to be hanged, I am to be burnt!".'

Petrie looked up, staring hard at Chirke. 'Nicholas,' he said softly, 'I wanted the mayor to leave because what I have to tell you is for no one else's ears.' He paused as he heard a sound from the house below. 'Soon, kinsman,' he said quietly, 'you will meet our guests. However, I was talking about . . . ?'

'Berisford's state of mind.'

'Ah, yes. On Friday last, the day before he disappeared, he was sitting by his parlour fire when a cloaked and hooded messenger arrived with a letter for him. The man refused to enter the parlour but stayed outside in the passageway for an answer. Berisford opened the letter and quickly read it. He then became very agitated, walking up and down, and told Mawsby

41

to dismiss the messenger, shouting, "I shall do what he says! I shall do what he says!" Later the same day, he attended a meeting of the vestrymen in the church of St Martin-in-the Fields, where he was keeper of the books. He settled all his accounts and, when asked why he was so sad, replied, "Any man about to be burnt would be melancholic." '

Chirke shook his head in puzzlement. 'Why should a justice involved in royal business be frightened of being executed as a felon?' he asked. 'Was there more between him and Vallence than just a few supplies?'

'No.' Petrie replied, a little too quickly. He wetted his lips with his tongue and went on with his story.

'On the morning of Saturday last, Berisford rose very early. Mawsby heard him going through chests and boxes in his study, where he burned an armful of papers in the fire. After that he washed and dressed in black breeches, black hose and leather boots. He had a broad, white linen band around his neck. He asked for his good ring and silver-plated sword and took a large sum of money in silver coin. He asked Mawsby to bring him his new camlet cloak, but then changed his mind and snapped, "I'll wear the old one! It will serve the day well enough!" He then picked up his gloves and walked out. When he reached the bottom of the lane, he suddenly turned. Mawsby saw him looking sadly back at the house, almost as if he knew he was leaving for ever. He did not return that night. Mawsby searched but nothing was found.'

'Was Berisford seen again after he left his house?'

'Yes, he was – on Saturday afternoon near St Sepulchre's Church opposite Newgate and then again, at about one o'clock, not far away, at the entrance to Black Pig Alleyway in the Vintry near the Thames. On both occasions he was described as wild-

eyed and haggard by the citizen who caught a glimpse of him.'
Sir Amyas shrugged. 'He was not seen alive again.' He tossed
a small scroll of parchment at Chirke. 'That's the coroner's
findings on his corpse. There's plenty of mystery about
Berisford's death. For one thing, it might not be murder.'

'What do you mean?'

'Well, given Berisford's melancholic state of mind and the
fact that he appeared to fall on his own sword, many people
claim it was suicide.' Petrie smirked. 'For reasons of state we
do not publicly dispute such gossip.'

'But surely,' Nicholas said, 'a man's corpse can't lie in a
ditch for five days and no one notice it?'

Petrie smiled. 'Ah, there is a mystery! A number of witnesses
at the inquest said they had passed the ditch on Monday,
Tuesday, Wednesday and even Thursday morning and there
was no sign of the cane or gloves. Indeed, the ditch was
proclaimed clear of its grisly burden as late as one o'clock on
the Thursday that Berisford's corpse was found. Moreover, the
weather had been foul; there was a savage rainstorm on
Wednesday yet Berisford's clothes were relatively dry.'

'So!' Chirke exclaimed. 'The corpse must have been put
there between one o'clock and . . . ?'

'Five that Thursday.'

'But who could do that? You can't very well ride through
London with a body over your saddlehorn and throw it in the
ditch without being detected.'

'Exactly,' Petrie replied smoothly. 'The coroner's report
shows, though, that Berisford must have been dead for days.'

'Are there any suspects? I mean, if it is murder . . . ?'

Petrie grinned. 'Oh, yes, there's even been an arrest.'

Chirke straightened in his chair. 'So, why do you need me?'

'Pause a while, kinsman! Sebastian Fromlich, a tanner, of Leathercote Lane, has been arrested. He stands trial for his life before the justices next Friday. Now Fromlich, a tanner of Flemish extraction, bought both wood and coal from Berisford. His trade fell off and he was unable to pay his bills to Berisford so he spent three days in the Marshalsea. After he came out he was heard often, in the alehouses and taverns throughout the city, swearing his eternal hatred of Berisford and his desire for revenge. Fromlich cannot, or will not, account for his movements either for Thursday afternoon or for Saturday. And the Crown has valuable evidence against him.'

'Such as?'

'Come, come, Nicholas! The master sergeant-at-law, Sir Joseph Janneux, swears that Fromlich's refusal to account for his movements will send him to the scaffold.'

Chirke groaned and looked away. He knew Joseph 'Bull' Janneux. Bald-headed, with the battered, square-jawed face of a pugilist, Janneux was more frightening than the hangman and had reduced many a plaintiff to a quivering wreck. He also knew the sergeant's methods – London was full of professional witnesses ready to swear a man's life away for a paltry coin and Fromlich, a foreigner, would have few friends.

'Fromlich's in Newgate,' Petrie continued. 'Apparently the only person to stand by him is a distant kinswoman.'

'And the judges?' Chirke asked.

Petrie's eyes narrowed. 'Chief Justice Popham, aided and abetted by Justices Dolpen and Scroggs.'

'Oh, for the sweet Lord's sake!' Chirke exclaimed. 'Fromlich will be lucky if he is even heard!'

'Oh, he will be! You, Nicholas, are to be his attorney! Now the Judge's rules maintain the accused must defend himself but

44

there's nothing against you advising him.'

Chirke stared down at the floor. He sensed he was being nudged gently into a trap.

'Why?' he exclaimed. 'Why this mummery, this hypocrisy? Fromlich will hang, you know that!'

'The king has asked me to intervene in this but to keep my hand hidden.' Petrie leaned across the desk. 'Of course, Fromlich will hang. But he is innocent; the real murderer is someone else.'

'Such as?'

'Blueskin for a start!'

'Who, in sweet God's name, is he?'

'Well, Berisford was a harsh justice. A year ago, during a visitation of the plague, a notorious grave-robber nicknamed Blueskin nightly skulked in cemeteries and churchyards and, like the cur he was, dug up hundreds of corpses to steal their shrouds. He actually kept a store of these in a pest house, selling them to the newly bereaved so that they might bury their kin. After hunting him for months, Berisford seized Blueskin himself and had the fellow stripped to the waist and flogged around one of the churchyards he'd desecrated. A few nights later Blueskin attacked Berisford but the justice, no mean swordsman, had him arrested, flogged again and thrown in prison. Blueskin left the Fleet just two weeks before Berisford's mysterious disappearance. We have not been able to track him down.'

Chirke studied the sheriff's sly, close face.

'But you don't believe Blueskin's the murderer, do you, Sir Amyas?'

'No, Nicholas, I don't. Berisford was no coward and the likes of Blueskin wouldn't frighten him. But there is someone else in London's underworld,' the sheriff gave a short cough, 'who even I would fear – a dark, sinister, anonymous figure who regards himself as the Captain of London's underworld. He issues orders, marks people down for death and controls the naps and foists who pilfer other people's pockets, the swindlers and the footpads. He receives and sells stolen goods. No one knows him; his identity is one of the city's most closely guarded secrets. He proclaims himself the Guardian of the Gates. Any law officer who crosses him suffers. Any felon who disobeys an order will either get his throat cut or be captured by the thief-takers and end up on Tyburn scaffold.' The sheriff's voice fell to a whisper. 'From my legion of spies I know the Guardian of the Gates is also searching for the secret Vallence carried. And there are others, perhaps even the French . . .'

'And, of course, there are the aldermen who were present when Vallence died.'

'Ah, yes.' Sir Amyas smiled. 'I heard the door below open. Both Sir Ambrose and Sir Oswald have now joined us. We should go down to meet them.'

'What do you think happened, Sir Amyas?' Nicholas asked.

The sheriff shrugged. 'I believe Lord Berisford's investigations opened old wounds. Someone powerful threatened him, then killed him. And Fromlich will hang for it.'

'And what is it you want, Sir Amyas? Vallence's secret?' The sheriff laughed and clapped his kinsman on the shoulder.

'Of course! But you are to defend Fromlich. Perhaps you can save him. Perhaps we can find the true murderer? Perhaps you can find the old queen's secret and, in doing so, win the eternal friendship of His Grace the King, not to mention myself. And—'

'And perhaps, Sir Amyas,' Chirke swiftly interrupted, 'I could be killed!'

'Yes, Nicholas, there's every chance you might be!'

They went downstairs and into the snug parlour. A pine-log fire flickered in the grate. Scathelocke sat on a stool next to it whilst Hobbedon lounged against a square-topped table gazing quizzically at a colourful tapestry depicting Mars chasing Venus. The two men on either side of him were not so calm but fidgeted nervously, barely concealing their anger at being summoned and having to wait. They rose as Petrie and Chirke entered. Like Hobbedon, they were dressed in the long, sombre gowns of aldermen, though theirs were of costly taffeta, lined with thick strips of miniver: around their necks glittered heavy silver chains of office. Petrie stepped forward, hands extended.

'Sir Roger, I thank you for waiting with our guests. They have been offered wine?'

'And courteously refused it,' Hobbedon replied.

The two aldermen coldly received Sir Amyas's handshake and nodded at Chirke as the sheriff introduced him. Sir Ambrose Venner was tall and angular, with a sallow, unhealthy complexion; his eyes were almost hidden in the white, puffy flesh of his face. He had a scrawny black beard which clashed rather incongruously with his greasy, grey hair. Sir Oswald Cooper was small and squat and completely bald. His cheeks were fat and well scrubbed and, with his snub nose, prim lips and tufted hair in the corner of each of his protuberant ears, he reminded Nicholas of a fat little piglet. Scathelocke was ignored as Petrie ushered everyone to seats, clicking his fingers at Chirke to join him.

Sir Amyas then questioned both aldermen about their visit to St Bartholomew's, but their accounts tallied accurately – a little too accurately, Nicholas thought – with that given by the sheriff.

'We told all this,' Venner complained, 'to Berisford.'

Sir Amyas then asked them where they had been on the day Berisford disappeared and on the Thursday his corpse was discovered. Huffing and puffing in their self-importance, both aldermen rattled out their answers then sat in prim-lipped silence. Sir Amyas sighed and dismissed them. They both threw Chirke a contemptuous glance and strode out of the room. Sir Roger spread his hands, shrugged and followed them. Petrie heard their footsteps fade down the passageway then the front door open and close.

'What do you think, Nicholas?'

'Vallence's death was a mystery, but Berisford's is the one to resolve. Are you certain about the aldermen's whereabouts on the Saturday Berisford disappeared and on the Thursday he was discovered?'

Petrie stretched, flexing the muscles in his back.

'Yes, Nicholas, I am, as I am about the whereabouts of Sir Roger Hobbedon. On the Saturday and the Thursday all three were at home in their great mansions on the Strand. They each have an army of retainers who would take an oath on it. They were not seen abroad; no servants brought their boots, hats or cloaks; no horses were saddled.'

'They could all be involved in a conspiracy to obtain Vallence's secret.'

'I doubt it,' Sir Amyas said. 'Sir Roger may be the aldermen's friend but he knew nothing about Vallence and he never met Berisford.' Sir Amyas played with a ring on his finger. 'And what could they hope to gain from such a conspiracy? They only accompanied me to St Bartholomew's as official witnesses. True, they may have been intrigued, but any involvement with Berisford would have been noticed. In any great house there is always some servant ready to sell his master for thirty pieces

48

of silver. No, I am sure that neither Venner nor Cooper, nor Sir Roger – and I only include him because he is here today – had any hand in the murder of Lord Berisford.'

Sir Amyas abruptly turned to where Scathelocke still squatted moodily in front of the fire. 'Master Scathelocke, you are well?' The servant hardly raised his head.

'Good!' said Sir Amyas sarcastically. 'If you meet Christopher Ratolier, you will give him my regards?'

Scathelocke averted his face, but Nicholas saw him tense as if he had been struck a blow. Sir Amyas turned back to Nicholas.

'You have your instructions, kinsman. You will defend Fromlich and seek to resolve these mysteries.' He laughed abruptly. 'Though God knows where you will start.'

'Perhaps Fromlich can fill in the missing pieces to this ingenious plot,' Nicholas said.

Petrie just shrugged and tapped a booted foot on the floor. Nicholas realized they had now outstayed their welcome. He gathered up his cloak, gestured to Scathelocke to do likewise, and they took their leave. Outside, darkness was beginning to fall. Children skipped and ran, carrying small lanterns in their hands; they looked like fireflies in the gloom. A group of raucous young men, fresh from some tavern, bawled out a rude song, ignoring the angry looks of passers-by. Nicholas waited whilst Scathelocke hired a link boy from the doorway of a nearby tavern to go before them down the Strand and up Fleet Street. Just before they reached their house in Poultry, Nicholas dismissed the link boy and turned to his servant.

'You are quiet, Henry.'

Scathelocke looked away. 'Like you, master, I have been thinking about what I saw and heard – and that was little enough.' Scathelocke scratched his beard. 'It's a twisted plot,' he murmured.

49

Nicholas grasped his arm. 'And it becomes even more twisted, Henry. To Hell with Sir Amyas's furtive secrecy! Listen to this sinister tale . . .'

In his little garret at the top of an old house in Red Ferret Alley of Clerkenwell, the cunning man Crabtree was thinking about rats. He stood, answering nature's call in the empty grate, for he considered it was too cold to go down four flights of stairs to relieve himself in the street. He loudly cursed as he heard fresh squeaking and, turning, he glimpsed two small, black-furred bodies on the table-top, gnawing on a piece of bread left there the previous evening. Crabtree washed his hands in a bowl and, opening a leather sack, broke his fast upon loaves and a small jug of canary wine he had stolen from a dingy tavern outside Smithfield Market.

Crabtree sat on his dirty trestle bed and chewed hungrily on the bread, keeping a wary eye on the two rats, now scurrying about looking for further provender. The previous evening, he reflected, had been pleasant enough, a welcome relief after the rigours and stench of the Marshalsea prison where he had spent a week because a shopkeeper had claimed, fantastically, that he had stolen something from his stall. Crabtree stared down at his ragged clothes, now filthy after his stay in prison.

'You do not,' he declared to the rags, 'befit my position as a gentleman and are most derogatory to my status.'

The rats, impervious to Crabtree's short speech, scurried down the table-leg to root amongst the rushes on the floor.

'Mind you,' Crabtree murmured to himself, 'things have improved.'

He stared lovingly at the russet doublet tossed over the room's one and only stool. The clothing had come into Crabtree's possession by a stroke of good fortune. On his way back to his lodgings he had stopped to speak to a baker held in the stocks in Turner Street and, seeing the poor fellow was so miserable, Crabtree had sat and given him some counsel. He pretended to be solicitous, one of those lozenges of humility like Crabtree's father but really nothing more than a white sepulchre of sanctified hypocrisy.

'So,' he had asked the baker, 'why are you placed here?'

The baker, his head held tight in the wood slats, rolled his eyes heavenwards.

'The wardsmen,' he moaned. 'They came into my shop and found a pot of steaming jakes I'd brought down from my privy chamber. Lord knows, as I told the guild, I meant to toss it outside.'

'Wretched man!' Crabtree shouted. 'Your punishment is not severe enough!'

Whereupon he had sprung to his feet, removed the baker's doublet as well as his boots and left him in the stocks to repent further upon his sins.

Crabtree sighed and looked around. 'Nothing for me here,' he murmured to himself. He dressed quickly in his new clothes, left the house and wandered the streets, bowing most civilly to anyone he thought might be able to further his interests. He thought of trying to find Nicholas Chirke, but shook his head. He liked the lawyer, but Chirke's insistence on personal hygiene and constant strictures against roguery had eventually driven Crabtree to his own devices.

Crabtree soon tired of his walk. The city was noisome and dirty, the streets icy and the kennels full of filth and excrement. Despite the cold and frost, the stench from the dunghills and privies stung his nostrils. Crabtree was a country boy. He had

51

spent most of his life poaching in the fields and woods of Essex and he would never grow accustomed to the stench of London. Once again he thought wistfully of Chirke and wondered where his erstwhile protector was lodged. He stopped and leaned against a house wall, trying to ignore the crashing of carts and the incessant screeching of hucksters crying out 'Hot Pies!' 'Hot Food!'. Above him, women and children screamed messages down from open windows to people they knew in the street. Crabtree retreated further down a squalid alleyway, hardly a yard wide; there wasn't even room for mourners to get a coffin out without turning it on its edge and carrying it lopsidedly to a waiting cart on the corner.

Crabtree wandered on, found himself near St Paul's so he went across to the print sellers and searched amongst the ballad writers and scriveners for information. There was little news except the finding of Lord Berisford's corpse on Primrose Hill so Crabtree decided to walk towards Westminster. He stole a venison pastry from a baker's stall but it stank like the devil and after one bite he threw it away. He felt his stomach clench with hunger. He wandered into a church and crouched at the bottom of a pillar, listening to a mealy-mouthed friar savagely inveighing against the pleasures of the flesh, until a pretty, modest-looking maid caught his eye. The girl stood on the other side of the pillar and Crabtree spent the rest of the sermon trying to take her by the hand. At first the girl giggled but, as Crabtree became more importunate, she took a large pin out of her purse and threatened to prick him if he tried again. So he gave a loud belch and swaggered out of the church. In the porch he picked up a cloak from one of the hooks but cursed its threadbare nature for it had grown colder and the chill wind reminded him of his hunger.

Crabtree decided to return home. He kept an eye alert for the devil's men who came out of their rat holes as darkness fell to steal from the unwary – although he had little enough to steal. At the top of Red Ferret Alleyway, a beggar resting on a gnarled cudgel, waved his hand.

'My wounds,' the fellow bawled. 'Got in the king's wars! At Crecy and Sluys!'

He stretched out an arm; under his rags the skin was blistered and the flesh appeared all raw. Crabtree paused and stared hard at the man.

'You're a bloody liar!' he bellowed. 'You're a ruffler, a pretend hero with pretend wounds. How did you get these injuries, eh? It's amazing what unslaked lime and soap can do to the skin!'

Crabtree slapped the fellow on the shoulder, noting how the blue eyes suddenly became more calculating and the well-fed face under the chalk-dust turned hard and resolute.

'Get a good wash!' Crabtree laughed. 'And place some brown paper smeared with butter over your wounds and you will be as right as rain! Old Crabtree knows a faker when he sees one.'

He continued down the dark alleyway. He heard the ex-soldier hopping behind, still whining for alms. He placed his hand upon the latch of the house then froze, wincing as the cold steel pressed into the side of his neck.

'Turn round, Master Crabtree!' a voice said.

Crabtree did so slowly. The 'soldier' now stood, two good legs apart, his cudgel in one hand and in the other a long stiletto pricking gently at Crabtree's throat.

Crabtree smiled thinly. 'A clever ruse. A false soldier pretending to be a cripple who, in fact, is an assassin.'

'Never mind that!' the fellow snapped. 'No trickery, Master Crabtree!'

53

Crabtree stared, but his opponent's face was hidden by a deep-cowled hood. Crabtree relaxed, spreading his hands out.

'What do you want?'

'I want nothing,' the man replied. 'I bring a message from the Guardian of the Gates. You have heard of him?'

Crabtree's blood froze. 'Who hasn't?' he stammered.

He considered himself a first-rate thief and counterfeit man but the Guardian of the Gates was in another class, a veritable warlord amongst the real rogues of London's underworld.

'What does the Guardian want with me?' he spluttered.

The fellow pressed the dagger point a little deeper into his flesh.

'The Guardian wants nothing of you except that if your friend, Master Chirke, visits you and asks you questions you tell him nothing!'

'Questions about what?'

'About Blueskin.'

Crabtree grinned in relief. 'I have nothing to do with that grave-robber.'

'Good!' the man said softly. 'And you will have nothing to do with Chirke. Now, turn around, Master Crabtree, and close your eyes!'

Crabtree did as he was ordered, trying to control the trembling in his legs and the fear that curdled his stomach.

'I have done what you asked!' he whispered. 'I have done what you asked!' he repeated more loudly.

Hearing no response he turned, to find the darkened street empty, and silent except for a long, mocking laugh which came from the shadows at the top of the alleyway.

Chapter 3

On their return, Chirke and Scathelocke found John had already cleared the stalls, brought down the shutters and finished the day's trading. The merchant was busy in his counting house, the table in front of him covered with pieces of parchment and heaps of coins. As they passed he smiled cheerily and waved. The twins had turned the warm kitchen into a bowling alley and shrieked with delight when Scathelocke appeared. They dragged him to a bench, clamouring at him to finish the story he had begun early in the morning. Nicholas found Catherine in the stillroom preparing jam, jars of quince and other preserves. She smiled, kissed her brother on the cheek and absentmindedly commented on how her day had gone.

'And is all well with you?' she asked.

'I have a position.' He grinned. 'Great preferment.'

Catherine wiped her hands on her smock and clapped her hands with joy. She pushed her brother back into the kitchen and made him iterate and reiterate the terms Sir Amyas Petrie had offered. The noise in the kitchen increased as she insisted on making Scathelocke corroborate everything her brother had said. Nicholas warned his servant with his eyes not to mention anything about their task. Catherine, her cheeks pink with excitement, hurriedly served Nicholas and Scathelocke deep-bowled cups of wine before hurrying off to tell John the good news. A maid laid the table for supper, trenchers were scraped, knives scoured, napkins folded and the great silver salt cellar placed and uncovered. John came back, telling his two sons to be quiet whilst, once again, Nicholas told the story of his meeting with Sir Amyas Petrie. Then John in turn told the apprentices and servants of Nicholas's good fortune when they were summoned around the long table for the evening meal. Nicholas hid his disquiet and just sat there, a pleasant smile on his face, accepting their compliments and good wishes. Nicholas watched Scathelocke hungrily eat the dinner of beef, loin of veal and hot meat pies.

'Oh,' Catherine looked up, her face red from serving the hot meal. 'You had a message from Father Thompkins, he has a rheumy nose and is ill humoured. The meeting of the singers has been postponed for a week.' She saw the disappointment in her brother's eyes. 'Never mind,' she concluded. 'Perhaps next week. You can sing then and there is always Sunday.'

Nicholas smiled back. He had been looking forward to the singing. The music would have been soothing and also it would have provided him with a rare opportunity of meeting Priscilla Prudhomme. Across the table Scathelocke grinned and quietly shrugged his shoulders. John Gawdy ended the meal, satisfying himself that all had eaten and drunk well. The twins read from their horn books, their skill being greeted by a chorus of approval. Chirke glowered at their scrubbed-clean faces, he considered his nephews imps from hell and kept a wary eye on them. Prayers were said, Psalm 149 whilst Scathelocke, at John's bidding, read from the Book of Ecclesiastes on the virtues of hard work. Nicholas half-listened, his mind going back to the plump curves and coy looks of Mistress Priscilla. The prayers finished, John herded the twins up to their attic chamber. Catherine busied herself, calling for the maid to bring the spice account. Scathelocke muttered something about a meeting and slipped his cloak on.

'Come, Henry,' Nicholas said, grasping his servant's arm. 'Perhaps one more drink.'

He picked up his cloak and, before Catherine could interfere, they were through the door and stepping gingerly across the darkening streets to the Jester's Quill. The place was hot and crowded, still full of traders and those not wise enough to go back to their homes. Nicholas and Henry sat near the great roaring fire and waited till the tapster served them huge frothing tankards of ale.

'You think there's mischief in this?' Henry suddenly asked.

'In what?'

'In Berisford's death.'

'Of course, I have said as much. But, what it is only the good God knows!'

'I mean,' Scathelocke continued, warned by Nicholas's angry look, 'that the sheriff wants to use us like dogs sniffing out some hidden prey deep in the undergrowth. I don't think he will let us go until we have unearthed it.'

'And if we don't unearth it?'

Scathelocke smiled. 'Then it's back to St Paul's, walking up the Mediterranean and looking for business.'

Nicholas sighed. 'Tomorrow, Henry, go to the houses of Sir Amyas, Hobbedon and the alderman. Be prudent and make enquiries amongst their servants.'

'About what?'

'Well, find out if they noticed anything suspicious in the last week, especially on the Saturday Berisford disappeared or the Thursday his corpse was found.'

Scathelocke drained his tankard and made to get up. 'I have to go,' he muttered.

Nicholas grabbed him by the wrist.

'Where, Henry? Where are you going? Come on, tell me. And where do you come from? Who is Christopher Ratolier? And what do you do in your room all by yourself? Why did what the sheriff said frighten you?'

Scathelocke pulled his wrist away.

'Don't hold me like that,' he said. 'You're always asking questions. I may be your servant but I'm my own man.' He tapped the side of his head. 'In here I have no master. I am as good a man as you, Nicholas Chirke.'

'Are you, Henry?' Nicholas felt his own temper break. 'Are you really? Then why not tell me everything?'

Scathelocke glared back, his eyes cold and hard with the rage inside him.

'If I told you,' he rasped, 'you might not like it. If you told me about yourself, I might not like it. You remember that, master!' The words were spat out. 'I bid you goodnight!'

Scathelocke swept through the fug of stale sweat and Nicholas, blank-eyed, watched him go. He looked around, relaxed now, and grinned to himself. Perhaps his manservant was correct – the more you knew about someone the greater the dislike. And did Scathelocke know of his master's secret vices – the cup of red claret, the attraction of the older woman and, above all, the joys of gambling, the heady excitement of hazard, even though you knew your opponent was a sharper, that the cards were spurred and luck heavily biased against you? Nicholas looked around, but there was no opportunity to sin tonight, no card games, only the solace of a deep cup of claret. Nicholas called the tapster over and ordered another cup. He drank greedily. What should he do about Berisford's death, he wondered? What would he find out? He yawned and, realizing how tired he felt, left the cup half-finished and wandered back into the cold night air. A party of watchmen marched by, staffs and lanterns in their hands. The night was particularly cold and there was no sign of a break in the weather. He found the house silent; John and Catherine had retired to their own chamber and the children had gone to bed. The kitchen was cleaned and swept, the fire burnt low and the apprentices in their pallet beds around the room were lost in sleep. Nicholas made his way up to his own chamber. Catherine had provided two new candles. He lit them and looked around, revelling in the homeliness of it all – the clean swept chamber, the silver warming pan thrust deep beneath the coverlets of his bed.

He sat at his table and unrolled the coroner's report on Lord Berisford's death. First came the description; Berisford had been a bachelor, fifty-five years of age, with dark, heavy-lidded eyes, a large, beaked nose and a sallow complexion. Then followed the reports Sir Amyas had mentioned about Berisford's agitation the Friday before he disappeared and the statements of witnesses who had seen him near St Sepulchre's in the Vintry. Nicholas noted the coincidence – this was very near the area in which Fromlich lived. He also noted that the ditch was certainly empty of any corpse before one o'clock on Thursday, yet the body, its clothes still dry, was found there four hours later.

He was fascinated by the number of people – local farmers, peasants, tinkers and pedlars – who had sworn that no stranger, let alone any mysterious cart, had been seen in the locality. So, he wondered, when had Berisford's corpse been moved and

59

arranged in the ditch to make it look like suicide?

Then there was the sworn testimony of a clerk, Peter Cranfield, who had been in a barber's shop on the Tuesday before Berisford's body was discovered. A person came in and cried, 'Lord Berisford has been found!' 'Where?' asked both the barber and Cranfield. 'He has killed himself upon Primrose Hill!' the man replied. A clergyman, Odo Lightfoot, curate of St Dunstan's in the West, testified that he had gone with a friend to a parchment-seller in St Paul's churchyard. Lightfoot stayed outside the shop reading whilst his friend went inside. Suddenly a young man, his hat pulled down over his head, clapped Lightfoot on the shoulder and asked, 'Have you heard the news?' 'What news?' asked Lightfoot. 'Lord Berisford has been found.' 'Where?' 'In Leicester Fields at Dead Wall with his own sword run through him.' After that this mysterious bringer of news had disappeared.

Nicholas paid special attention to the conclusions of the physician, Jonathan Skillard, who had examined the cadaver:

Primo – There was no sign of blood on Berisford's clothing. So, Nicholas asked himself, had Berisford been stripped, killed and the corpse then dressed? If so, why?

Secundo – There was a swelling just under Berisford's left ear, as if a knot had been tied there.

Tertio – Blue-black bruises were on Berisford's face and covered his chest and stomach, showing that he had been stripped and beaten before being killed.

Quarto – Berisford had been dead for days. 'For,' Skillard reported, 'he had begun to putrefy and the flesh was so decayed it hung upon the incision knife.' So where had the corpse been kept? And how could it have been moved out to Primrose Hill and dumped so carefully in a ditch without anyone noticing?

Quinto – The neck was broken and so distorted that it had been possible for the doctor to take the chin and set it on either shoulder.

Sexto – There were two sword wounds in the chest. One stopped at a rib whilst the other cut right through the body, as if the killer had struck twice, his first sword thrust being blocked by the bone. Moreover, the absence of blood demonstrated that Berisford had already been dead when the sword thrusts occurred.

Septimo – Berisford had been strangled, hence the corpse's face was blotchy and the blood vessels of his eyes full to bursting.

Octavo – The linen band that Berisford had worn around his neck was missing.

Nono – Apart from the neck band, all of Berisford's possessions were on him, including the silver coins, so the motive for murder was not robbery.

Nicholas put the coroner's roll down.

'What,' he asked himself, 'had frightened Lord Berisford so much? Where had he been between the Saturday and the Thursday when his corpse was found?'

He stared into the guttering flame of the candle and, suddenly, remembered something. He went back to the coroner's roll and turned to a description of Berisford's black hose. Yes, there it was. Candle wax. Drops of beeswax candle had been found upon the dead man's clothing. Nicholas shook his head. A man like Fromlich, he mused, could hardly afford such expensive candles. A tanner would have to be content with greasy tallow light. He smiled thinly – such an observation would not save Fromlich from the hangman's noose.

He drummed his long fingers on the table top and speculated

61

on the other mysteries posed by the coroner's report. Who were these strangers who knew so much about Lord Berisford's whereabouts? Both had reported that Berisford had committed suicide but why had one given the right location whilst the other had mentioned Leicester Fields? And the physician's evidence was confusing. What were those black bruises all over Berisford's chest and abdomen? Why the bruise under his left ear? Had he been strangled or hanged?

Nicholas went back to the coroner's evidence, but this only confused rather than clarified matters as he picked out further items, such as the state of Berisford's boots – they were clean and polished, which proved that Berisford had never walked on the muddy fields of Primrose Hill. So he must have been taken there by carriage or horse. But surely someone would have seen this? Nicholas's tired brain spun like a top. And the murderer? Chirke smiled thinly. The list of suspects, he thought, like the devils in the gospel, were legion. Was it the alderman? Was it Blueskin settling a score? Or some other rogue from the cesspool of London's underworld? Or the mysterious Guardian of the Gates?

'Why stop there, Nicholas my boy?' he murmured to himself. 'What about the powerful ones? Did the king really want Berisford to find something? Or did the sheriff have a hand in it? Or the mayor? And why was it so important for Fromlich to hang?' Nicholas's eyes closed. Tomorrow, he thought grimly, he must visit Fromlich in the death cell at Newgate. He opened his eyes suddenly and gazed around the darkening chamber. And what about Isabella, the dead queen mother? Had she communicated some great secret to Vallence, verbally or in writing? If it was the latter, where could it be? Why had the dying Frenchman summoned Berisford over? What did he mean by St Denis? Was Berisford, in some subtle way, connected to the dead queen's secret? And why was the king so insistent on its discovery?

For a while Nicholas stared into the darkness. '*Primo*,' he whispered, 'Vallence did not want to be taken alive. Any secret he held must have been committed to memory, hence he resisted, fearful of torture. *Secundo*, the king, or rather Sir Amyas on his behalf, tried to discover that secret but achieved no success. *Tertio*, they remembered Vallence's plea to Berisford so they commissioned him to continue their search – or did they just hope to frighten him? *Quarto*, what was Berisford so terrified about?' Nicholas scratched his head. What else? 'Ah, *quinto*, who visited Berisford the evening before his disappearance? What message did he bring? *Sexto*, Fromlich – he is a sacrificial lamb, but why? *Septimo*, how is a rogue like the Guardian of the Gates involved?' A shiver ran up Nicholas's spine. He truly felt he was about to enter the shadows of the Valley of Death.

Nicholas Chirke got out of bed the next morning. He looked through the small casement window and groaned. In the half-light outside, the fog was as thick as steam in a bath-house. He lit a candle and slowly began to dress. All around him the house was still quiet. He opened his door and listened, thanking God the twins were still in bed. He had heard Scathelocke come back late so he decided to let him sleep and to make up their quarrel later. He buckled on a broad sword belt, making sure both rapier and dagger would slip easily in and out of their sheaths, and went downstairs. The fires in the kitchen were still banked. A sleep-laden servant girl was busy preparing the table. Nicholas seized bread and some dried meat from the scullery and hurried out. The roads and alleys of Cheapside were quiet in the freezing cold morning; lantern horns still winked their light and an occasional torch spluttered vainly in the gloom. The people he met were like wraiths; they slipped silently by, cloaks tight about them, their hoods pulled close. Most of them were officials or members of the court, with the occasional lady of the night, flitting like a bat back to her nest before dawn. Carts rattled by, all the more sinister as the horses were urged on by dark, muffled figures. Chirke slipped and slithered down the frosty track between the houses up to where Newgate loomed gloomily through the mist opposite St Sepulchre's church.

Newgate was a foul, noisome gaol. The great towered gateway, battlemented and fearsome, stared out over Snow Hill, where the guts, dung and blood from the butchers' stalls poured down refuse-filled gutters to Fleet Street. Nicholas stopped and stared up at the noisy windmill above the gate, which churned feebly to provide fresh air – Newgate was such a narrow place that there was very little chance for air to circulate. Even in broad daylight, its runnels were lit by link lights. Nicholas pulled at the bell and, after a sharp quarrel with a guard, a postern door was opened. Nicholas stepped into the porter's lodge, a great flagstoned chamber lit by greasy lights and smelling worse than a pig sty. He was questioned by the head gaoler, a narrow, yellow-faced fellow dressed completely in black, with gloomy eyes and skull-like features. Nicholas recognized him from his nickame, 'the parson'. The man's lizard eyes hardly flickered in a face devoid of expression as Nicholas explained his errand. 'The parson' examined the warrants Sir Amyas had signed, nodded, snapped his fingers and led Nicholas down torchlit passageways. They crossed the Press Yard where felons who refused to plead were crushed to death under a huge, metal-embossed door. Nicholas caught a glimpse of this and his stomach lurched at the dark red bloodstains which coated the crushing side of the great slab of wood.

They went through the common side where felons, male and female, awaited trial. The stench was terrible, composed of unwashed bodies, tallow candles, and that most dreadful of odours, anger and despair at imminent death. Eventually they turned down a passageway, and guards, their faces black with dirt, their 'uniforms' nothing more than motley collections of gaudy rags, unlocked thick doors. 'The parson' led Nicholas down a dark tunnel, past a row of grill-faced doors. He stopped before one of these, took a key from his belt, unlocked the door and ushered Nicholas into a cell that was really nothing more than a cavern. The air was fetid. There were no windows and two buckets full of human excrement stood just within the door. A man loaded with chains around his ankles and wrists staggered to his feet. In the dim light Nicholas caught a glimpse of black-ringed, staring eyes, straggly hair and beard and a haggard, despairing face.

'Who are you?' the man grated.

'Nicholas Chirke, lawyer. And you?'

'Sebastian Fromlich.'

Chirke turned to 'the parson'.

'As I have said,' he explained, 'I am here on the orders of those who can make their influence felt. I want candles brought, the best wine and those buckets removed, now!'

The death-head's face of the gaoler remained impassive.

'Well, sir, I am waiting!'

The fellow stared coolly back.

Nicholas dipped into his purse and handed over two coins. What passed for a smile crossed the gaoler's face. The coins disappeared, orders were shouted and a trail of dirty servitors cleared the cell. A jug of wine and two cups were brought, together with thick, heavy tallow candles in brass holders. Nicholas pronounced himself satisfied. Then, as an afterthought, he said, 'I'll need a chair as well.'

This, too, was brought, though Nicholas looked suspiciously at its cracked legs and splintered wood. Nevertheless, aware of Fromlich's growing nervousness, he wanted to get rid of the gaoler, so he made no complaint. At last the cell was cleared, the gaoler locking the door behind him, though Nicholas, through the grille, saw that he remained standing outside. Nicholas gestured to Fromlich to sit quietly whilst he dragged the chair alongside him, so close that any spectator would have thought he was a priest preparing to hear the man's last confession.

'I have come to help you,' he said. He saw hope flare in the prisoner's eyes. 'And believe me,' he added quickly, 'you need all the help you can get! You stand accused of the murder of Lord Stephen Berisford.'

The man nodded anxiously.

'I am innocent!' Fromlich exclaimed.

Nicholas caught the faint trace of a foreign accent in the man's voice.

'Did you make threats against Lord Berisford?' he asked, leaning so close that his face was only a few inches away from that of the prisoner. 'I want the truth.' He rasped. 'Lie just once and I will walk from this cell and leave you to the hangman.'

'I made threats,' Fromlich replied sullenly. 'Berisford may have been a just man but he was a harsh one.'

'Did you threaten to kill him?'

'Yes, I did.'

'Did you kill him?'

66

'No, I did not.'

'Do you know anything about a man called Vallence?'

Fromlich looked puzzled and shook his head. Nicholas studied him closely. He felt the man was telling the truth.

'Where were you on Saturday night?'

'Which Saturday?'

'Last Saturday?'

Now Fromlich looked away. 'I can't tell you,' he mumbled.

'Why can't you?' Nicholas snapped.

'I can't remember.'

'Where were you on Thursday last, late in the afternoon?'

Again the man shook his head. 'I don't know. I can't remember.'

Nicholas stood up. 'Then, Master Fromlich, you will hang and there is nothing you, I, your kinswoman or the good Lord in heaven can do to save you.'

'Wait!'

Nicholas turned.

'I'll tell you. But my kinswoman must not know,' Fromlich pleaded. 'On both occasions, on the Saturday and the Thursday, I was in my shop, but it was closed up.'

'Can you produce any witnesses to that?'

'Yes and no.'

'What do you mean?'

Fromlich put his face in his hands and quietly sobbed before raising his tear-stained face.

'You promise,' he pleaded. 'You will not tell anyone?'

'For God's sake, man. What's so dreadful?'

'I remember both days well,' Fromlich said haltingly. 'On the Saturday I was in my workshop when I saw this beautiful girl in the street outside. Master Chirke, she had a face like an

67

angel; her hood was half-pulled back and I glimpsed golden curls. She wore a bottle-green dress with crisp white linen around her neck. She was delicate, pretty in all her movements.' Fromlich licked his lips. 'I could see she was no street walker or common whore. I went out and asked her business. She talked most prettily and claimed she was interested in buying strips of leather. Well, the street was cold and deserted and, although I live in a small house in Budge Row, I have lodgings behind the workshop.' The man sighed. 'To cut a long story short, the girl – she said her name was Lucy – tarried and grew flirtatious.' He shrugged. 'You know the way of the world, master lawyer. A touch led to a kiss, a kiss to other things.' Fromlich stared bleakly around the cell. 'She was unlike anything I have ever seen before. Her dress, her stockings, her garters were pure silk.'

Nicholas stared at him in disbelief. 'Master Fromlich, you expect me to believe that some high-class courtesan turned up at your workshop and, without gold or silver, served you so well?'

'Oh, there's more, Master Chirke,' Fromlich replied sourly. 'I begged the girl to return and she said she would but that it would have to be most secretly because she was the mistress of an old merchant with a great house in West Cheapside.'

'And she came back?'

Fromlich nodded. 'On Thursday, about noon. I made sure my apprentice had gone to the market in Aldgate Street.'

Nicholas groaned and got up, kicking the chair away from him.

'Master Chirke,' Fromlich said, 'the girl can surely be found!'

Nicholas rubbed the side of his face, turned and bent over the haggard-faced prisoner.

'Oh, for God's sake, Fromlich, can't you see? You were

trapped. There'll be no Lucy. There'll be no old merchant in Cheapside. The girl was probably some high-class whore. On the day Berisford disappeared you say that you were with a beautiful girl behind the locked shutters of your workshop. On the Thursday afternoon, when the Crown will prove Berisford's body was dumped in a ditch on Primrose Hill, you were again locked in your workshop with this mysterious wench. For God's sake, man, who will believe you? What proof do you have? And,' Nicholas continued despairingly, 'if you deny the girl and say you were in your workshop, the prosecution will produce witnesses, as they surely will, Master Fromlich, who will claim they went to your workshop and found it empty.'

Fromlich sagged to his knees, hands clasped together.

'Master Chirke, I beg you to help me! Whatever I did, whatever I said, I did not kill Justice Berisford!'

Nicholas sat down again on his chair. 'Sit up, Fromlich,' he ordered. 'For pity's sake, sit up. Look at me.'

Fromlich raised his head and Nicholas saw the tear streaks on the man's grimy face.

'Do you have a cart?' Nicholas asked wearily.

'Yes, yes, of course I do!'

Nicholas's heart sank and he stared up at the black stone ceiling. Fromlich, he concluded, had both the motive and the means to kill Berisford. The fool had announced his intention and could produce no real evidence of his whereabouts either for the day Berisford had disappeared or the afternoon his corpse was found.

'Can you help me?' Fromlich wailed.

'Yes, yes,' Nicholas lied and patted him on the shoulder. 'I shall return.' He smiled down at Fromlich. 'Let me make my own enquiries.'

69

Nicholas hammered on the door. 'The parson' let him out and took him silently along the disgusting runnels back through a postern gate in the main door, which he slammed shut behind the lawyer.

'Master Chirke, you are the lawyer, Chirke?'

Nicholas leaned against the brickwork. The woman addressing him was petite; her skin was white as snow, her large eyes kind, even saucy. She moved closer and Nicholas forgot his troubles as he smelt her heavy, musky perfume. The woman was swathed in a cloak from her neck down to just above her shiny brown leather boots. He glimpsed a golden rose on the instep and the white linen of her petticoats.

'Who are you?' he asked.

'Helen Fromlich.'

She looked around uneasily at the throng outside Newgate – pickpockets, knaves and other disreputables as well as the families of bankrupts and other people trying to gain access to their loved ones.

'I would like to talk to you about my kinsman,' she murmured. 'But not here.'

Chirke glanced about. He understood the woman's unease and realized that it was not due entirely to the unsavoury people around them. He felt sure they were being watched. He stared across the street.

'Over there.' He indicated with a nod of his head the dingy Devil's Cauldron tavern, which stood on a corner opposite St Sepulchre's church.

He took her gently across the muddy lane, avoiding the carts and the gout-legged horses who pushed their way to Smithfield. Outside the tavern a pedlar stood on a small plinth of stone, bawling out that he had cures for corns, glass eyes for the blind, and ivory teeth for broken mouths. A party of young bloods in resplendent colours, the sleeves of their jerkins puffed out, stood around him, their small cloaks hanging jauntily from one shoulder as they shouted abuse at the poor fellow. They turned as Nicholas tried to push through them and there were murmurs, catcalls and whistles of approval as they saw Mistress Fromlich. One young gallant turned, moving obscenely to display his extraordinarily large codpiece. Others blew kisses from carmine-painted lips. Nicholas's hand felt his sword hilt, but a bawd slipped between him and the group, her dyed red hair piled high on her head, a small monkey sat on her shoulder dressed in cap and bells, its dirt staining her sagging bodice. The young men now turned their attention to her. Nicholas sighed with relief and entered the warm, sombre taproom, Mistress Fromlich tripping breathlessly behind him. They secured an empty table in the far corner. Mistress Fromlich ordered a glass of warm cordial but Nicholas took wine, his stomach still queasy after his visit to Newgate.

'You are Fromlich's kinswoman?'

She nodded.

'Why do you want to see me, mistress?'

He studied the woman carefully as she folded her hood back to reveal an unruly mop of red curls. Mistress Fromlich, with her elegant dress and carefully painted face, was a toothsome wench. He felt a stir of excitement in his loins just staring at her and wondered if he should visit his widow friend, Mistress Sachet, in her cosy little house near Rolls Passage off Eastcheap.

'You're staring, sir.'

Chirke smiled apologetically.

'I did ask you a question. You want my help?'

'Yes, to prove my kinsman's innocence.'

71

'What makes you think he is guiltless?'

'I know he is.'

'How do you know that I have been visiting your kinsman in Newgate?'

She smiled wanly. 'One of the gaolers told me.'

'And how do you think I can help?'

'No one else will.'

'Who else have you asked?'

'Chief Justice Popham.'

Chirke groaned. Mistress Fromlich had indulged in the increasingly popular practice, frowned upon by the authorities, of securing a private interview with a royal justice in the hope of influencing him. But Popham, who was to try Fromlich, was a florid-faced bully with a savage dislike of women. And he delighted in issuing the death sentence with as much relish as a priest a benediction.

'And what,' Nicholas asked, 'did Justice Popham say?'

The woman blushed. 'I saw him in his private chamber. He offered to help, if . . .' She paused.

'If what?'

'If I first let him discipline me.' The woman's eyes filled with tears. 'And I had to agree.'

Chirke squirmed on his bench. Popham was a bully, a shrewd but cruel and vindictive judge. He had once interrupted some poor lawyer whose plea he thought to be taking too long and sentenced him to walk around Westminster Hall with his documents slung around his neck.

'Popham,' Nicholas observed, 'likes to humiliate people. My advice, Mistress Fromlich, is to stay well away from him. I believe your kinsman is innocent.' He was glad to see relief soften the woman's expression. 'However,' he continued hastily, 'there have been other developments and proving his innocence is a totally different matter. Your kinsman has yet to account for his movements last Saturday and Thursday. He cannot, at least not openly in court.'

'Tell me.' The woman's eyes fluttered. 'What is behind all this?'

Nicholas moved his wine cup aside and leaned across the table.

'Lord Berisford disappeared last Saturday. His body was left on Primrose Hill some time in the afternoon the following Thursday. On both occasions your kinsman, Mistress Fromlich, cannot produce one witness to account for his movements.'

He caught the worried expression in his companion's eyes.

'There is worse. Everyone knows about your kinsman's threats against Berisford. Witnesses will come forward to offer testimony.'

'They are liars!' the woman exclaimed.

'Can you prove that?'

'No,' she whispered. 'What else can my kinsman face?'

'God knows,' Nicholas answered with mock cheerfulness. 'But there are a number of interesting questions he can ask to create doubt in the jury's mind. First, we have the testimony of two witnesses that Berisford's death was well known in the city. Secondly, how could your kinsman transport the justice's corpse to Primrose Hill and not be seen? Thirdly, if Master Fromlich – and I say "if" – killed Lord Berisford, why not just throw the corpse into the river? Finally, mistress, if your kinsman did plan Berisford's death, his lack of a subtle defence could prove a saving grace.'

'But you think he will hang?'

Nicholas studied the woman's pretty face.

'Yes,' he murmured. 'Unless we find other evidence, and I doubt if we will, your kinsman will hang.'

The woman sighed deeply and rose. 'Well, Master Chirke, do what you can. You will have my undying gratitude. I shall never forget.'

Nicholas swallowed hard. Mistress Fromlich clasped his hand in hers and, gathering her skirts, daintily picked her way around the table and out of the door.

Nicholas sat and watched her go. He hired a candle, because the tavern was dark, drew out the coroner's now greasy report and once again studied it. He was still puzzled by the elaborate lengths taken to abduct Berisford, torture him, kill him and leave the corpse in the most unlikely place. It seemed that the murderer had wanted to extract some information from Berisford and had then arranged for Fromlich to be incriminated. Nicholas had no doubt that the courtesan sent to entertain Fromlich in his workshop had been paid by Berisford's murderer. And who could afford her services? Someone very wealthy as well as cunning? Some lord? Or the Guardian of the Gates?

Nicholas sat back on the bench and wondered whether Scathelocke had carried out the errands he had asked him to do. He regretted their quarrel the previous evening and quietly vowed to make amends for the ceaseless questioning of his hapless servant. Finally, there were Catherine's constant silent reproaches. Nicholas's eyes half-closed. Should he forgive his brother Robert for winning the heart of Beatrice, the love of Nicholas's life? Should he go back to Norwich and make his peace with Robert and the rest of his family? Perhaps settle there? Since the quarrel, Nicholas had felt himself floating, letting circumstance dictate the tenor of his life. Now there was this business. He had no doubts that Sir Amyas Petrie was using him. Would it lead to preferment? Or disgrace? Or worse?

Nicholas shook himself free of his reverie. Sir Amyas had mentioned Blueskin and perhaps it was time he made enquiries about whether the grave-robber had had a hand in Berisford's murder. Then he started as a hand clutched his arm.

'Master lawyer, do you remember me?'

Chirke looked down at a dwarf of a man, no more than four foot high, whose crimped hair framed a wizened face covered in cheap paint. The man was dressed in cheap, garish clothes – his jerkin and hose were of vari-coloured tawdry taffeta and his codpiece was of unbelievable size. His fingers were covered in a shimmering mass of cheap stones. Nicholas stared at the grinning face and the huge tankard the mannikin held in his right hand.

'Of course, Bogbean!' He sighed. 'How could I forget you?' He nodded at the tankard. 'What are you doing, supping from it or having a bath?'

Bogbean laughed, a deep rich sound, surprising from someone so small.

'I have been watching you, lawyer,' he said. 'You look troubled?'

'You are a perceptive man, Bogbean.'

'And I know why.'

'Oh?'

'A man has been watching you. Now he has left and is waiting outside for you.'

'Do you know who he is?'

Bogbean shook his head. Nicholas pushed a coin towards him.

'There you are, Bogbean. Something for your trouble. When I leave, make sure my mystery pursuer does not follow.'

75

Bogbean smiled and skipped away. Nicholas got up and pushed his way out of the tavern. Outside the cold air hit him like a blast from a trumpet. He shivered and made his way down Holborn. He grinned as he heard a crash and a yell. He looked swiftly back; Bogbean was dancing furiously around a cloaked figure lying prostrate outside the tavern door. The little man was screaming and screeching, peppering his questions with coloured oaths and filthy words as he told the fallen unfortunate to take more care where he walked.

Nicholas hurried up the street and down a darkened alleyway that led into Dyer Lane. He felt tired and cold. He stopped, wondering whether he should return to Catherine and put her mind at ease about Robert. He leaned sideways to scratch his leg, certain he had picked up fleas in the dingy taproom. He felt a brush of air pass his right ear and a broad-bladed throwing dagger sank deep into the timber of the house beside him. He stared around, terror replacing fatigue.

'When in doubt,' he whispered to himself, 'run!'

And, gathering his cloak about him, he charged down the alleyway, knocking beggars aside. He ran until he reached Dyer Lane, then walked quickly along Bowyers Row and into Fleet Street, where he hired a ride from a carter. He did not feel at ease until he stood outside a tall old house in Rolls Passage near the Inns of Court. He wondered whether the recent attacker was a common footpad or whether the assault was linked to the matter he was investigating. Who had been pursuing him – a Chancery spy or a minion of the Guardian? He did not really care. He was tired and cold. He wanted to hide and sleep. Tomorrow he would think and scheme.

He tapped gently on the door of the house and, as footsteps sounded on the stone-vaulted passageway beyond, he silently drew his dagger. The woman who opened the door was tall, with black hair betraying silver, greyish tints. Large dark eyes gazed solemnly out of a creamy, heart-shaped face; sensuous lips, half-parted, displayed white even teeth. The woman's dress was of dark taffeta with linen-edged cuffs. Above her dark thick-soled shoes Nicholas glimpsed a white kirtle.

'What do you want, sir?' she asked, her eyes rounding in alarm. Nicholas pushed the door open and stepped inside, his dagger only a few inches away from the woman's full bosom. She stepped back.

'What do you want?' she cried again. 'I have but little silver.'

'I want you.'

'Oh, sir, please!'

Nicholas pushed the dagger closer. 'Your choice is clear, mistress.'

The woman stepped back, her hands to her lips.

'You have been watching me,' she murmured. 'My maid has gone. The manservant is out on errands.'

Nicholas heard a sound from the room at the end of the passageway. He smiled and shook his head.

'I think you lie, mistress. So, quietly, up the stairs.'

The woman, softly protesting, led Nicholas up into a spacious bedchamber made cosy by the rich woollen tapestries on the wall. Small rugs covered the polished floor and the oaken furniture gleamed with reflections from the fire burning merrily in the grate. Nicholas pushed the woman towards the great four-poster bed with its gold-edged bolsters and heavy green tester.

'What do you do, sir?' she cried.

Nicholas sat on the bed, cradling the dagger in his hands.

'Undress!' he ordered.

'No, sir, I will not!'

'Undress!' he snarled.

Slowly the woman undid the belt and buttons of her dress, shrugging it off.

'Everything!' Nicholas ordered, not content until the woman's Junoesque body, white as pure marble, stood in a circle of taffeta.

'Now,' Nicholas said thickly. 'Come here!'

The woman, her hands clasped before her, walked slowly towards him.

'Let your hair down!'

The woman's hands went up, plucking out her silver comb so that her dark tresses fell like a veil to her shoulders. Nicholas stood and embraced her, pressing her softness against him.

'Mistress Sachet,' he murmured through the perfumed tendrils of her hair, 'I have missed you dearly!'

The woman's arms went around his neck and she grinned mischievously.

'Nicholas,' she murmured. 'I have missed you, too!' She stroked his face. 'Last time you'd been drinking and stood outside singing a love song.' She giggled. 'What next?'

Chapter 4

Afterwards Nicholas lay on his side, staring into the darkness, listening to the woman's gentle breathing beside him. Outside the wind had picked up, rattling the horn-covered windows and making the old timbers creak and groan. Nicholas smiled to himself as he thought of Mistress Sachet and the comforts of her warm, plump body. He had known her since he had been a ragged-bottomed student at Pegasus grappling with the finer points of English law. They had become lovers and close friends. He found her the most selfless person he had ever met – asked for nothing except for companionship. He always teased that when he became Lord Chancellor she would be the grandest lady in court. He stirred as the bells of St Etheldred's chimed for compline and quietly got out of bed. He kissed the sleeping woman, dressed and stole silently down the stairs. He stepped out into the street, gazing warily around. He knew he was in danger and, in that moment, sensed his own weakness. As always, he was refusing to grapple with the central problem: he had drawn no pattern to explain the killing of Berisford and, in his mind, Nicholas still refused to accept that his own life was in danger.

Keeping close to the shadows, he made his way back through

the silent streets. He was about to turn a corner when he recoiled in fright as a figure slipped out of the darkness before him.

'Peace, master!' Scathelocke's cheery voice sang out.

'For God's sake!' Nicholas snarled. 'Must you creep around like a thief in the night?'

Scathelocke grinned, the harsh words of the previous evening now forgotten.

'I have missed you, master.'

In using the word 'master', Scathelocke was, Nicholas realized, being gently sardonic.

'My name is Nicholas.' He protested. 'And I have just had a knife thrown at me.'

Scathelocke, suddenly grim-faced, loomed closer. He caught the fragrant smell of Mistress Sachet and forgot his teasing. In the poor light Nicholas's face looked ghostly, drawn and white.

'Well, there's no comfort back there,' Scathelocke said, indicating with his head. 'Mistress Catherine has declared war on the twins. Even Master John has gone into hiding.'

He coaxed Nicholas further up the street and into a small alehouse.

'So, you have been attacked?' he asked as he gently directed his master to a stool and pulled another up close to him. 'Was it a footpad or is it connected with Berisford's death? For I have news on that.'

Chirke drank the wine Scathelocke ordered, then rubbed his eyes.

'It's all connected,' he said, 'but the knife thrower could be anybody – an assassin sent by God knows who?' He forced a smile. 'Well, what's your news?'

'Fromlich is dead,' Scathelocke replied simply, 'and so is his kinswoman.'

The cup slipped from Nicholas's hand. He felt himself sway and gripped the table-top.

'How can that be?' he asked.

'A message came about an hour ago from Sir Amyas Petrie. Fromlich was visited in prison by a friar, an elderly man, who said he had been sent by you to give Fromlich some comfort. He apparently bribed a gaoler to bring some wine. He talked a while and, when he left, Fromlich was still alive. The gaolers brought some food round and found Fromlich dead in his cell. The poison in his wine cup would have killed an ape from Barbary.'

'I sent no friar.'

'Of course not!'

'When did this happen?'

'At about four o'clock. About an hour later, according to an eyewitness, Mistress Fromlich was visited at her house in Candlewick Street by an old lady who said she had a present and a message from you. Shortly after the old lady left a neighbour went up and noticed blood seeping under the door of Mistress Fromlich's chambers.' Scathelocke sighed. 'The door was eventually forced. Mistress Fromlich was found slouched in a chair, her throat gashed from ear to ear.' He picked up a goblet and sipped from it. 'Now who would want to kill a poor prisoner, probably innocent of any crime other than cursing Berisford, and murder a middle-aged spinster apparently just because she was the prisoner's kinswoman?'

Nicholas jerked upright on his stool.

'What is it, master?' Scathelocke asked anxiously.

'Mistress Fromlich!'

'What about her?'

'You called her middle-aged, a spinster?'

81

'That's how Sir Amyas described her – as quite old and rather deaf.'

He saw the colour drain from his master's face.

'I met a woman outside Newgate this morning,' Nicholas stammered, 'who claimed to be Fromlich's kinswoman. She was young and very pretty.' He put his face in his hands. 'Oh, God save you, Nicholas Chirke, you are a fool!' he exclaimed. 'Fromlich told me that on the day Berisford disappeared, and on the following Thursday when the corpse was discovered, he was being entertained in his workshop by a young courtesan. The woman I met outside Newgate was probably the same person, only this time she pretended to be Fromlich's kinswoman. I told her everything I knew.' Nicholas gritted his teeth. 'I was so certain,' he breathed. 'She acted the part so convincingly.'

Scathelocke leaned over and patted his master on the shoulder.

'Well, at least it proves one thing. The woman who entertained Fromlich and the woman who duped you this morning were the same artful courtesan. Only the Guardian of the Gates is capable of organizing such deception. Ergo, he must have had a hand in Berisford's death. *Quod est demonstrandum*!'

Chirke stared into his cup. 'You're right,' he groaned. 'The Fromlichs were used. When their usefulness came to an end, Fromlich was murdered in case, somehow or other, he should escape the hangman's noose. His poor kinswoman died to cover this morning's deception and to warn me that the Guardian controls this city.'

'I also made another discovery,' Scathelocke declared.

'Which is?'

'The two aldermen and Sir Amyas Petrie have great houses in the Strand. Venner and Cooper are married. Petrie is a

widower – his wife died some years ago of a malignant disease.'
Scathelocke sighed. 'All three are very wealthy men – their
houses are three or four storeys high and have gardens that
stretch down to the Thames. I mingled with their servants,
talking to ostlers, grooms, retainers in the nearby taverns.'
Scathelocke grinned. 'I drank a little and learnt a lot. Venner
and Cooper were both at St Albans on the Saturday Berisford
disappeared.'

'And Petrie?'

'He was in his chancery all day. I talked to his groom as well
as his clerk of the chamber.'

'You are sure of that?'

'As I am sitting here.'

'And on the Thursday Berisford's body was discovered?'

'All three dined in a tavern, the Broadsword, in Feltop Lane
just off the Strand. They returned much the worse for drink.
They were scarcely capable of lifting a glass, much less of
carrying a corpse through St John's Wood to Primrose Hill.'

Scathelocke stared into his goblet. 'Master,' he continued
softly, 'I am sorry we quarrelled last night.'

Nicholas smiled and shrugged. 'No, Henry, *I* apologize. I
have a lawyer's inquisitive turn of mind. Your secrets are your
own – though I am still curious.' He saw the anger flare in his
servant's eyes and continued quickly, 'But *quieta non movere*
– "let sleeping dogs lie".'

Scathelocke took a deep breath. 'So where now, master?'

Nicholas grinned. 'I don't know, but let's drink to the truth,
as well as to friendship!'

Much later than they had intended, Nicholas and Scathelocke
staggered out of the tavern, all their problems forgotten as they
lurched home, trying to sing in harmony the new madrigal Father

Thompkins had introduced. They had forgotten all about Catherine, but she had not forgotten them. She sat in the kitchen, bright-eyed with anger, and studied the two swaying men, arms around each other's shoulders, as they blinked vacuously at her.

'You stink of wine!' Catherine cried. 'You wander around the city late at night. We don't know where you are. You arrive home at a God-forsaken hour!' She dabbed her eyes with a napkin. 'And I, your sister, am sick with worry.'

Scathelocke tried to intervene but Catherine turned her full fury on him.

'You, sire!' she roared, 'will keep your mouth shut!'

Scathelocke pulled a face and stepped hastily back. Nicholas tried to retreat to his bedchamber. Even though he was full of rich claret and good cheer, Nicholas knew his sister; usually mild-mannered, she now bore down on him like a vengeful warship. At last, he just sat near the inglenook, Scathelocke like a shadow beside him, whilst Catherine gave him a sharp-tongued lecture on what was wrong.

Why didn't he make his peace with their brother Robert? True, true, Beatrice had married Robert but was that the end of the world? Weren't there other fish in the sea?

'I don't want a fish.' Nicholas made the terrible mistake of interrupting.

Catherine stamped her foot in anger. 'You are impossible!' she snapped. 'Absolutely impossible!'

And she flounced off to bed.

Nicholas, smiling benignly, waved her goodnight. Looking round, he saw that Scathelocke had already fallen fast asleep.

'A good idea,' Nicholas slurred to himself.

He settled himself more comfortably in his chair and drifted into a wine-enriched sleep.

The next morning, they both woke cold, hungry, thick-headed and contrite. Catherine, however, apart from a few dark looks and vague mutterings about the foolishness of men, left them alone. Nicholas and Scathelocke fled the house like two truant boys. They didn't even dare look at each other until they were round the corner and under a barber's awning, where they burst into peals of laughter as the surprised barber trimmed their hair and beards. After that they walked down Cheapside and into a tavern in Fleet Street to break their fast.

'Tell me,' Chirke asked, remembering his conversation with Scathelocke the previous evening. 'Where did you learn the Latin tag, *quod est demonstrandum*?'

'At school.'

'Which school?'

Scathelocke tapped the side of his nose. 'Here we go again, master. You have your secrets, so have I.'

'Thanks to my sister's tirade last night, I have very few left.'

Scathelocke laughed. 'So your lover left you for your elder brother? What's so secret about that? Brothers have been fighting since Cain and Abel. There are darker secrets and greater mysteries, including' – Scathelocke added bitterly – 'the death of Berisford. Your beloved master the sheriff, Sir Amyas Petrie himself, will want you to render an account.'

Nicholas took a roll of parchment from a leather bag he carried under his cloak and hired a quill and ink-horn from the landlord.

'Come, dear Scathelocke, let's see what we have now, eh?' He began to write.

'Item, one dead justice – though who killed him and why is

a mystery. The same could be said about how Berisford's corpse, dry as a bone, was discovered in a ditch outside London.

'Item, Fromlich and his kinswoman, also murdered.

'Item, a French squire, Vallence, mortally wounded whilst trying to escape on board a Venetian galley. All he babbles in his death throes is "St Denis! St Denis knows it all!"

'Item, Vallence was carrying some dark secret entrusted to him by the dead Queen Isabella. What was this secret? Was Berisford party to it?

'Item, the king, through Sir Amyas Petrie, wants this secret.

'Item, so does the king of London's underworld, the Guardian of the Gates. Why? To blackmail the Crown? Was the Guardian responsible for the recent attack on me?

'Item, the murder of the Fromlichs. Did the Guardian send the woman who accosted me outside Newgate? Did he use the grave-robber Blueskin to murder Berisford?'

Nicholas studied what he had written and stared at Scathelocke.

'Where to now, eh?'

'We could visit Mawsby, the dead justice's clerk?'

'Possibly,' Nicholas replied. 'But he's probably told the authorities all he knows. I doubt if a man like Berisford would confide in a mere servant.'

'So, where can we go?' Scathelocke asked.

'We stand at a crossroads,' Chirke concluded. 'We can ignore Berisford's death and try and discover the great secret Vallence was carrying. Or we can fight the Guardian of the Gates on his own ground. However, to do that we need a man who knows the alleys and fetid runnels of London.' He grinned. 'And who better than the cunning man, Crabtree?'

'Who?' Scathelocke asked.

'Oh, you'll see. So, Scathelocke, which path shall we take?'

'What about returning to Newgate and making enquiries about Fromlich's assassin or the circumstances behind his kinswoman's death?'

Nicholas shook his head. 'I don't think there is any profit in doing that. As I said last night, the Fromlichs were murdered by a professional assassin. We'll get no joy at Newgate.'

'A visit to Primrose Hill?' Scathelocke queried.

'To see a ditch and view where the corpse lay? What will that tell us? No, no!'

Nicholas began to put away his scraps of parchment. 'What we have to do, Scathelocke, is to visit one place we've so far never mentioned in our discussions – Queen Isabella's tomb at Greyfriars!'

They left the tavern and went along Cheapside. The place was packed with carts, their drivers lashing the horses. Fat merchants, full of pomposity, swaggered around greeting each other in high-pitched voices. Gallants, fresh from feasting in a tavern, their purses now as empty as their brains, pushed through the crowds.

'Stand aside!' one of these barked at Nicholas.

Nicholas stared at the brawny, well-dressed oaf. The man's face was flushed from drink, his lips slobbery, his eyes red-rimmed. Nicholas shrugged and shoved by him, kicking him on the shins before he and Scathelocke disappeared into the crowd. They went down Friday Street, keeping close to the house walls, forcing their way past apprentices yelling, 'Mackerel, mackerel, six to a penny!'

The stench of rotting fish curdled their stomachs and, as they turned a corner, Nicholas saw the ward beadles pushing a woman to the tall, blood-soaked whipping post in the middle of

87

Fish Street. They clapped her hands in the manacles and stripped her to the waist. The parish beadle began to lay on with strips of leather, criss-crossing the whore's broad white back with bloody streaks. A small crowd gathered. Nicholas made to move on – after all it was none of his business. He looked away as the whore began to blubber and shriek.

'She's got children,' Scathelocke whispered.

Nicholas turned and glimpsed the two beggarly, skeletal children clinging together like frightened puppies, eyes large and dark in thin, pallid faces. Beyond them Nicholas noticed a beggar, clothed in rags, his face seamed with grime. Nicholas gave no thought to the man – until he saw that the fellow was watching him, a cold, calculating look on his face. Nicholas shivered – once again he was being followed.

The whore was flinging her head back in pain as the beadle continued to lash her. At last he stopped and turned his sweaty, plum-coloured face to the small mob to receive their plaudits for a job well done. Then he released the whore, who stood, head bowed, arms across her chest. Nicholas, ignoring Scathelocke's muttered protests, was about to walk on when the beadle contemptuously pushed the whore away. Nicholas, in disgust, turned back and confronted the beadle. He pressed the heel of his boot down on the bully's toes. The fellow shrieked, his eyes watering in pain.

'You did that on purpose!' the beadle bellowed.

'In which case,' Nicholas said, smiling, 'I do apologize.'

The beadle tried to grab him. Nicholas pushed him away, deliberately shoving him against the beggar. Both men crashed to the ground. The rest of the crowd, fickle as ever, gathered round to kick both. Nicholas winked at the whore, put a coin in her hand and hastened away down Fish Street.

'Why did you do that?' Scathelocke asked breathlessly, coming alongside him.

'First, I don't like beadles. Secondly, I don't like to see women whipped. Thirdly, I don't like being followed!'

'Followed? Who by?'

'A man pretending to be a beggar. Now he's busy fighting the beadle.'

They entered Carter Lane, where the great mass of St Paul's loomed over them. In the open spaces in front of the cathedral a frost fair had been set up with booths, huts, cookshops, barbers' stalls and drinking sheds. All were doing a roaring trade as apprentices, freed from their morning work and armed with sticks, played a rough game, chasing a polished shin bone across a broad expanse of ice. Nicholas and Scathelocke skirted the crowd. A drunk lurched by, a dog yapping at his heels. An old woman pleading for alms hurried towards them. They avoided her and entered the grounds of Greyfriars through a small postern gate. A lay brother, who stopped and asked their business, showed them to the church, which lay to the right of the friary cloisters.

'There's no service going on,' he said. 'And Father Prior won't object.'

Nichola. thanked him and pushed open the door. He and Scathelocke went through the incense-filled porch into the church. They found themselves in a long, dark nave with round, squat pillars separating it from shadowy aisles. They walked the length of the nave, went under the rood screen and genuflected before the high altar. Then Nicholas led Scathelocke into the Lady Chapel, which lay on the left.

'I didn't realize you knew where Isabella was buried,' Scathelocke whispered.

Nicholas grinned and pointed to the long, elaborately carved tomb of Purbeck marble.

'The mighty princes of the world, Scathelocke, always like to be buried in some holy place. They believe the soul doesn't leave the body till long after death. Once it does, a terrible battle ensues between the angels and the devils for the possession of the dead person's soul. If the person is buried in a holy place, the demons cannot invade it and the soul journeys direct to God.' He grinned. 'Well, that's what they think.'

As Scathelocke wandered off to explore further, Nicholas stared back across the main sanctuary at the ornately carved stalls where the brothers would chant divine office. Although dedicated to poverty and the rule of St Francis, Greyfriars church was already beginning to be patronized and favoured by the wealthy. The altar was of pure marble and the sanctuary lamp gold-encrusted. On the bare walls artists had painted brilliant scenes in a fine array of colours. In the apse, behind the high altar, a fresco in blue, green and russet depicted David with a lyre singing psalms; next to it a golden lion, the symbol of St Mark, turned to face the figure of Christ in Majesty. On the vaulted roof a large painting of St Catherine showed the wheel on which she was martyred breaking asunder and the flying pieces scattering the pagans who were torturing her. The walls of the Lady Chapel were similarly painted, with scenes from the Passion cycle and the life of St Christopher. Nicholas stared up at the marble, serene face of the Virgin holding the boy-child Christ then back at the huge, tomblike chest which had been erected above the burial place of Queen Isabella.

'There are royal tombs in the other chapel,' Scathelocke whispered as he came back. 'But I can't see anything untoward, can you?'

Nicholas studied Isabella's tomb. The marble effigy on top was of a woman clothed in the robes of a nun. The cowl, however, was crowned whilst between the joined hands lay a sceptre fashioned out of lilies. The queen's face was peaceful, sensuous-lipped; the closed eyes, slightly upturned, gave a Moorish cast to her features.

'What was it?' Chirke whispered. 'What terrible secret did you hold?'

He scrutinized the sides of the tomb. On one side were shields bearing the arms of England, France and Navarre. On the other, the soul of the deceased queen was depicted as a small, naked figure being carried by angels into heaven. On both ends of the tomb-chest strange beasts had been sculpted and carved angels kneeling in prayer held up small heraldic shields.

Scathelocke and Nicholas went round and round the tomb.

'The king did his mother full justice,' Scathelocke remarked, resting against the marble top.

'It's easy to honour the dead!' a voice boomed out.

Nicholas turned in alarm. Scathelocke half-drew his dirk.

'It's easy to honour the dead!' the voice repeated hollowly, the words echoing through the empty church.

Nicholas gazed up at the winking sanctuary light and steadied himself, breathing in deeply to control his panic. Was he having a vision? Was there someone hidden in the church?

'Who are you?' he called out.

'I am the living dead!' the voice replied.

'It's coming from the wall,' Scathelocke whispered, pointing to what looked like a buttress near the entrance to the Lady Chapel.

Chirke walked over and saw that there was a small, wooden door built into the buttress. Looking up, he saw eyes peering at him through a hole higher up.

91

'Who are you?' he asked.

'My name is Edmund. I am an anchorite doomed to a life of penance. The good brothers nourish me whilst I stare out at God's altar praying and fasting to atone for my sins.'

'What sins?' Nicholas asked curiously.

'Many years ago,' the anchorite replied, his voice hollow and distant. 'I killed my brother whilst hunting. The Angel of the Lord pursued me; I bore on my head the mark of Cain. Now I spend the rest of my life in atonement.'

Scathelocke came and stood beside Chirke, staring up at the wall. 'I have heard of these places, but never seen one,' he whispered.

Nicholas said, 'Every church used to have one – a small chamber carved out of the wall where a holy man or woman could spend a life of prayer.' He pointed to the hole from which the voice had come. 'They call that a leper's squint. Through it, the anchorite can see Mass celebrated at the high altar.'

'Quite right!' came the anchorite's voice.

Nicholas smiled quietly.

'Don't grin, young man! I may be old but my sight and hearing are good.'

'And what did you see and hear the day the queen was buried?'

'Oh, the usual obsequies. On the night before the requiem, the queen's coffin lay before the high altar in its leaden casket, ringed by purple candles. I prayed for that woman's soul all night, wrestling with the Angel of Darkness. Stand in front of the high altar! Go and see the cause of her wickedness!'

Nicholas obeyed. He went through the Lady Chapel into the sanctuary and read aloud the words on the carved stone that lay before the high altar.

'Roger Mortimer, Earl of March.'

'Aye!' the anchorite shouted back. 'Roger Mortimer, the queen's paramour. I was here, almost thirty years ago, when they brought his bloody, tattered remains from Tyburn. A Mass was sung and his remains were buried there, quick and abrupt as if he had never lived. The queen mother was treated no differently.'

Nicholas walked back to the leper's squint.

'What do you mean?' he asked.

'Well, the corpse arrived late in the evening,' the anchorite replied. 'It was laid before God and ringed by candles, but no one came for the coffin watch.'

'No one? Not the king, her son, or any other members of the family?'

'No one,' the sepulchral voice answered.

'And the next morning?'

'Solemn High Mass was sung. Only the king and his family attended. They sat in the choir stalls and you could see from their faces that they wished to be elsewhere. The king was most agitated. He kept looking down the church and beckoning to Sir Amyas Petrie, the sheriff of London – time and again, even during the bishop's homily, he beckoned him forward.'

'And then what?'

'Sir Amyas would look down the church.'

'For what reason?'

The anchorite chuckled, though the sound curled the hair on the nape of Nicholas's neck.

'I see things,' he replied. 'I, Edmund of Abingdon, see things. And the brothers tell me the rest.'

'What do they tell you?' Scathelocke asked. 'And how do you know Sir Amyas Petrie?'

'The brothers told me who everyone was. They said that after the service the king refused to stay, even to break his fast in their refectory. He and Sir Amyas left. The king's soldiers, knights in chain mail and full armour, were looking for someone amongst the guests. They could not find him, so they too left.' The anchorite sighed. 'But isn't that the way of the world? Once dead soon forgotten? The king's masons came and erected that tomb. Since then no one has come back except you. Oh yes, and one other.'

'Who?' Nicholas asked.

'A tall, thin fellow, constantly dabbing at his nose with a rag. Like you, he stood before the tomb. I asked him his business. He said he was Lord Stephen Berisford, a justice; he asked if the tomb or the Lady Chapel, or indeed the church itself, contained anything connected with St Denis.'

'St Denis!' Scathelocke exclaimed, looking at Nicholas.

'St Denis,' the anchorite repeated. 'But I told him, no. I know this church like the back of my hand. Every candle-holder, nook and cranny. Why should an English church pay tribute to a Frenchman who lost his head?'

Nicholas recalled the legends of St Denis and smiled.

'Now be gone!' the anchorite ordered. 'Leave me to my orisons!'

'One final question?'

'It will cost you!'

'What!' Nicholas exclaimed. 'Money for a man of God?'

'Aye, a man of God. But I have a terrible passion for cheese, soft and creamy.'

Nicholas placed a coin on the ledge of the leper's squint. It promptly disappeared.

'Do you know of a man called Vallence?'

94

'Never heard of him!'

'You did not see a young Frenchman attend either the death vigil or the Mass itself?'

'I told you, I saw nothing. Now be gone!'

Nicholas shrugged. He genuflected towards the tabernacle. Scathelocke, more clumsily, followed suit and they walked back down the nave.

Nicholas sat down on a bench, gesturing to Scathelocke to join him. He stared at the crucifix which hung down before the high altar.

'I don't understand this,' he murmured. 'Isabella dies of the pestilence and is buried hastily. Her son, the king, becomes very worried during the Requiem Mass. It must have been that he discovered Vallence was missing and so ordered the hunt: hence the constant distractions during the service.'

He blew on his cold fingers.

'But two other matters intrigue me. First, Vallence. He was a faithful retainer of the old queen. He was prepared to lay his life down on her behalf. So, why didn't he at least attend her death vigil?' Chirke rubbed his hands together. 'I can understand him not attending the Mass itself. He would use that as a pretext to slip away, to get down to Queenshithe and board that Venetian galley. But why didn't he pay his last respects to his mistress?'

'More importantly,' Scathelocke interrupted, 'if he wasn't here, why didn't he try to slip away the night before?'

Nicholas shrugged. 'Perhaps the Venetian galley wasn't ready for sea.' He gnawed at his lip. 'Secondly, Lord Stephen Berisford. He came here looking for St Denis. So Vallence's dying words were more than mere babbling – that saint, or rather his name, may hold the key to all this mystery.' He sighed and got to his feet. 'But enough of this. We have reached an impasse. Let's seek out Crabtree. He could lead us to Blueskin and perhaps guide us through this tangle of lies!'

Words between the pilgrims

The man of law paused in his story-telling as the friar, his brown-berried face flushed with excitement, sprang to his feet.

'You tell no fable!' he exclaimed. 'I have been to the church at Greyfriars. Edmund of Abingdon was an anchorite there. Mortimer's bones do lie before the high altar.'

'Well, everyone knows that,' the monk scoffed, glaring jealously at his companion.

'What every one doesn't know, though,' the friar continued pompously, wetting his sensuous lips, 'is the mystery of the queen mother's tomb.'

'What do you mean?' the wife of Bath queried before digging her face into a deep bowl of claret.

'What I say!' the friar snapped. He gestured at the story-teller. 'The tomb is, as our honourable friend describes, ornately carved and stands in the Lady Chapel.'

'So, where's the mystery?' Harry the taverner asked.

The friar sat down. 'Perhaps not so much a mystery,' he replied, 'as a great silence. No one goes near the tomb. No visit is ever made by Isabella's children or grand-children. No Masses are sung there for the repose of her soul.'

'Well, that's because she was hated,' the pardoner said. He

looked round, fingering his flaxen hair. 'She was hated,' he repeated in a loud whisper.

'But there have been no Masses?' the merchant asked.

'None,' the friar declared. 'When I was last there I was so intrigued I inspected the Book of the Dead.' He paused for effect. 'For the last ten years, no Masses have been ordered.'

The merchant rose to refill his goblet from the jug of wine the franklin had brought. 'I had colleagues who traded in Norfolk before Isabella died,' he said. 'They sometimes tried to enter Castle Rising but found it nigh impossible. The countryside around was thronged with the king's bowmen. Very few people could get in and everyone who left was always rigorously searched.'

'The same is true of the Norfolk ports,' the shipman spoke up.

The man of law clapped his hands. 'I hear what you say,' he declared, with a half-smile, 'but I'll come to that in a minute . . .'

PART III
Chapter 1

Nicholas Chirke and Scathelocke made their way through the streets to the stinking slums of Alsatia around the monastery of Whitefriars. Soot hung heavy in the air, children were begging on street corners, women lay drunk in alleyways along with the corpses of dead cats and dogs. Pigs gorged themselves on offal heaped in the gutter. A madman was selling invisible parchment and a woman with a growth in her throat offered to drink a gallon of water and vomit it up for a penny. Even the spots of rain from the clouds overhead seemed like drops of brimstone. Nicholas, his hand on his sword, pushed his way through the rogues and vagabonds who lurked there, far enough away from the officers of the law. The 'Anglers', men and women who poked sticks through windows to take out valuables. Rufflers who would pretend that they had fought in the recent wars and dress up as crippled beggars, crying out it was a sad thing that old soldiers should have to beg for maintenance while young men rode on horses. Scathelocke looked at these. Chirke had told him about them, men who could paint terrible sores and injuries, even pretending they had lost a foot or hand though they returned home full-limbed at night to share their booty out. He put his hand in his purse searching for a coin to give one of the beggar women who swarmed around, children clinging to their dusty skirts. Chirke seized his wrist.

'They're Paliards!' He whispered. 'Women with their children, they cover these with artificial sores and send them out to beg! And look at that!' He pointed to where a stark-naked madman danced up and down. 'I'll wager he is as sane as you or I – feigned madness can be a lucrative way of earning a living.'

Opposite the sprawling buildings of the Carmelite monastery, Nicholas and Scathelocke picked their way over the cobbles, went through a ruined archway and down an alleyway to a dingy tavern. Its windows were all boarded up, its paintwork was flaking and its sign, depicting a drunken bishop on a donkey, hung askew. Nicholas swept into the gloom of its taproom and peered around at the motley gang of rogues gathered there.

'Crabtree!' he shouted. 'I know you are here, you lying bastard!'

Scathelocke stood transfixed, appalled that his master dared to issue such a challenge amongst this collection of villains. But a man appeared, as if from nowhere. He was dressed in a garishly coloured jerkin, pantaloons and a pair of garish boots. The fellow was a born villain though he had a wholesome face, sly eyes and a merry mouth. Jet-black hair framed his sunburnt face and hung down to his shoulders. Grinning, he said, 'Master Chirke, my saviour, welcome to my humble abode.'

'Crabtree,' said Nicholas, 'you are the cheekiest scapegrace under God's heaven! My servant, Henry Scathelocke.'

Crabtree's eyes, a strange pale blue, met Scathelocke's. He stretched out a warm, strong hand.

'Henry, you are most welcome.'

Scathelocke gripped the outstretched hand. He instinctively liked the fellow.

100

'Come!' Crabtree gestured with his hand. 'Landlord,' he bawled, 'a flagon of your best and three cups. Master Chirke will pay the bill!'

He led them across the taproom, stilling any alarm or disquiet caused by the arrival of the two strangers with a brilliant smile and gentle assurances. Scathelocke noticed that the table he chose was at the far end, quite separate from the rest, just beside a small rear door. As they sat down, Nicholas pointed to the door.

'Your habits never change, Crabtree. Always ready to run!'

Crabtree pulled a pious face and spread his hands.

'Misunderstandings, Master Chirke, misunderstandings. They haunt my dreams and plague my life.'

They fell silent as the landlord brought the wine and cups. Crabtree served them as delicately and courteously as if they were supping at high table in the Inns of Court.

'Let me introduce Master Crabtree,' Nicholas began, smiling at Scathelocke. 'As he says, Crabtree is a most misunderstood man. He is not a thief, he just finds it hard to distinguish between his property and everyone else's.'

'True, true,' Crabtree sang out as he leaned back against the wall, basking in what he thought was appropriate flattery. 'I am your servant, Master Chirke. At times I have even been tempted to take up the offer of entering your service, though' – he shot a dazzling smile at Scathelocke – 'I see that vacancy is now filled.'

Nicholas abruptly leaned across the table and grasped Crabtree by the arm. 'This is rent day,' he said. 'I have come to collect my debt.'

Crabtree forced a smile and eased his wrist gently from Nicholas's grip.

'Anything you wish, Master Chirke, anything at all.'

'Do you know anything about Berisford's death?'

'Nothing.'

'Well, have you heard of a rogue called Blueskin?'

'I know the name but nothing of the man. I rob from the living, Master Chirke, not the dead.'

'So it seems you cannot help me?'

'No, Master Chirke, I can't.'

Crabtree rose to his feet. He tossed his threadbare cloak over his shoulder and stalked towards the tavern door, where he turned, his face now a mask of anger.

'Piss off, Chirke!' he shouted. 'I'll see you in hell before I speak to you again!'

He was through the door before Nicholas could reply.

'If it is rent day,' Scathelocke murmured drily, 'you leave as poor as when you arrived, Master.'

'Shut up, Scathelocke.'

'Of course, master.'

Nicholas gulped down his wine and strode out into the cold, gathering gloom. He was angry and, if he admitted it, hurt that Crabtree could dismiss him so easily. Behind him Scathelocke shuffled along, talking to himself. Nicholas knew he was cursing under his breath. Then, at the mouth of an alleyway, near the entrance to Whitefriars, a pebble thrown from one of the narrow runnels splashed into a puddle in front of him.

'Stay where you are, Master Chirke!' a voice hissed. 'I mean no ill, but the frumpery you have just witnessed was necessary. No, don't come any nearer. Stop and act as if you are talking to your servant.'

Nicholas turned, almost colliding with a wide-eyed Scathelocke. He winked at his servant.

'Stand, Henry,' he whispered, 'as if we are talking quietly together.' He turned and looked into the alleyway. 'Go on, Crabtree,' he said softly.

'You know the Guardian of the Gates?' Crabtree's voice was almost inaudible.

'I have heard of him.'

'He's involved in Berisford's death.'

'How do you know?'

'I don't have any evidence. For God's sake, Master Chirke, this is not a court of law, I just know it!'

'And Blueskin?'

Crabtree chuckled softly. 'Go to the Cormorant tavern – it's in an alleyway near the Temple. The landlord there keeps curiosities. Ask him to show you his Morisco.'

'What's that?'

'You'll find out. Just go. I'll see you soon.'

'One other thing, Crabtree.'

'What?'

'Find out all you can about Berisford. I'll pay you well.'

Nicholas put his hand on Scathelocke's shoulder and they walked on together. Crabtree watched them go and laughed softly to himself. He leaned against the urine-stained wall and stared up at the darkening sky.

'I don't like to be threatened,' he whispered to himself. 'Even by the Guardian of the Gates, God damn him!'

Nicholas and Scathelocke walked to Fleet Street, where they hired a link boy who, for a penny, took them to the Cormorant. The tavern was a ramshackle four-storeyed affair. Its top storeys jutted out so far that even in the darkness it looked as if the whole edifice might come crashing down into the street. Its big taproom was packed with whores, pimps and cut-purses and felons, the scum and froth of London's underworld. They sat around wooden trestle tables gambling, arguing or noisily eating from huge bowls of rancid meat cooked in cheap oils and garnished with spices. They hardly spared a glance for Nicholas and Scathelocke. Their attention seemed fixed on a fevered game of hazard taking place in the centre of the room, where a group of gamblers squatted amongst the dirty rushes, eyes intent on the dice falling from a cracked pewter cup.

'Master,' Scathelocke whispered. 'Look around!'

Obeying, Nicholas gave a gasp of astonishment. Displayed around the walls was a collection of curiosities. A stuffed porpoise was labelled 'A Sea Monster'. A huge conch shell was described as an ivory turret from the lost Island of the Blessed. An embalmed head, dark and wizened, was, a dirty scrap of parchment proclaimed, the head of Goliath. A blood-soaked flag, its blue and red colours now faded, had been carried by Saladin when he took Jerusalem. Pride of place, however, was given to a figure standing in a battered wooden case and described as a Morisco from the gold mines of Trebizond. Nicholas went over to examine it. The dark brown body, clad only in a loin cloth, was perfectly mummified. The eyes were half-open, the mouth kept shut by a thin metal bar shoved between chin and breastbone and a bright scarlet turban covered greasy black hair. Nicholas wrinkled his nose in disgust. He looked carefully at the shoulders, where the stain had begun to fade, and at the sunken cheeks, mottled with dark-blue patches.

'What is it, master? Is it the Morisco?'

Nicholas shook his head. 'We are looking at the mortal remains of the grave-robber Blueskin, hanged or killed in some tavern brawl. His body has been stuffed with herbs, painted and presented as this curiosity.'

'Can I help you, masters?'

Behind them the landlord, a greasy barrel of a man with a bald head shaped like an onion and the milky-blue eyes of an old cat, watched them suspiciously. Nicholas slipped a coin into the man's calloused hand.

'I have heard of your curiosities, and I came to see for myself. This Morisco is most peculiar. How long have you had him?'

The landlord shrugged his shoulders, 'Two, three weeks, but he's not for sale.'

'A wise decision. But he's been here for at least two weeks?'

'Yes, yes, why?'

Another coin changed hands.

'Nothing, taverner, except I leave a much wiser man.'

Nicholas, followed by a disgusted Scathelocke, turned and left the tavern as quickly as he could.

'Well,' he said when they stood outside, 'we have learnt three things, Henry. First, Fromlich is not guilty. Secondly, Berisford's killer is probably the Guardian of the Gates. Finally, Blueskin had gone to his well-deserved reward long before Berisford ever did.'

Words between the pilgrims

The man of law stopped speaking. He stared round the now silent tavern.

'I think the rain has stopped,' the chantry priest said. He looked at the man of law and shook his head. 'Such evil deeds! So many terrible murders! The preacher is correct when he says that power breeds wickedness.'

'The love of money is the root of all evil,' intoned the pardoner, playing with his flaxen hair.

The knight, sitting by the inglenook, was fascinated by the prioress, who now crouched over her little lapdog. The man of law's story had created a tense stillness – it had reminded them all of the power the great ones of the land carried in their wallets and scabbards.

'Continue!' the cook cried. He scratched the open ulcer on his leg, making it even sorer.

The man of law shook his head. 'Perhaps it's best to pause for a while, now that the rain has stopped.'

He let his sentence hang in the air, shaking his head as his audience pressed him to continue. He rose, pulling his multi-coloured coat close around him. He pushed his thumbs into the silken-lined pockets of his doublet and walked out into the herb garden behind the tavern. The manciple followed.

'Must you tell that story, Nicholas?' he asked when they were alone.

The lawyer kept his back to him.

'I need to tell it,' he said quietly. 'Last year Sir Roger Hobbedon and Sir Amyas Petrie died. The old king is also dead and I am released from my bond.'

The manciple shrugged and walked back into the tavern. The man of law stood waiting for the lighter footsteps to come and when they did he did not even bother to turn his head.

'Nicholas.'

'Madam Eglantine!'

'To me you will always be Nicholas. I thought to you I would always be Beatrice.'

Now the man of law turned, his strange-coloured eyes brimming with tears.

'For me, Madam Eglantine, the Lady Beatrice died many years ago.'

The prioress took a step forward.

'By Saint Aloy!'

The man of law snorted. 'For God's sake, madam, drop these pretences! Talk to me in plain English, not the courtly French you picked up in some Stratford convent.' He took a step forward. 'Look at you,' he said softly, 'feeding your dog roasted flesh and the finest manchet bread soaked in milk. Your grey wimple all pleated! Your golden brooch and amber rosary beads!' He blinked furiously. 'To think that I and my brother Robert, God assoil him, fought over you!'

The prioress's blue eyes stared back at him.

'Robert's dead,' she said.

'Aye, he should be. You broke his heart!'

'I waited for you. I was sure you'd come back,' the prioress said. 'And, when you didn't, I was in hell.'

'That's strange,' the man of law snapped. 'I was there too, but I didn't see you!'

'What happened?' the prioress asked, ignoring the insult. She stepped forward, her soft white fingers clawing at the man of law's wrist. 'Nicholas, what happened?'

'Listen to my tale, madam.'

She stepped back. 'You've become hard,' she said. 'Your heart has turned to stone.'

The lawyer bowed. 'Madam, as the proverb says, "If you sleep with wolves you wake up howling".' He looked away, watching the swifts who nested under the eaves of the tavern swoop and dive above the herb banks. 'I'm not hard,' he told her, 'but the world is. As a knight carries a shield, so must Every Man protect his soul.'

The prioress turned and walked slowly back into the tavern. The man of law watched her go.

'What's the use?' he whispered. 'What's the use of singing if no one listens? Or smiling if no one responds?'

He walked down the yellow-paved path, savouring the smell of the mint, thyme, rosemary, parsley and fennel that grew there. Amongst the dark-green trees behind the tavern a cuckoo began to call and, for a minute, the man of law closed his eyes and was a boy again. He, Robert and Beatrice were playing in a flower-filled glade in a copse near the ruins of Bigod Castle.

'Sir?'

Once again the man of law did not bother to turn.

'Yes, sir knight!'

'I know you now.'

'Do you?'

'I had no part in what happened,' the knight said. 'I was carrying out orders. Something terrible happened, didn't it?'

'No, Sir Godfrey. Only the little ones were oppressed, those without power or protection.'

The man of law stood, crushing some mint in his fingers. He raised his hand to his nose to sniff. He did not turn until he heard the knight walk back up the garden path.

Then he saw Harry the taverner standing at the door waving at him to come in. 'It's going to rain again,' he shouted, pointing to the sky. 'We wait for you to continue your tale.'

The man of law looked up at the clouds now closing again to block out the weak sunlight. He looked once more around the yard. Everything was fresh. Marshalling his thoughts, he walked slowly back towards the tavern door. He sucked in the clear spring air and realized he had to be careful. If he told his tale he would feel as if he had been purged, shriven. Nevertheless, he was astute enough to know that the secret he carried was still jealously guarded by those in power. Oh, the old king was dead, buried in his coffin in Westminster Abbey, but his sons still lived, powerful young hawks, as steeped in blood as their elder brother, Edward the Black Prince, whose corpse, rotten with syphilis, now lay before the high altar in Canterbury Cathedral. The man of law's pilgrimage was not simply to pay homage at Becket's tomb but also to pray for the prince and the evil he had done. The man of law paused and took off his coat and, as he did so, the summoner, a goblet of wine in his fat paw, staggered through the door. He had a garland on his head as large as any tavern wine bush and his normally red face was further inflamed by the claret he had drunk.

The man of law looked in disgust at the red boils and white pimples that ran down either side of the man's nose, at the leering wet eyes under the black scabby brows and the scant beard which covered a pock-marked chin.

'Yours is a good story,' the summoner slurred, his breath reeking of wine, garlic and onions.

The man of law hid his distaste and made to go past. As he did so the summoner moved sideways to block his path, the bonhomie draining from his fat, ugly face.

'The Guardian of the Gates sends his greetings,' he whispered. 'Be careful what you say!'

PART IV
Chapter 1

Nicholas and Scathelocke leaned back in their chairs before the fire, their boots cast off, sipping the claret Catherine had served them. She was now on the upper floor trying to keep the children in bed whilst John was busy in his counting house. Nicholas felt sleepy; he was reflecting on what they had learnt. Now and again he would glance sideways at Scathelocke and idly wonder what he was dreaming about.

'Scathelocke,' he began without thinking, 'just where do you go to?'

Scathelocke's face creased in annoyance. He was about to reply when there was a loud rap on the door. Scathelocke sighed with relief, rose and padded across the flagstones.

'Is Master Chirke in?' a voice bellowed from the darkness.

'Come in, Crabtree!' Nicholas shouted. 'Wipe your feet and keep your hands off anything valuable!' He stretched out a foot and pulled a stool closer. 'Sit down here. If you behave, you'll get something to eat and drink.'

'Most generous, master, most generous,' Crabtree replied, sitting on a stool between Nicholas and Scathelocke.

'I am not your master!' Nicholas snapped.

'Yes, you are,' Crabtree replied, stretching his fingers out to the blaze. 'Please, master, at least until Michaelmas. I am starving.'

Nicholas glanced across at Scathelocke, who shrugged.

'Why didn't you want to be seen with us in public?' Nicholas asked.

Crabtree's elfish face broke into a grin. 'It was for a good reason. However, give me a shilling a quarter, pennies for my food and board, and I'm your man.'

'Why should I hire you?'

Crabtree stretched his hands towards the fire. 'For a cup of wine and a scrap of bread, master, I can tell you all – or at least something – about the mystery that now confronts you.'

Nicholas nodded at Scathelocke, who lumbered to his feet and headed for the buttery.

'Some wine,' Crabtree called out, 'the best bread, some cheese, nice and soft, and a strip of dried bacon. Perhaps an apple . . . ?'

Scathelocke muttered something unrepeatable but eventually came back with everything except the bacon. He thrust the platter into Crabtree's hand and placed a pewter goblet beside him.

'There's no bacon,' Crabtree moaned.

Nicholas looked surprised. Catherine had at least three hams hanging from the rafters to be cured. Scathelocke ignored his glance and sat down, staring into the fire.

'Tell your tale, Crabtree,' Nicholas ordered.

But Crabtree was busily pushing the food into his mouth. Nicholas sat and watched as the platter was cleared of every crumb. Crabtree burped, picked up the wine goblet and smiled into the fire.

'I won't tell you a tale,' he said. 'But I'll answer your questions.'

'Who is the Guardian of the Gates?'

Crabtree sipped from his goblet. 'God knows, master. Everyone, from the gangs of rifflers south of the river to the footpads of Hounslow and Clerkenwell, is afeared of him, but no one knows who he is.'

'But I thought he was the King of the Underworld? The Thief King?'

'No, no,' Crabtree replied. 'He is what he styles himself, the Guardian of the Gates. No thief is allowed into London without his permission. No crime is committed in the city without him knowing. A very dangerous man, the Guardian. If you offend him the bailiffs collar you and you are off to Newgate. He's like a farmer, he allows the harvest of thieves to grow thick and fast and, when he wants to, orders in the reapers. Many a man who has gone up against him wishes he hadn't when he is standing at the scaffold at Smithfield.'

Scathelocke made a rude noise.

'If you don't believe me,' Crabtree said, 'go out and talk to the pickpockets of Alsatia or the foists and Palliards around Whitefriars.'

'But how does he control them?' Scathelocke jibed.

'How does rumour spread?' Crabtree snapped back. 'He makes his presence felt. Like the Lord, he works mysteriously. I do not wish to be the object of his spleen.' He pulled a face. 'He has already warned me off helping you.'

'Why should he do that?' Nicholas asked.

'Oh, master, come. We have all heard of Justice Berisford's murder, of Vallence's death as well as Fromlich's sudden demise in Newgate.'

Nicholas slipped his dagger from its sheath and gently grazed Crabtree's cheek with it.

'Master Crabtree, I suggest you tell us all you know.'

Crabtree slurped from the goblet, licked his dirty lips and drew a deep breath.

'Slowly!' Nicholas warned.

'The old queen has died,' Crabtree began. 'Stiff as a board out at Castle Rising in Norfolk. Everybody mourns and the body is brought along the Mile End Road to be given fair housing beside the high altar in Greyfriars church.' He stared quizzically at Nicholas. 'You know, where her lover, Roger Mortimer, Earl of March, is buried? He had his neck stretched at Tyburn for ploughing the king's mother as well as for ordering red-hot pokers to be stuck up the arse of the king's sodomite father.'

'Go on, Crabtree.'

'Well, a young squire called Vallence, sent by the old queen, attempts to board a Venetian galley in the Thames. Vallence is caught, he puts up a fight and is wounded. He is taken to St Bartholomew's hospital in Smithfield, where he is visited by our old sheriff, Sir Amyas Petrie, and by two aldermen. But Vallence is hurt badly. He coughs his blood out and dies. He is given nothing for his pains but a pauper's grave beneath the yew trees by St Bartholomew's.'

'And what else?' Nicholas asked.

'The king's warships seal the Thames. The galley is stopped and searched, but allowed to continue. The quayside is likewise combed, because Vallence's package, or whatever he was carrying, is lost. Now, Justice Stephen Berisford also visits the late lamented Vallence – he has been ordered by the sheriff to investigate what secrets the French squire might have been carrying. Some days later Berisford is found foully murdered on Primrose Hill and no one knows who did it. His death looks like suicide, but how can a man undress, fall on his sword,

116

dress himself again, then go and lie in a ditch on Primrose Hill, eh?'

Nicholas nodded, remembering the coroner's report.

'Tell me, Crabtree, Justice Berisford was badly bruised and beaten up before he was killed and his death was made to look like suicide. Who would do that?'

'Master, I could think of a hundred lusty fellows now roistering in the taverns along Southwark bank who would, for the right price, do that to their mothers!'

'No, no, who'd do it?' Nicholas insisted. 'Somebody enjoyed that – there are other ways of killing a man besides stamping him to death.'

Crabtree licked his lips.

'You know, don't you?' Scathelocke gripped him by the shoulder.

Crabtree spread his dirty paw. 'Master, a shilling?'

Nicholas pressed his dagger more firmly against the man's neck.

'Don't whine,' he said softly, 'it doesn't suit you. You've eaten and drunk here. Now tell me.'

'Your promise?'

'Tell me!'

Crabtree sniffed. 'Wormwood!'

'Who?'

'Wormwood. A professional assassin. One of the Guardian's bully-boys. He frequented the Locked Heart tavern off Pig Alley near Chick Lane. He loved to torture. He was sly and cunning. He used to be a skinner – owned a small shop and cellar off Aldersgate until he began to use his knife on people rather than the pelts of animals.'

'How do you know all this?' Nicholas stared at this cunning

man who might be spinning him fairy tales.

Crabtree smiled and tapped the side of his nose. 'Crabtree moves, master, like the wind. Free and blithe. No one notices me. But I listen and I remember.'

'Perhaps we should talk to this Wormwood?' Scathelocke interrupted.

'I don't think so,' Crabtree murmured, 'Wormwood's gone the same way as Blueskin. A few nights ago he was fortunate enough to win the favours of a lady of the night. They hired a special chamber and she took his heart all right, straight through with a dagger.' Crabtree smiled at his own joke.

Nicholas re-sheathed his knife and let his head fall back against the chair. He stared up at the beams.

'So, Wormwood was murdered by a woman. A lovely young woman met me outside Newgate claiming to be Fromlich's kinswoman.'

'He had no such kinswoman,' Crabtree said.

'I now know that!' Nicholas snapped. 'But who, in God's name, is she?'

Crabtree slapped his hands together and roared with laughter.

'Nightshade!' he whispered. He grinned at Nicholas. 'Oh, that's what we call her. A lady of the night, a high-class courtesan. You have to pay for her favours. Pay her a little more and she'll make sure whoever sleeps with her sleeps for ever. Many a wife and jealous lover has hired her. No law officer has ever captured our Nightshade.'

Nicholas rocked himself gently in the chair.

'Only one person, master,' Crabtree continued, 'can buy the services of people like Wormwood and Nightshade. The Guardian!'

'Let us,' Nicholas said, 'try to make bricks out of these

118

straws. *Causa disputandi*, for sake of argument. Vallence is killed, or rather dies, at St Bartholomew's. Whatever secret he is carrying is lost. Justice Berisford is commissioned to discover it. The city authorities are engaged in this, urged on by the court. The Guardian of the Gates senses a profit, so he orders Wormwood to murder Berisford. Wormwood does this, in his usual cruel way, but Nightshade then kills him, to keep his mouth shut.'

'That would make sense,' Scathelocke interrupted. 'But what happened to Berisford's body? Apparently he had been dead for days. Many people must pass that ditch on Primrose Hill, but no one saw the corpse until the two workmen discovered it.'

Nicholas drummed his fingers on the arm of his chair.

'I agree,' he snapped. 'It's all a mystery.'

'And then,' Scathelocke persisted, 'there's this business of Fromlich, and the strange reports of Berisford being seen alive in different parts of the city.'

'Oh, that's easy,' Nicholas replied. 'The Guardian would deliberately spread rumours, putting the blame on Fromlich, and muddying the water so it's difficult to distinguish between truth and falsehood.' He leaned forward and tossed a log on to the fire. 'What concerns me is why was Berisford so terrified? What did he mean by declaring he was to be hanged or to be burnt? On the day he died he must have gone to meet his killer, the evil Wormwood. But why should an upright justice and merchant of this city agree to go within even spitting distance of a man like Wormwood?'

'And there are other questions,' Crabtree crowed, eager to air his knowledge.

'Such as?' Scathelocke teased.

'What was Vallence carrying that was so important? And where did he hide it?'

'Whatever it was,' Nicholas said, 'it was something to do with the old queen. Perhaps a message? The Venetian galley Vallence sought passage on was to visit a French port. But what could an old dowager queen have that was so harmful to the interests of this kingdom?'

'What's all this, then?'

Nicholas whirled round.

Catherine stood in the doorway, staring narrow-eyed at Crabtree who sprang to his feet, nervously scratching his codpiece as he hopped from foot to foot. Catherine took one look at the rogue's slightly twisted nose, cunning eyes and merry mouth and her colour deepened.

'I didn't know you had visitors, Nicholas.'

'An old friend.' Nicholas rose and walked towards his sister. 'Catherine, may he stay? I need him.'

Catherine nodded, her eyes never leaving Crabtree.

'There's a room at the end of the passageway,' she said. 'What's your name?'

'Crabtree, mistress.'

'Aye,' Catherine's face relaxed, 'and I'm the Queen of France. I'll get the room ready for you, Master Crabtree.' She wagged a finger. 'You are my brother's guest and, as long as you keep your fingers to yourself, a welcome one.'

She bustled off. Crabtree scratched his head and breathed a sigh of relief. Then held out his hand.

'Master, my shilling?'

Nicholas fished into his purse and handed over one of his precious coins.

'Be mindful of my sister's words, Crabtree. Your knowledge

might be precious, but so is my sister.'

'And remember, Crabtree,' Scathelocke interposed, 'a little knowledge can be a dangerous thing!'

'Yes it can be,' Crabtree quipped back. 'And just you remember it, Master Scathelocke, next time I ask for a piece of bacon.'

And, grinning, Crabtree scampered after Catherine whilst Scathelocke, muttering under his breath, stomped off upstairs.

Nicholas roused Scathelocke and Crabtree early the next morning. Tip-toeing around the kitchen, Nicholas ignored Crabtree's moans about his empty belly. They snatched some ale, bread and cheese from the buttery and made their way down to the riverside. The mist was thick and cloying, swirling through the narrow alleyways, drowning the rumble of the carts. Only the candlelight from the occasional casement window and the lantern horns of the watch pierced the gloom. Nevertheless, the city was waking. At Fish Wharf six pick-pockets were already in the finger stocks, the bailiffs tightening the vice-like clasps over the felons' fingers and thumbs. Two drunks were stripped and doused in filthy river water before being chained into barrels of the same water and forced to stand on the quayside till noon.

The wharves were busy with the fishing smacks which had just returned. Their catch, still silvery, wriggled as it was piled on to the dockside, where ragged, young urchins, their arms soaked in blood, chopped off the fish's heads before throwing the carcases into tubs of brine and salt. A ship was preparing to sail on the morning tide. Men-at-arms in chain mail and basinets jostled with leather-clad archers as sergeants tried to impose order. In a corner, just within the door of a warehouse, men queued up for a cowled and hooded friar to hear their confessions and shrive them. Two whores flounced by, their dyed hair glowing red. The archers whistled and cat-called. One whore pulled her skirt up, exposed her grimy buttocks, and fled up an alleyway before a bailiff could intervene.

Chirke and his companions fought their way through the throng, went down the wet, slippery steps and hired a skiff. The boatman pulled out into the middle of the river, well away from the other craft and ships turning on the tide, and sped down to Westminster. Nicholas felt as if he was being rowed by Charon across the river Styx: for the wherryman sat, hood drawn over his ears against the cold as he pulled at the oars. They glided down the river, through the cloud of stench where the Fleet, the great sewer of the city, emptied into the Thames, on past the Temple, its beautiful tower glowing eerily white, round the river bend and down to Westminster. Scathelocke and Crabtree remained silent – the mist was stinging cold and by the time they reached King's Steps at Westminster their cheeks had turned blue and their teeth were chattering. They took a path round the palace and into the small hamlet which had grown up around the abbey. A link boy, carrying a torch, showed them to Berisford's house for a penny. Nicholas looked up, glimpsed lights at the windows and heaved a sigh of relief that his journey had not been fruitless. A balding, bleary-eyed servant answered his vigorous knocking.

'Nicholas Chirke. I'm here to see Mawsby, Justice Berisford's clerk.'

The old man dabbed red-rimmed eyes with his fingers and took them into a small, comfortable parlour where a grimy-faced maidservant was busy building up the fire. Nicholas and his companions stamped their feet on the rushes on the floor. Crabtree was so cold that he shooed the girl away, seized the bellows and began vigorously to fan the flames. Soon the logs, covered with a sprinkling of coal, caught light and all three gathered round to thaw their fingers and seek some warmth.

'Which of you is Master Chirke?'

Nicholas spun round. The old servant had reappeared, bringing with him a thin man with a hooked nose, rheumy eyes and a cod-like mouth. He stood in the doorway, nervously fingering the woollen wrap across his shoulders.

'I am Matthew Mawsby.'

He walked across the room and indicated the stools round the fire. 'Please be seated.' He snapped his finger at the servant. 'Oswald, bring our guests some mulled wine.'

The old man lumbered off as they took their seats. 'He was my master's servant,' Mawsby exclaimed. 'He and the maid still come in for a few hours every morning.'

Nicholas showed Mawsby his letters of accreditation from Sir Amyas. Bending forward to catch the glow of the fire, Mawsby scrutinized them closely before handing them back.

'I can throw no light on this matter,' he said, noisily clacking his tongue. 'A terrible business! A terrible business!' He extended shaking hands towards the fire and looked, eyes brimming with tears, at Nicholas. 'Lord Stephen was a good man, a good man, he lived an honourable life; he deserved a more honourable death.'

'Tell us what happened, from the beginning,' Nicholas urged, then paused as Oswald returned with the mulled wine. All of them sipped at the wine, relishing its warmth.

The old clerk smacked his lips. 'At the end of August,' he said, 'there was a great commotion in the city. A courier from Sir Amyas Petrie, the sheriff, arrived at our house demanding my master's presence. A fugitive had attempted to board a Venetian gally and, when prevented, had attacked the royal

123

archers. He had been wounded and taken to St Bartholomew's hospital in Smithfield. My master was to go there and meet Sir Amyas and two aldermen, Sir Ambrose Venner and Sir Oswald Cooper.' The old man shrugged and hitched the woollen wrap closer round his shoulders. 'It seemed a simple enough matter. Lord Stephen was a justice, and his presence was necessary for the prisoner to be examined.' Mawsby paused and blinked at the fire. 'But when he returned he seemed perplexed and worried.'

'Did he tell you the reason?'

'Not immediately. He said only that the prisoner, a young man, had died of terrible wounds. He went into his writing office and stayed there for hours, sitting at his desk, poring over a piece of parchment. I went in to ask him what was the matter. He whispered, "God help poor Vallence!" '

'So he knew the dead man?'

'Yes, he did,' Mawsby replied. 'And it was then he told me what had happened at St Bartholomew's.' Mawsby drew a deep breath. 'The good brothers had taken Vallence into a small chamber and placed him on a cot bed. It was apparent he was dying, from a terrible wound in his stomach. The blood was soaking the bed. His face was white and there was blood on his lips. Sir Amyas and the two aldermen were standing over him.' The clerk licked dry lips. 'According to Lord Stephen, they were all very angry, Sir Amyas in particular. Vallence's clothes lay around the chamber and it was obvious that they had been searched.'

'Why was Sir Amyas so angry?'

'I don't really know. According to Lord Stephen, he was shouting at Vallence, sometimes in French and sometimes in English, but always with the same questions – "Where is it?"

124

"What were you carrying?" "What did Queen Isabella give you?" '

Nicholas glanced at Scathelocke and raised his eyebrows. Sir Amyas Petrie and the two aldermen had been most economical with their account. Nicholas leaned forward.

'Did Lord Stephen say what answers Vallence gave to the interrogators?'

'He just kept shaking his head and pleading with them for a priest. Sir Amyas replied that he could have a priest as soon as he had answered their questions.'

'And your master?'

'He claimed he was very nervous and stayed near the door. Vallence saw him and called him over. He whispered something, then his head fell sideways. His eyes were still open, but a thin trickle of blood snaked out of the corner of his mouth. He was dead.'

Nicholas was fascinated. 'Surely the others questioned your master?'

'Of course. Lord Stephen knew the young man because he'd sold coal and timber to the old queen's household. Sir Amyas was most insistent. What, he asked, did the young man whisper? Nothing, my master replied, he just muttered something about St Denis.'

'Did your master know Vallence very well?'

'He came here sometimes, but only to order supplies.' Mawsby shrugged. 'He was just one amongst many. And, before you ask, I do not know why he mentioned St Denis, nor did Lord Stephen.'

The clerk plucked at a loose thread in his thick woollen hose.

'Some time later, much later, Sir Amyas ordered my master to investigate the circumstances surrounding Vallence's death.'

Nicholas put his goblet down. He scowled at Crabtree, who was lolling on a stool half-asleep. Scathelocke had pushed his chair back into the shadows, his hand half-way across his face.

Why, Nicholas wondered testily, was his servant so secretive? 'And did Lord Stephen discover anything?' he asked abruptly.

Mawsby shook his head mournfully. 'He visited Greyfriars and the quayside where Vallence was injured. The royal archers on guard there claimed they stopped Vallence before he reached the Venetian galley. Vallence drew his sword, a fight ensued and the young man was injured.'

Nicholas moved in his chair. 'So nothing untoward really happened until the Friday before Lord Stephen disappeared? Sir Amyas says a stranger came to the house.'

'Yes,' Mawsby replied. 'Lord Stephen was sitting here. For the previous few days he had been agitated, refusing food and drink. Now and again he would mumble, "I am to be hanged". Or, "I am to be burnt". Anyway, the messenger arrived.' Mawsby waved a scrawny hand. 'No, I did not see him; he was cloaked and hooded and stood just inside the doorway. Lord Stephen took the message, brought it back in here, read it, then tossed it into the fire. He then told me to dismiss the messenger, shouting, "I shall do what he says! I shall do what he says!" '

'Whoever that messenger was,' Nicholas intervened, 'the letter he brought disturbed Sir Stephen's mind?'

'Oh, yes,' the clerk replied. 'That very evening Lord Stephen attended a parish council meeting at St Martin's-in-the-Fields. He was sad and, when I asked him why, he replied. "Any man about to be burnt would be melancholic." The next morning he rose early, unlocked his secret coffer and burnt a pile of parchment. He then left, still looking very sad.'

Nicholas rubbed his finger round his lips. 'And you have no

idea about the messenger or the message he brought?'

Mawsby opened and closed his mouth.

'Please,' Nicholas insisted. 'However stupid it may appear to you. Anything at all!'

The clerk chewed his lip. 'I have considered that, before God I have! When I opened the door the man just asked for my master, who met him in the passageway. Lord Stephen waited until he thought I was out of earshot. All I heard was one phrase. I think the messenger said, "I have told no one of this, but I am a friend of Patricius".'

'Patricius?' Nicholas repeated.

'Yes, yes, I think it was that. I heard the "Pat . . ." and, from the ending of the word, I'm sure it was a Latin name.'

Nicholas looked at his two companions. He tapped Crabtree with his boot to stir him awake.

'I wasn't asleep,' the fellow protested, rubbing his eyes. 'Just enjoying the warmth.'

'Did Sir Stephen burn all his manuscripts?' Scathelocke abruptly asked.

'Yes, he did. I have been through everything.'

'And you found no reference to anyone called Patricius or Patrick?' Nicholas asked.

'None whatsoever.'

'Had Lord Stephen become involved in anything? Had he . . . ?' Nicholas paused to choose his words carefully.

'What are you implying?' Mawsby snapped.

Too quick, too quick, Nicholas thought. He was sure the clerk was hiding something, even if it was just unworthy suspicions.

'My master was a kindly man,' Mawsby declared, 'a shrewd merchant, an upright justice, well-loved and respected. He liked books and manuscripts and was a regular visitor to the libraries at Blackfriars and the Temple. And he enjoyed walking,' he added. 'Lord Stephen used to walk for miles round the city. He said it helped him to think more clearly.'

Nicholas nodded. He was about to ask if he could search Lord Stephen's writing office, but knew that would be a futile waste of time. The justice had burnt most of his manuscripts, for whatever reason, and Mawsby the loyal clerk would have sifted through them again to remove anything damaging.

He got to his feet and extended his hand, which Mawsby limply took. 'I thank you, sir, for your kindness and hospitality. I do hope your master's murderers will be brought to justice.'

A now sullen clerk led them to the door. Outside the mist was beginning to lift, though it was still thick enough to conceal the figure in a doorway further down the alleyway who had been watching the house since their arrival. Crabtree, still half-asleep, slipped on the icy cobbles and if it had not been for Scathelocke he would have ended up in a frozen sewer. No sooner was he on his feet than a casement window was flung open and a potful of steaming jakes and urine narrowly missed his head. Crabtree, jumping up and down, shook his fist and screamed curses until a laughing Nicholas and Scathelocke manhandled him gently further down the alleyway. They stopped at a pie shop, just outside the gate of Westminster Palace. Crabtree ate like a starving man. Scathelocke refused to eat. Nicholas's hunger was soon blunted by a large piece of bone in the middle of the pie, so he tossed it at the mongrel who had been purposefully following them and led his companions into the Bishop and Hoop tavern to break their fast on pots of ale and chicken stew. The latter was heavily garnished with herbs to hide the fact, as Crabtree pointed out, that this particular chicken must have been very old when he was a young boy. Nevertheless, the tavern was clean and sweet-smelling. The ale was tangy in its tastiness and the fire strong enough to fend off the cold draughts seeping through cracks in the wooden shutters across the windows.

'Well, well, well!' Crabtree leaned back, licking his pewter spoon. 'One thing is certain, master. Lord Stephen Berisford was not murdered by his clerk. Mawsby does not have energy to break wind!'

Nicholas laughed, then stared curiously at a tinker who came into the tavern and sat opposite them.

'If you tell us one thing, Crabtree, I'll tell you another. If you can find Patricius or whatever he calls himself, we'll find the reason Berisford was so terrified.'

'Why,' Scathelocke asked, 'was Berisford brought into this business in the first place? I mean, if Sir Amyas wanted secrecy . . . ?'

Nicholas pulled a face. 'Probably a mistake. Perhaps they thought Vallence might talk to a justice he knew, however slightly. Or, more probably, Sir Amyas Petrie wanted to give Vallence's death some appearance of legality. He thought it would be easy to discover Queen Isabella's secret – and that,' Nicholas concluded grimly, 'proved to be a costly and fatal mistake.'

Chapter 2

They left the tavern and hired a ride on a cart going up Fleet
Street. The day was cold but the thoroughfare was packed with
carts fighting to get in or out of the city. Pedlars with packhorses
and sumpter ponies and wandering priests and scholars thronged
around them. Crippled beggars, clutching makeshift wheel
barrows, hurried into the city to take up their usual positions
for the day. At Fleet prison, just past the stinking city ditch, the
execution cart was being prepared to take convicted felons up
past Farringdon into West Smithfield. The prisoners were bound
hand and foot and some – a woman sentenced to be boiled for
poisoning her husband with burnt spiders, a footpad guilty of
stealing a silver crucifix from a church in Clerkenwell, a river
pirate and two counterfeiters – had placards slung around their
necks advertising their crimes. The red-masked executioner tried
to drive off the bystanders and onlookers with his whip, helped
by the sheriff's men with their tipped staves. A drunken bagpipe
player had to be helped to his feet so that he could give the
death cart a musical accompaniment to the execution ground.
At last the cart moved off, the crowd following it, and Nicholas
and his companions were able to go through the old city gate
and into Bowyers Row.

'Where are you taking us, master?' Crabtree asked.

'Wait and see!' Nicholas snapped.

They went along Paternoster Row, past the Bishop of London's palace and under the dark mass of St Paul's. Nicholas looked at it, smiling wistfully. If this present business hadn't occupied him, he'd be strolling the cathedral's middle aisle looking for clients. He smiled quietly at his own self pity.

'But I'd still be grumbling,' he consoled himself, 'at being unable to obtain a fat fee!'

They passed one of the gates leading into St Paul's graveyard. Nicholas stopped and looked through.

'Many of your friends here, Crabtree?'

Grinning, Crabtree strolled just within the gateway. Nicholas and Scathelocke followed. They stared at the small bothies, stalls and makeshift dwellings erected against the graveyard wall. Crabtree was immediately recognized by many of the felons and wolvesheads who lurked there, protected by the Church's sanctuary laws from the city's law officers. A hail of good-natured abuse followed which Crabtree answered with colourful language. Suddenly a sharp-eared man with a pockmarked face sprang forward. He was dressed in brown leather from head to toe and, on his head, had a fool's cap with small bells sewn on it.

'I know you,' the fellow yelled, pointing a grubby finger at Scathelocke.

'Piss off!' Scathelocke hissed. 'You wouldn't even know your own mother!'

The fellow's hand fell to the sharp knife pushed into his ragged belt. His narrow, close-set eyes flickered.

'I am sure I know you,' he repeated, his mouth bared into a wolfish grin.

Nicholas flinched at the yellow rotting teeth jutting out from inflamed gums. He saw the 'F' brand burned into the man's cheek, the mark of a forger.

But the man had caught sight of Nicholas's robes and recognized him as a lawyer. He stepped back, made a rude gesture with his fingers and disappeared into the throng.

Scathelocke walked out of the gate and back into the street. Crabtree stood drinking in the sights and sounds.

'I wonder,' Nicholas said to him, 'if anyone here would know about the late departed, if not lamented, Wormwood.'

Crabtree's cheeky grin died. 'Lord, no, master, never ask! By all that's hallowed, you'd get a knife in your gizzard. And how do you know you would be told the truth? I know where Wormwood lived. Let's go there.'

Nicholas nodded his agreement. They rejoined Scathelocke and walked up into Westcheap. The Shambles was busy. Muscular, leather-aproned slaughterers hacked open the cadavers of sheep, cattle and pigs. The air was fetid and the cobbles underfoot slippery with blood. On the steps of the College of St Martin le Grand, a relic-seller and a pardoner were both yelling at a small crowd of amused onlookers; as Nicholas passed, both men gave up arguing and tried to settle their differences by throwing dice. Outside the Goldsmith's Hall, Crabtree abruptly stopped and looked over his shoulder. He stared down the narrow street, studying the people thronging there.

'What's the matter?' Scathelocke asked. 'Do you recognize someone?'

'We are being followed,' Crabtree said. 'I think there are two of them. They take turns. One leads, the other follows. Ah well, if they mean danger they'll show their hand.'

They crossed St Martin's Lane and went up into Aldersgate.
An urchin selling dried cat skins eventually directed them
towards Wormwood's house which was a narrow, mean, two-
storeyed tenement that seemed to have been squeezed between
the houses on either side. The woodwork was flaking, the plaster
was dirty and hadn't been painted for years. The arrow-slit
windows were all shuttered. Scathelocke tried the door but it
was locked. Crabtree told him to stand aside and produced from
some pocket a piece of wire, hooked at each end.

'Wormwood might not have taken care of his house,' he said
as he bent down, 'but I am sure he bought the best lock and
they're always the easiest to pick.' He worked the wire in the
keyhole whilst Nicholas and Scathelocke stood between him
and the passers-by, trying to conceal what he was doing.

'Hurry up!' Scathelocke muttered.

'I am doing my best,' Crabtree retorted. 'Which is more
than I can say for you, No-skin.'

Nicholas looked at Scathelocke. 'What does he mean?'

The manservant blushed and looked down at his feet.

'He knows what I mean,' Crabtree sang out. 'There's not
much old Crabtree doesn't know. Ah . . .'

Nicholas looked round. Crabtree was already pushing the
door open.

'There's little I don't know about locks,' Crabtree boasted.
'Every day I thank the good Lord for those miserable years
spent as an apprentice to a locksmith.'

They walked down the stone-flagged corridor. There were
three rooms on the lower floor – a kitchen, a buttery and a
small parlour. They looked as if they hadn't been inhabited for
years. The walls were dirty, the rushes dry and rotting and
Nicholas glimpsed rat droppings on the greasy, shabby furniture.

They went up the stairs, wrinkling their noses at the foul smell, disturbing the rats which scampered away into the many cracks and gaps in the walls. The upper chambers contained ramshackle beds with dirty soiled sheets; candle grease lay thick on battered furniture. Crabtree stared around what must have been Wormwood's bedchamber.

'Once the news of Wormwood's death becomes public, this place, full of muck and dirt as it is, will be cleaned out,' he said. 'Thieves will take whatever they can move and destroy the rest. What do you hope to find here, master?'

Nicholas pinched his nostrils and leaned against the wall.

'Wormwood undoubtedly killed Berisford, on the orders of the Guardian of the Gates. Berisford was seen near St Paul's. I am sure Wormwood murdered him here. But such violence would have left some trace. Berisford may have been old but he wore a sword and mightn't have given up his life easily. But let's start downstairs. It's unlikely that they came up here.'

They walked downstairs. Nicholas went into the dirty kitchen. He stared around and saw what he had not noticed before, a trapdoor in the far corner. Opening it, he found wooden steps leading down into darkness. He told Crabtree to find a candle and, when he had done so, Nicholas led the way down the steps. At the bottom he stopped and held up the candle. The cellar was small and musty. There were sconce torches on the walls which Scathelocke lit from the candle. The cellar flared into light. Nicholas espied a small cot bed, a stool, a cracked pitcher full of brackish water and a cup. There were bloodstains on the bed, and at its head a set of manacles was screwed into the wall.

'It looks as though I was right,' Nicholas said. 'I am sure if we carefully examined the cellar we'd find traces of poor

Berisford.' He picked up the remains of a small beeswax candle and recalled the coroner's report. 'I was wrong about that!' he murmured. 'I thought only the rich used beeswax.' He tossed the scrap to the floor. 'Apparently Wormwood used only the best when he was engaged in his murderous practices!'

Crabtree hunched down and began to sift amongst the rushes. After only a few moments he gave a cry of satisfaction and held up a blood-soaked neck band. 'Look!' he said. 'It's of good quality!'

Nicholas examined it closely. 'It's Berisford's. The coroner's report said it was missing.' He looked around and whistled under his breath. 'For God's sake, let's get out of here!'

They left the cellar. Crabtree said he had forgotten something upstairs, but Nicholas knew that he wanted to search the house once more for anything valuable to take. Crabtree joined them outside in the street. A freezing rain had begun to fall so they walked back into St Martin's Lane and stopped in a tavern behind the Guildhall. Nicholas sat staring moodily for a while. Crabtree, nervous, mumbled that they were still being followed; Nicholas told him to shut up and then leaned back, gazing up at the rafters. Scathelocke excused himself and, before Nicholas could say anything, drained his tankard and slipped out of the tavern on one of his mysterious errands.

'Crabtree, what do you know about Scathelocke?' Nicholas asked.

The cunning man just tapped the side of his nose. 'Not now, master. Far be it from me to fish in other men's pools. Scathelocke will tell you himself, eventually.'

Nicholas drummed his fingers on the table.

'What have we found out, Crabtree?'

The landlord came back with the ink-horn, quill and

parchment Nicholas had asked for.

'Well?'

'I don't know, master. Except Wormwood killed Berisford. He tortured him in that cellar, took the corpse and tossed it into that ditch on Primrose Hill.'

'But how and why?'

Crabtree shook his head mournfully.

'Master, you're the lawyer!'

Nicholas sighed, took the quill and began to marshal his thoughts.

In a tavern farther up the lane, really nothing more than a dingy alehouse, two French merchants were also discussing what they had found. Both men were hooded and cloaked; they leaned close together over the grease-covered table.

'Do you think,' the elder, grey-bearded one asked, 'that our lawyer will discover anything?'

'He's only a pawn,' the other replied. 'But who knows? He can stumble about and discover what we want.'

'If only Vallence had boarded that galley. If only that pouch had been handed over.'

The younger one shrugged philosophically. 'We do not know if he was even carrying a letter.'

Greybeard wiped his mouth on the back of his hand. 'Vallence knew something damning. But what?'

The younger man finished his wine and got to his feet.

'Stay there,' he said. 'I'll go and clean the tavern yard by pissing on its cobbles.'

He strode down the passageway and went out into the stable yard. He undid the points of his hose and urinated in a cloud of steam. Once he had finished he turned round, did up his points and walked towards the pump to wash his hands. A young woman was standing there, a leather bucket in her hand. She turned as he came up. Golden curls framed an angelic face and the man's heart leapt at her beauty. He pointed to the bucket.

'If I could have some water?'

The young woman smiled and offered him the bucket. The man thanked her with his eyes and took it. The woman walked to his side. The fellow turned.

'No, just some . . .'

His words were cut off. The young woman moved closer and, still smiling, slipped the long dagger she had concealed in her hand straight between his ribs.

The man groaned and staggered back, dropping the bucket and scrabbling at the dagger hilt protruding from his chest. The woman stood her ground and smiled slightly as the man stumbled towards her before crashing down on to the cobbles. Then she turned and slipped quietly across the yard and back into the tavern.

In the taproom the older man sat finishing his drink, drumming his fingers on the table. He stared around and remembered the proverb warning that 'the hunter must be careful not to become the hunted'. He and his companion had followed the lawyer ever since he had left his house early in the morning, downriver to Westminster and now back into the city. Yet, all the time, they had had the feeling that someone had been following *them*.

The Frenchman stared appreciatively at the golden-haired young woman who passed through the taproom, stopping to talk to the landlord. The woman went out and the greasy-aproned taverner came over to him.

'That young woman asked me to give you a message, sir,'

he said. 'She will join you soon. Meanwhile, she sent you this as a gift.'

He placed the wine goblet brimming full of claret down before the old merchant, who sniffed at it appreciatively. He lifted it up and began to sip carefully, unaware of the poison Nightshade had placed in it.

Nicholas and Crabtree were still struggling to understand what they had discovered in Wormwood's cellar. Time and again Nicholas would write down a conclusion, then he would scratch it out in a splutter of ink as he reflected further.

'It doesn't make sense,' he grumbled. 'Berisford disappears. Wormwood has him in that cellar, he tortures him, pummels him and eventually kills him. But then, somehow, he transports the corpse to Primrose Hill.' He glanced up as Scathelocke re-entered the tavern.

'Welcome back!' Crabtree sang out. 'You are like the mist, Scathelocke, going where you wish.'

The manservant glared at him and sat down. He dug inside his jerkin and tossed a soiled piece of green canvas on to the table.

'Where have you been?' Nicholas asked.

'I went back and broke into Wormwood's house. I know now how Berisford's corpse was moved. Wormwood was a skinner, yes?' He picked up the piece of canvas. 'I cut this from a roll hidden in a corner of that cellar. When I unrolled it, it smelt like a charnel house. And it has bloodstains on it.'

Scathelocke looked up and clicked his fingers for some ale. He waited until the potboy had brought it before continuing.

'Wormwood wrapped Berisford's corpse in that canvas, took it out to Primrose Hill and hid it at the bottom of the ditch. The canvas would protect the corpse from the elements and wild animals. Some time on that Thursday afternoon, Wormwood went out and unwrapped the canvas. He left the body so that it would appear to have been mysteriously just placed there.'

'Was that possible?' Crabtree asked.

Scathelocke smiled triumphantly. 'On the other side of the canvas are clots of mud, grass and brambles. I am sure if we go out to Primrose Hill we'll find the ditch where Berisford's corpse lay to be very deep.'

'But why all this subterfuge?' Crabtree asked.

'I can answer that,' Nicholas put in. 'Those behind Berisford's death wished to confuse everyone – by spreading rumours round the city, by concealing the corpse and by putting the blame on poor Fromlich. Hiding the body also gave the Guardian more time. He knew the authorities would be too busy looking for Berisford to continue their own search for what secrets Vallence might have been carrying.'

Scathelocke pointed to the parchment Nicholas had been writing on.

'Does that help your conclusions, master?'

Nicholas grinned. 'Yes, it does. It's another piece in the puzzle. In August Queen Isabella dies at Castle Rising. Vallence leaves the fortress and comes into London, probably accompanying her corpse. His real destination, however, was a Venetian galley. Vallence was the bearer of some great secret the authorities wanted. He is arrested on the quayside, puts up a fight, is seriously wounded and taken to St Bartholomew's hospital. He is interviewed by the sheriff and two aldermen. Berisford is in attendance. Dying, Vallence whispers something about St Denis to Berisford, whom he apparently recognized. Some time later Berisford is commissioned as the investigating justice; he spends the next ten days in a state of agitation. On the Friday before he disappears, he receives a mysterious visitor and his melancholy increases. He exclaims he is to be hanged or burnt, but apparently agrees to meet someone in the city. We know that that someone was Wormwood, who killed him but kept his body concealed for a week and spread confusion in the city before leaving the corpse on Primrose Hill.'

Nicholas tapped the quill against the side of his face. 'The king of London's underworld, the Guardian of the Gates, is responsible for Berisford's death as well as that of the hired assassin Wormwood. He spreads rumours around the city, blames poor Fromlich and then has him killed.' Nicholas cleared his throat before continuing. 'Other murders are committed. Blueskin disappears – we were supposed to waste more time searching the city for him. Fromlich's kinswoman is killed, to protect Nightshade, as a warning to me or even because Fromlich might have told her something.' Nicholas stared at his two companions. 'So, where are the gaps?'

'First,' Scathelocke replied, 'why did Vallence come into London? Castle Rising is on the Norfolk coast. He could have taken a ship from Bishop's Lynn or one of the eastern ports.'

'I know why,' Crabtree said. 'Before she died the old queen probably told Vallence not to act suspiciously or impetuously.' He grinned mischievously. 'I am sure if we examine the records of the old bitch's funeral, we'd find Vallence was in attendance. Once the Requiem was over, it was simply a matter of slipping through the side streets to Queenshithe Wharf.'

'It was Queen Isabella's secret,' Nicholas said. 'That is why the authorities were waiting for him. They knew the old queen held a secret and believed that once her funeral was over, her faithful retainer would try and slip abroad.'

'I agree.' Crabtree leaned over the table. 'I am sure we will discover that all eastern ports were being watched during the last days of the queen as well as for some time after her death. Vallence hoped to escape from London.'

Chirke rubbed his eyes. 'What other gaps are there? Why did Vallence recognize Berisford?'

His two companions just looked askance. Chirked sighed.

'And, above all, what secret did Vallence carry?'

He broke off as shouts and the sound of running feet came from outside the tavern door. Cries of 'Harrow! Harrow!' showed that the hue and cry was being raised. Crabtree got to his feet and went out to investigate. He returned a few minutes later.

'There've been murders!' he exclaimed. 'At a nearby tavern. Two men. One stabbed, the other poisoned.'

Nicholas shivered and crossed his arms. '*In media vitae sumus in morte*,' he murmured. 'In the midst of life we are in death. The Red-Handed slayer stalks us on every side.'

'Where shall we go now?' Crabtree asked. 'What can we do, master?'

Nicholas hid his smile at the way Crabtree had inveigled himself into his company, making Nicholas's task his own. He tossed the quill back on to the table.

'We have no guarantee the Guardian of the Gates has not already discovered what Vallence was carrying.' He stared at the doorway, where the clamour had now subsided. 'What loose threads are there for us to pick up? Fromlich is dead. Berisford is dead. Vallence lies rotting in a pauper's grave. The only morsel of new evidence we have is that given us by Berisford's clerk. Who is this Patricius? Why did he terrify Berisford?' Nicholas got to his feet. 'There must be something Mawsby has forgotten.'

He stared at his companions. 'You needn't come if you don't want to, but I am going back to Westminster.'

Scathelocke and Crabtree groaned. 'What else can we do? Where else can we go?'

'I have other business,' Scathelocke announced.

'Well, I can go,' Crabtree said.

As they were leaving, they had to stand in the doorway to let the death cart go by. It contained two corpses, covered by a rough horse blanket. Chirke glimpsed the boots of the dead men jutting out and wondered what had happened.

'Death's common,' Crabtree murmured. He glanced nervously about. 'No one knows if this is their last day in this vale of tears.'

Nicholas told him not to be so gloomy and they went down an alleyway, across Old Fish Street into Vintry and hired a wherryman to take them to Westminster, where the palace was now bustling with lawyers in their striped robes, judges in their scarlet, tipstaffs, plaintiffs and defendants. A myriad of hawkers and pedlars thronged about, hoping to make a profit from the business of King's Bench, or the courts of Common Pleas, Chancery and Exchequer. Nicholas and Crabtree pressed on until they reached Berisford's house. Nicholas knocked vigorously at the door.

'Perhaps Mawsby has left?' Crabtree wondered.

'The servants would certainly have been gone by now,' Chirke said. He drew his dagger from his belt and pounded once more on the door with the pommel. Still no reply.

'There's a rear entrance,' Crabtree observed.

They went down a narrow alleyway and found the shabby gate at the end standing slightly open. They pushed it back and entered a long garden enclosed by a high yellow-stone wall.

Beyond the raised flower beds Nicholas caught a glimpse of water. He climbed on to one of the flower beds to get a better view.

'What is it?' Crabtree asked.

Nicholas narrowed his eyes. 'A stew or carp pond.'

He saw then the flash of colour floating in the pond and jumped down and ran as fast as he could along the narrow, twisting path. The carp pond was broad, the water cold, icy to the touch and, in the middle, floating face down amongst the lilies was Mawsby. Followed by Crabtree, Nicholas waded into the water and together they pulled out the swollen corpse, heavy in its water-drenched robes. They laid the corpse at the edge of the pond and stared down at the white-blue face, popping eyes and gaping mouth. A garrotte string was still twisted tightly around the old man's neck, biting into the soft skin of the throat. Crabtree took one look at the swollen tongue, its tip caught between the yellowing teeth, and turned to retch and vomit on the frozen grass.

'Hell's teeth!' he gasped. 'Mouse's tits!'

Nicholas also felt queasy. He pulled the corpse further from the edge of the pond and stared around the garden. He could see nothing untoward, no sign of any struggle or violence. Both house and garden were eerily silent. He knelt and turned Mawsby's dead face towards him. The skin was icy, fish-like to the touch. He stared at the clerk's slender, ink-stained fingers.

'How long has he been dead?'

'God knows!' Nicholas stared down at his hose just above his own boots. 'The water's freezing.' He rubbed his leggings. 'There's nothing we can do.'

They walked back along the garden and through the back door of the house. A part-filled cup of mulled wine stood on the kitchen table; it was warm to the touch. The fire in the scullery still blazed merrily. Followed by Crabtree, he wandered through the rooms. He found no sign of violence – none of the chests or coffers had been disturbed. In the small writing office scraps of parchment, thinning with age, littered the table alongside an ink-horn and a quill knife which Nicholas picked up and examined carefully. He told Crabtree to light a candle, then held the pieces of parchment up against the glow of the flame.

'What is it, master?'

Nicholas screwed up his eyes, wishing the light was better. Each scrap of parchment bore one word, presumably written by Mawsby.

'Patricius,' Nicholas read aloud. He picked up another piece. 'Here it has changed to Patroclus.' He threw the scraps down. 'Let's make sure there's nothing else.'

They searched the house, going through papers, looking for some secret hiding-place. Darkness fell and they lit more candles but after a while Nicholas confessed they could find nothing and said they should leave. They doused the candles, made the door secure and returned on foot to the city. Nicholas stopped at the Guildhall to leave a message about Mawsby's corpse for the coroner and then returned home.

They found the house in commotion. The twins were screaming, chasing each other with wooden swords. John and Catherine were deep in conversation, sitting close, arms clasped, heads together. Nicholas felt a pang of jealousy. He was cold, hungry and lonely and beginning to regret that he had ever accepted Sir Amyas Petrie's invitation. Crabtree also had had enough of 'trailing in the city' as he put it and disappeared out of the door, heading like an arrow for the nearest tavern.

* * *

145

'Have you seen Scathelocke?' Nicholas asked his sister.

Catherine smiled and shook her head. 'Do you want some food?'

Nicholas remembered Mawsby's icy, white-blue face and shook his head.

'No, just a goblet of wine.'

He went over to the dresser, filled a goblet to the brim and stumped off upstairs, ignoring both John's bemused glances and Catherine's advice that he should change his clothes and get a hot meal inside him.

Once in his own chamber, he gulped the wine down, took off his boots and lay on the bed, staring up at the ceiling. The blankets beneath were warm. Nicholas relished the heat from the warming-pan full of burning charcoal Catherine had kindly slipped between the sheets at the bottom of the bed. He heard sounds from below – the children shouting, Catherine and John telling them to be quiet. His mind whirled as he tried to make sense of the day's happenings. His eyes grew heavy. He slipped into a sleep, plagued by nightmares. He was standing on the wild desolate heathlands outside Norwich, but the grass was covered by a fine white sand and, above him, the sky had turned purple-red. In the middle of this heath was a black, gaunt manor house which looked as if it was built of steel. Its windows were empty. Across a slime-filled moat, where rats and mice bobbed and swam amongst black lily stems, a massive door kept swinging open and shut.

In his dream, Nicholas went across the moat through the door and along darkened passageways until he found himself in a broad chamber. He thought the walls were lined with velvet but, on closer inspection, discovered that the wall-covering was the living bodies of rats massed together. He sat down at the table, so long that the far end seemed to stretch into infinity. In the middle of the table stood a huge glass jar filled with water, large enough to take a man's corpse. Mawsby was floating there, his face pressed against the glass, eyes staring, wisps of hair streaming round him like some shabby halo; the dead clerk's thin, bloodless lips opened and shut like a carp's. He was shouting at Nicholas but Nicholas couldn't hear. He tried to free him, then found he couldn't move. Mawsby's hands were now beating against the glass, his face taking on a mottled hue. Nicholas felt every gasp of the drowning man as if it was his own. He woke and sat up, his body dripping with sweat, even as he realized he had overlooked something.

'The cup of mulled wine!' he said aloud. 'The cup of mulled wine!'

He sat on the edge of the bed, arms crossed. Was Mawsby drinking the wine when the murderer came? Or did he prepare it for his visitor? Nicholas closed his eyes and tried to picture the scene. Mawsby was scrawling on those pieces of parchment. There was a knock on the door. Mawsby answered and let his killer in. He offered the visitor a cup of mulled wine. So the visitor must have been someone Mawsby respected or liked enough to offer hospitality. He must have gone into the scullery to prepare the wine, leaving the visitor to read the parchments. The assassin then went into the kitchen and tasted the wine. But why should they go into the garden? Perhaps the visitor wanted to show Mawsby something? Or discuss something where no eavesdropper or spy could overhear? Whatever the reason, Mawsby went out, the assassin slipped behind him, the garrotte string was produced and Mawsby was killed.

Chapter 3

Nicholas was about to wash his hands and face when he heard footsteps on the stairs and a pounding on the door. He opened it to find Scathelocke standing there, grinning. Scathelocke thrust a yellowing piece of parchment into his hands.

'A boy gave it to me,' Scathelocke said. 'He was waiting for me outside in the alleyway. What is it, master? A lover's note?'

Going back into his room to take advantage of the candlelight, Nicholas carefully unrolled the parchment. The writing, in blue-green ink, looked strange. The parchment, coarse and rather thick, was of the sort used by public scriveners outside St Paul's. It bore his name and a simple message: 'The Joy of Jerusalem, Southwark at noon. Vallence.'

'It's no love note,' he told Scathelocke, 'but an invitation to The Joy of Jerusalem.'

Scathelocke whistled under his breath. 'If there was a hell on earth, master, that dingy tavern would be part of it. I'll go with you.'

Nicholas shook his head. 'No. If you came, whoever was waiting would just fade away.'

Scathelocke made to protest but Nicholas shook his head and the manservant continued up the stairs to his own chamber, grumbling under his breath. Nicholas remembered the cup of mulled wine and, going downstairs, asked Catherine to prepare him one.

'Of course.' She wiped the sweat from her brow with the back of her hand – she had been busy, baking tomorrow's bread. Then she looked at Nicholas, eyes narrowed in concern. She went up to him. 'What's the matter, Nicholas?' She touched the side of his face. 'You look tired and drawn.'

Nicholas grinned and shrugged. 'A cup of wine will put it right.'

'You shouldn't drink wine on an empty stomach!' she snapped, but she went to the fire and re-kindled the flames. She poured some wine into a pewter cup, placed it on a small stone in the inglenook then pushed two thin pokers into the fire.

Nicholas sat and watched them until they glowed red hot, then he took them out and plunged them into the pewter cup. Catherine offered to help, but Nicholas shook his head. He waited until the pokers glowed red hot again then dipped them once more into the wine. The cup became hot to the touch. He took a rag, wrapped it around the cup and carried it back to his own chamber. He winked at Catherine, asking her to excuse the madness of her brother and would she be so kind as to douse the fire?

Once back in his own chamber, he placed the mulled wine on the table. He took an hour glass and turned it over to start the sand trickling through. Then he sat, watching the level of sand fall and now and again testing the temperature of the cup as it cooled. When it was only as warm as the one left by Mawsby in Berisford's house he checked the hour glass carefully. Only a quarter of the sand had trickled through.

'Lord save us!' he muttered. 'If we had arrived fifteen minutes earlier, I could have saved Mawsby and trapped his murderer!'

He remembered the suspicious old clerk. Whom would he allow into the house without a second thought? For whom would he prepare a cup of posset? Then walk out into the garden, totally unsuspecting? Sir Amyas Petrie, the sheriff? One of his minions? Nicholas shook his head. No, Mawsby would not do that. It was apparent from their earlier conversation that the clerk had no liking for the city authorities, whose mysterious tasks had led to his master's murder. So who? Someone sent by the Guardian of the Gates? A man like Wormwood? Again Nicholas shook his head. He heard Catherine call from downstairs. He smiled, picked up the cup and sipped from it. Of course, a woman. Nightshade, the poisonous name given to that fair-faced, innocent-eyed assassin. But why would the Guardian want Mawsby dead?

Nicholas lay down on the bed. A few minutes later he was asleep. Scathelocke tip-toed in, extinguished the candle, placed a blanket over his master and quietly slipped out of the room.

Nicholas stirred. He glimpsed Scathelocke leaving, cloaked and booted, and sleepily wondered where his enigmatic manservant was off to now. He recalled Sir Amyas's enmity towards Scathelocke and, before he fell asleep again, a wild thought occurred to him. Could Scathelocke be in the employ of the Guardian of the Gate? Was he really some wolfshead in disguise? Was that why he had been recognized in St Paul's graveyard and why he had left so abruptly? What did Crabtree know? Nicholas vowed that, when this business was over, he would confront Scathelocke once and for all; he'd either tell the truth or be dismissed.

Nicholas slept late the next morning. When he woke, refreshed and very hungry, the streets below were already noisy

151

and thronged as a weak sun began to dissipate the mist. Remembering his meeting at Southwark, he hastily stripped, washed, shaved and dressed again. He snatched something to eat from the buttery, downed a small jug of ale and, armed with sword and dagger, hurried out towards London Bridge. The causeway was packed, thronged with carts to-ing and fro-ing, so he went down the steps beneath the bridge along the quayside where he hired a boatman. The fellow took his coins and, as he rowed him across the Thames, regaled him with a string of stories about merry monks, fornicating friars and naughty nuns. Nicholas listened with half an ear, smiling now and again out of politeness. The water was choppy and fast-running and the clinging, cold mist seeped through every article of his clothing. He landed at the Fish Wharf in Southwark and, despite the cold, pushed his cloak back over his shoulder, allowing all comers to see the sword and dagger strapped to his belt.

Southwark was a veritable hell-hole. Its narrow streets were packed with all the denizens of the underworld – sham beggars, relic-sellers, footpads, whores, pimps, cut-purses, forgers, counterfeiters and murderers. Many were men who would kill another human being for the price of a pot of ale. Once away from the quayside Nicholas stopped and stared round. He felt uneasy, certain someone was staring back at him. Nevertheless, he could see no real danger except from the occasional rogue or footpad lounging in a tavern doorway He entered the narrow alleyways made almost impassable by the stalls and booths set up on either side which sold baubles, cheap food or other items, usually stolen from shops across the river. Prostitutes flocked, thick as starlings on a freshly ploughed field. Every dirty corner and filthy alleyway had its own gang of rifflers eager to strike, even in daylight, against the unsuspecting. Thin, ragged children scurried around like mice in a hayrick, shouting and screaming, dashing in and out of the small houses, even swinging from the ale-stakes pushed under the eaves of the shabby inns. The air stank with a mixture of pungent smells from the open sewers, which ran rank and foul, as well as the stench from the tanners, skinners and brick-burners who plied their trade in a host of small rooms and wooden sheds.

Every second house seemed to be a tavern and Nicholas had some difficulty in finding the Joy of Jerusalem, which stood on a corner of a darkened alleyway patrolled by mangy, thin-ribbed cats who fought angrily over heaps of rubbish. They even climbed on to the corpse of a beggar lying in a frozen puddle at the mouth of the alleyway. Nicholas murmured a prayer to St Andrew and went inside the tavern. The taproom was surprisingly clean. Its small windows let in little light, making it an ideal den for any man hiding from the law. Two gamblers sat dicing in a corner and did not even bother to look up when he entered. A fat woman, her face pock-marked but merry despite a scar which ploughed across her right cheek, came bustling up, shouting, 'What do ye lack? What do ye lack, sir?'

Nicholas settled himself on a stool behind a rickety table and stared around. Scrawny-necked chickens were roosting on the edge of beer barrels. He did not wish his ale to be spiced with their droppings so he paid heavily for an unstoppered flagon of wine.

'And make sure it's claret, the best the house has!' he ordered.

The ale wife thanked Nicholas as if he was her long-lost son and quickly returned with a flagon still sealed, and a cup. Nicholas carefully poured out the wine. He sipped slowly; he didn't wish to become drunk. The bells of a distant church chimed for the noon Angelus, but no one approached him. People

153

came and went. An old crone became so drunk that she almost crawled out of the door. Only the gamblers stayed. The afternoon drew on. Nicholas became restless; he was heavy-eyed from the wine and the cloying warmth of the tavern. At last he stood up, preparing to leave, convinced that he had been sent on a fool's errand. At the same time, the gamblers rose and walked slowly towards him.

Nicholas's hand went to his sword. But, even as he faced them, he recognized that the gamblers were not the usual visitors to such a place. He smiled suddenly.

'You find us amusing, sir?' one of them asked.

Nicholas stepped back, tossing his cloak over a stool. He clutched the hilt of his sword.

'Yes, I find you amusing,' he replied. 'You are dressed shabbily enough. A man can hide his face, let his beard grow, tousle his hair and wear untidy, ill-fitting clothes, but he is always betrayed by his hands.' He flicked his fingers at them. 'Yours are clean and soft, your nails are carefully manicured.'

Both men smiled, one stretched his hand out in a gesture of peace.

'Monsieur Chirke, we wish you no ill.' He pointed to the table behind Nicholas. 'Let us share the rest of your wine.' The gambler smiled lopsidedly. 'Perhaps we can also share a problem.'

Nicholas shrugged and sat down. The strangers pulled over stools and squatted opposite him, smiling as if they were old friends. One was tall and thin, his face white and gaunt under a bush of fiery red hair. The other was smaller, fat and bald. He looked as cheerful as Friar Tuck in some story about Robin of the Greenwood. They were dressed in tattered, patched robes fastened at the neck but, as they sat down, both of them moved a little to accommodate the long, stabbing daggers concealed underneath. The woman brought two cups. The small, fat one, without any bidding, refilled all three cups to the brim. He toasted Nicholas and sipped gratefully at the wine.

'I hope you enjoy my claret,' Chirke observed sarcastically.

'It's better to be alive and drinking wine,' the small fellow quipped, 'than drowned in cold water like poor Mawsby.' He put his cup down. 'Let us introduce ourselves. I am Eudo Epingall and this' – he turned to his red-haired companion – 'is Robard Clerrier.'

'Was it you who killed Mawsby?' Nicholas asked.

'No! But it is we who have been following you round the city,' Eudo Epingall said. 'There used to be four of us, but our two companions are dead. One was stabbed, the other poisoned. You must have heard the clamour their deaths caused yesterday when you were supping with your own companions near the Guildhall.'

Nicholas stared at them open-mouthed. 'Who are you?'

'Gascon merchants. Well, not exactly merchants – though we carry letters saying we come from Bordeaux, bringing our beautiful wine to your country. More the servants of Our Master.'

'And who is he?'

Epingall smiled. Nicholas leaned across the table. 'You're French spies! You are here to collect information. What do you know about Vallence?' He pushed his stool back. 'It could be treason just to talk to you.'

Robard Clerrier touched Nicholas's wrist gently. 'Monsieur, please, listen to us. We are not here to bait or threaten but to tell you a story you probably already know. Last August Queen Isabella died. She harboured some great secret. Before she died, she committed this secret to Vallence, who slipped away from her funeral ceremony at Greyfriars and tried to board a Venetian galley. He was stopped, wounded and later died at St Bartholomew's. Since then, the king and his eldest son, the Black Prince, have used their powerful friends in the city to discover what Vallence was carrying and where he might have hidden it. We also know that the King of the Underworld, who styles himself the Guardian of the Gates, is making a similar search.'

Clerrier smiled thinly. 'We have a similar person in Paris. He calls himself *le Roi de Gueux*, "the King of the Beggars". Oh, we've heard all about Berisford's death, and Fromlich's.' He paused and sipped from his goblet. 'Now, you will say, Monsieur Chirke, that what concerns the French should not concern you. But, have you considered, monsieur, what might happen to you when you discover Vallence's secret?'

Nicholas felt the hair on the nape of his neck curl. He quietly cursed; he hadn't thought of that. If this secret was so dangerous, so important, what would happen if, and when, he found it? He picked up his own wine cup to mask the concern Clerrier's words had caused him.

'What are you proposing?' he asked.

'Tell us what you know. We'll reward you. Never again will you have to search for a fee or live off the kindness of your sister.'

'I am not a traitor!' Nicholas snapped.

'But you might be a fool,' Epingall jibed. 'All we are asking is that you tell us what you know and we will reward you. Go back to your masters. Tell the same to them and say you find the whole matter most perplexing, beyond your capabilities. You would not only be rich but grow old enough to enjoy it.' He clapped his hands softly. 'Come, monsieur, tell us.'

Nicholas sucked in his breath. He bitterly regretted that neither Scathelocke nor Crabtree was with him.

'I know very little, except how Berisford died – he was killed by an assassin called Wormwood. Fromlich was falsely blamed for the murder. Both he and Wormwood were murdered by a female assassin hired by the Guardian of the Gates. She probably killed Mawsby too. Before you ask, the only thing Mawsby told me was that Berisford knew Vallence even before they met at St Bartholomew's. Also, the night before Berisford disappeared a mysterious messenger arrived at his house carrying a letter from someone called Patricius.'

The two Frenchmen listened intently.

'Is that all, monsieur?'

'That is all. Oh yes, Vallence said something about St Denis.'

He watched for some reaction but the Frenchmen stared impassively back. Nicholas shrugged.

'That's all I know.'

'Patricius?' Epingall asked, with a sigh.

Nicholas nodded.

'No,' Epingall said. 'I don't think it was Patricius. I think it was Patroclus.'

'Who, in God's name, is he?'

Clerrier smiled. 'Come, monsieur, don't you know your Greek history? Patroclus was a friend of Achilles, whom Hector killed.'

Nicholas sat, looking puzzled.

Epingall's grin widened.

'Don't pose riddles!' Nicholas snapped.

'Achilles loved Patroclus,' Epingall explained. 'It was an unnatural love, they were sodomites. Patroclus is the name taken by a coven of homosexuals here in London. Berisford was a member of that coven and so was Vallence.'

157

Nicholas rubbed his hand across his mouth and smiled apologetically.

'Of course,' he breathed. 'Berisford sold wood and coal to Vallence for the old queen's household. Such men have their own signs and secret rituals.'

The two Frenchmen nodded.

'And the Guardian of the Gates discovered Berisford's secret and blackmailed him,' Clerrier explained.

'Which is why,' Nicholas said, 'Berisford kept muttering about being hanged or burnt. Sodomites caught in the act, if the case is proven against them, are hanged at Smithfield above a slow-burning fire. So, Wormwood probably sent that message to Berisford's house and Berisford had no choice but to agree to meet him, otherwise his secret would have been made public.'

Nicholas stared across the tavern at the old beggar who had shuffled in the doorway and now sat on the floor, his back to the wall, shouting at the ale wife for something to drink.

'But why should the Guardian of the Gates blackmail Berisford?' he asked. 'He hadn't discovered anything. Or had he? Did Vallence whisper something else to him before he died?'

Nicholas pushed his cup away. Epingall went to refill it.

'No, I have drunk enough!' Nicholas exclaimed.

'Can't you see what will happen if you do discover Vallence's secret?' Clerrier asked. 'Do you think those who hired you, will allow you to live on peacefully? The Guardian of the Gates is no less dangerous – he wants that secret so he can blackmail others, secure privileges, riches, increase his own power and wealth.'

Nicholas shrugged. 'But how can they threaten me, a poor, needy lawyer?'

'You have a brother, who is married to the woman you love,'

Epingall replied softly. 'You have a sister, Catherine and her merry, yeoman husband. They have children. You have your life, Monsieur Chirke. So, if you proceed in this matter and find this great secret, come to us at the sign of the Moon and Sickle in Lothbury.' Epingall gripped Nicholas's hand and squeezed it tightly. 'We are warning you, monsieur, for your own sake. Ignore us and you do so at your peril!'

Nicholas stared at the Frenchmen, trying to curb the lurching in his stomach and the increased beating of his heart. He admired their cleverness – whichever way he jumped he would face danger, and they were offering him a way out. But what would it mean? Exile in France? Would John, Catherine, their children and his brother be safe?

'Who is your leader?' he asked.

'Come to us at the Moon and Sickle tavern and find out. Ask to play a game of hazard.'

Nicholas stared past them through the doorway. The day was drawing on. He glanced at the beggar. The fellow was one-eyed, his nose was rotting with corruption and a drool of saliva ran from one corner of his mouth, but Nicholas wildly wondered if the man was a spy – someone sent by the Guardian of the Gates or by those other powerful ones in the city.

'I must go,' he said.

'Not by the doorway.'

Clerrier rose and called the woman who had served them. She bustled across. Clerrier whispered to her, dropping a coin into her calloused hand. She smiled and beckoned, leading them over to a far corner of the tavern behind high-stacked beer barrels. She plucked a key from her belt and unlocked a side entrance which led into an alleyway. Epingall and Clerrier stepped through, Nicholas behind them. The Frenchmen stood, hoods up over their heads, cloaks tightly wrapped around them. Clerrier moved forward. His hands were held out in farewell to Nicholas when the crossbow bolt took him full in the mouth. Nicholas heard a whirr like that of a kestrel swooping for the kill and glimpsed something black as it skimmed past his eyes.

The Frenchman had no chance. The crossbow bolt smashed into his face and he crashed to the cobbles. Epingall, pulling Chirke by the cloak, shoved and pushed him down the alleyway.

'Run!' he whispered hoarsely.

They did, even as a second crossbow bolt smashed on to the cobbles between them. Epingall glanced back at his fallen comrade. He looked pleadingly at Nicholas.

'I cannot leave him,' he whispered.

'No! No!' Nicholas shouted hoarsely. 'He's dead!'

Epingall shook his head. He drew his dagger and, keeping to the alley wall, edged back to where Clerrier lay face down in an ever-widening puddle of blood. Turning the body over, Epingall cut the wallet from the dead man's belt and hurried back.

Nicholas pressed against the wall, away from the hidden marksman. Epingall had nearly reached him when the whirring sound came again. The Frenchman leaned towards Nicholas like a swimmer, his hands out, eyes staring, mouth opening and closing, gasping for air. He stumbled against the piss-stained wall. He glared painfully at Nicholas, whispering 'Jesu, Mercy, Mercy', and dropped like a bundle of rags. The crossbow bolt, with its iron jagged point, was embedded firmly between his shoulder blades.

Nicholas fled even as another crossbow bolt whirled, hitting the wall above his head. Despite his panic, he realized that there must be two assassins, not one. He ran blindly, away

160

from the death-strewn alleyway, hiding amongst the beggars, pimps and bawds thronging the streets of Southwark. He gazed wildly about, trying to glimpse the hunters. He was safe from any crossbow, but not from the subtle assassin who could sidle up and slip a dagger between his ribs. He reached the riverside. Muttering and cursing, he jumped into a boat, hastily pressing a coin into the wherryman's dirty hand.

'Pull, man, pull!' he roared.

The boatman leaned over his oars, rowing away from the bank. Nicholas stared back through the gathering darkness, but neither the fading daylight nor the huge spluttering torches on the river bank revealed any sign of his pursuers. The boatman pulled lustily at his oars; he studied Nicholas closely from under his heavy-lidded eyes, curious at this well-dressed man's white face, sweat-soaked skin and obvious look of terror.

'You shouldn't really go there,' he muttered.

'Shut up!' Chirke snarled. 'And pull!'

The boatman landed Nicholas between Dowgate and London Bridge. He staggered through the streets, eager to reach safety. He kept his hand on his dagger hilt and every so often he paused at the mouth of some foul alleyway and looked back over his shoulder. When he arrived home, John and Catherine were busy and the children were playing outside in the frozen garden. Nicholas made his way to his own chamber, where he lay, arms crossed, on the bed, staring up at the ceiling.

'What,' he muttered, 'what caused so many deaths? What was so precious about what Vallence knew?'

He counted the number of people who had died. Vallence, because of what he carried; Berisford, tortured to death to reveal what he knew; Wormwood; the Fromlichs; and now four French spies. Was the Guardian of the Gates responsible for all these deaths, or was it someone else? Should he go back to see Sir Amyas Petrie and Sir Roger Hobbedon and tell them their task was too dangerous, beyond his strength and capability?

There was a tap on the door. He ignored it, thinking it might be the children, but it was repeated more insistently.

'Come in!' he shouted.

Scathelocke and Crabtree sidled into the room.

'We've been looking for you, master.'

Scathelocke stood near the bed and studied his master's white face.

'We've been looking for you,' he repeated.

'I wish to God you'd found me!' Nicholas said.

Without waiting for an invitation, he told them what had happened. He saw the fear in Scathelocke's eyes. Crabtree, squatting on a stool, moaned to himself and clutched his stomach.

'Two spies.' The cunning man whispered. 'Killed just like dogs.'

'You are not to go to the Moon and Sickle tavern,' Scathelocke said eventually. 'If you do, you could be arrested for treason. England's at war with France. You might be killed, or executed, for just talking to such men.'

Nicholas pulled himself up on the bed. 'I could go back to Sir Amyas.'

'Oh no,' Crabtree wailed, 'not to that flint-hearted bastard. Anyway, he might believe we have discovered what Vallence was carrying.'

'And what was that?'

'I also wondered about such a secret,' Scathelocke replied slowly. 'So I went to see some friends in Lombard Street.'

'I didn't know you had friends,' Crabtree crowed.

'Shut up, you little bastard!' Scathelocke snapped. 'Now is not the time for droll stories or funny witticisms. All three of us are bound by this secret.'

He scratched his beard. 'As I have said, I went to see friends – people who knew the old queen. Well, everyone knows Isabella had her husband Edward II murdered at Berkeley Castle and played the two-backed beast with her lover Roger Mortimer until they both fell from power when our present king was a young man. Afterwards, Isabella was kept at Castle Rising, trotted out now and again for state banquets and important festivities, but really living the life of a recluse.'

'So?' Nicholas interrupted.

'Whatever the secret was, it didn't originate in her last years. It came from the time when she ruled the kingdom with Mortimer – or even before. Now I asked my friends how Isabella fared before she fled from her husband. They told me that Edward II, her husband, was a sodomite who fell deeply in love with one of his noblemen, Hugh de Spencer. It was this unnatural lust that drove Isabella into exile. Before that she was a noble queen and dutiful wife and there was no hint of scandal.'

Scathelocke paused to gather his thoughts. 'When Isabella and Mortimer fell from power they were arrested at Nottingham Castle. Mortimer was actually in the queen's bedroom at the time. So was their close confidant, Henry Burghersh, Bishop of Norwich. Isabella's son, Edward, reached that chamber by a secret passageway. He burst in with a group of knights and ordered Mortimer's arrest. Isabella fell to her knees shrieking, *'Ayez pitie! Ayez pitie à gentil Mortimer!'*

'Then what happened?' Crabtree interrupted.

Scathelocke shrugged. 'Well, my friends only know this from rumour. Mortimer shouted abuse at the young Edward before

163

being dragged out. He was sent under close guard to be tried at Westminster. During his trial he was not allowed to speak, not even to make his plea known. He was gagged throughout his trial. Once sentence was pssed, he was taken to the Elms near Tyburn's tree, hanged, drawn and quartered. His mangled remains lie buried in Greyfriars.'

'And?' Nicholas asked testily.

Scathelocke grinned. 'Apparently the old bitch wanted the best of both worlds, in death as well as in life. She was buried beside the high altar next to her lover with a silver casket containing her husband's heart in the coffin beside her.'

Nicholas looked through the gap between the shutters. Darkness had fallen.

'I have never heard of a man being gagged throughout his trial,' he murmured. 'So what was it that Mortimer knew and could not be allowed to reveal?'

'Is it possible,' Crabtree suggested, 'that our present king, Edward III, is not a true King of England but the illegitimate by-blow of Mortimer and Isabella?'

Scathelocke looked thoughtful. 'It is all rumour, scandal, gossip, proving nothing. Nevertheless, you may be right, Master Crabtree. Certainly it would appear that Queen Isabella may have had a hand in the promotion and protection of Mortimer before she fled from her husband. However, that does not mean Mortimer begot children upon her.'

'But her husband was a sodomite,' Crabtree insisted.

Nicholas shook his head. 'He was bisexual. Many men are.' He shrugged. 'Of course, that does not apply to any of us!'

'I am not too sure,' Scathelocke growled, glancing sideways at Crabtree, who made a rude sign with his middle finger.

'Nevertheless, Scathelocke, I thank you,' Nicholas said. 'The gossip you've gleaned supports our theory that Queen Isabella possessed a secret which she tried to pass on to her friends in France. However, her son, our present king, closely guarded his mother, wary lest she play some mischief.' Nicholas swung his legs off the bed, rose and stretched.

'Revenge is a dish best served cold,' he said. 'Isabella kept her secret during her lifetime but arranged for it to be revealed when she was dead. What a legacy to leave, eh?'

'So, what do we do?' Crabtree asked.

'Get out of London,' Nicholas replied, 'even though we have very little money. We'll go to Norwich – old Burghersh is still alive. Then, on to Castle Rising, to snoop amongst the household there, see what we can discover.' He rubbed his face. 'Who knows? By the time we return, Vallence's secret may be found. We'll collect our bag of coins and go back to strolling the aisle of St Paul's, touting for business.'

'Whom shall we tell?' Scathelocke asked.

'No one!' Nicholas snapped. 'Not even Catherine and John.'

He went to the window and looked out at the gathering night.

'Though I suppose,' he murmured, 'it will make little difference.'

He stared down at the doorway opposite, where a lantern glowed on its hook. He glimpsed the shadow move and realized they were still being watched from the darkness.

Chapter 4

They left late the next morning, just as the city bells tolled for Mass, their clanging cutting like a knife through the cold winter air. Crabtree had been busy, spending Nicholas's precious monies to hire horses and a nasty looking sumpter pony. The 'beast', as Crabtree christened it, had a will all of its own as well as a spiteful way of biting and kicking anyone foolish enough to approach it unwarily. Nicholas told his sister little, except that they might be away for days. Catherine, anxious-faced, kissed him on both cheeks and stared sadly at him.

'Are you going to Norwich, Nicholas? Will you call in to see your brother? Robert would be so pleased to see you.'

Nicholas mumbled that he would try. 'Look after yourself, sister.' He pressed her closely. 'Take care of John and watch the children.'

'Why?' Catherine pulled herself away. 'Nicholas, what's happening?'

Her brother refused to meet her eye. He squeezed her hand and went out into the street, where Scathelocke and Crabtree were holding the horses. John came out of his shop to wish them a fair journey; his broad, generous face smiling, he sidled

167

up to Nicholas and pressed a small purse of coins into his hand. Nicholas would have refused.

'No, brother, take it,' John insisted. 'Eat well.' He looked up at the grey, leaden sky. 'Those who know say we will have snow. Keep warm and may God bless you on your journey.'

The children ran out to say goodbye, as did Catherine. She refused to let Nicholas go until he promised to pin the St Christopher medal she'd brought onto his threadbare cloak.

They left the street and made their way up Bishopsgate through the old city walls and across the stinking ditch. Nicholas hated the place. Beneath the dirty coating of ice he glimpsed the cadavers of animals and, despite the cold, the place still stank like a sewer. They passed St Mary of Bethlehem, taking the road north to Holywell. The thoroughfare was busy with peasants bringing their produce into the city as well as the usual stream of travellers – ragged students, hedge priests with their wheel barrows, mountebanks, landless men hoping the city would provide them with wealth and soldiers marching down to reinforce the garrison at the Tower. A royal messenger, dressed in the blue, red and gold of the court livery, galloped by. The occasional noble, resplendent in silks, his horses gaily caparisoned with colourful heraldic devices, swept splendidly along.

As the day drew on, however, the road across the wild heathland north of London grew emptier. They stayed the night at a small tavern, spending most of the time awake – the beds were infested with fleas and the noise from the taproom below, where a group of tinkers were carousing, persisted most of the night. Such discomfort and the freezing weather kept conversation to a minimum. The leaden skies seemed to press down on them and the countryside was often hidden by driving winds which carried a freezing rain to lash their faces. They passed through small, squalid hamlets, staying at miserable inns where the one topic of conversation was the war against the French and the Crown's insistent demands for more supplies. The peasants they passed, trying to break the hard frozen soil, were often dressed like scarecrows. Some had even given up such work to scavenge like kites for something to eat.

'Jesu have mercy on them,' Crabtree murmured as they passed through one small hamlet. 'Their lot is most pitiable. The young men are pressed into the king's wars. Only the crippled return, unable to fend for themselves.'

Nicholas agreed and stared out across the broad, frozen brown fields. 'In times of peace,' he said, 'the peasants are heavily taxed. Royal purveyors move like the plague from village to village collecting produce. After them come the tax collectors, followed by the bailiffs and serjeants of the local lords.'

Now and again, they met families trudging the roads. Nicholas distributed pennies, which were taken without thanks by cold, grasping hands. They passed corpses decomposing in ditches, gibbets and scaffolds heavy with their rotting human fruit. On one occasion they were attacked by outlaws, a group of desperate men covered from head to toe in tattered rags. These were poorly armed and posed no real danger; their bows were so makeshift and badly sprung that their arrows fell far short.

After a week's travelling they reached the outskirts of Norwich. Nicholas decided they'd recover from their journey in a large spacious tavern just within the city walls – a vast, noisy building with the golden 'I H S' carved above the entrance supported by angels with innocent, smiling faces. Inside, the cobbled yard, bounded by galleries and staircases, was full of travellers seeking rest as they passed to and from the great ports on the eastern coast. Nicholas smiled as he looked around. He remembered the place from his youth; his father had stayed there on a number of occasions. As he walked along the passageways and up the narrow, spiral wooden staircase of the tavern, he recalled snatches from his youth and wondered, once again, whether he should try and make his peace with his brother Robert. He decided that would wait; first he had to rest and seek an audience with Henry Burghersh, bishop of the city.

Once they had hired a room, unpacked their panniers and seen to the stabling of the horses, Nicholas wrote a short letter to the bishop. He requested an audience, 'because of urgent business which held the interest not only of the sheriff and mayor of the city of London but also the king himself'. The following morning he was surprised to receive a swift reply. The bishop, so his clerk wrote, would be pleased to meet Master Nicholas Chirke in his chambers at the bishop's palace after midday Mass.

'I'll go,' Chirke announced. He glanced at Scathelocke and Crabtree warming their fingers over a charcoal brazier. 'I doubt if the bishop will talk with any witnesses present, so you had best stay here. Make enquiries about the best routes to Bishop's Lynn and Castle Rising.'

Crabtree, protesting loudly at the cold rigours of the journey, now moaned at the prospect of more travelling. Nicholas, however, hurriedly prepared for his audience. He told Scathelocke and Crabtree that they were to stay in the tavern, carry out his enquiries and take careful note of any other travellers who showed more than a passing interest in them. After that he made his way through the narrow, winding streets of Norwich and into the cathedral precincts. A servitor took him into the episcopal palace, where the bishop's arrogant

170

chancellor led him through a maze of draughty passageways into a great chamber. After his wanderings through the cold, fetid streets of Norwich, Nicholas was astonished at the grandeur of the bishop's room. Sweet-smelling rushes covered the floor and these had been covered by fragrant herbs so every step he took filled the air with a delightful fragrance. The walls were draped in multi-coloured tapestries from Bruges. Nicholas glanced at these and fought to keep his face straight – the tapestries dealt with themes certainly not to be found in the bible or the writings of the Fathers. Around the room, beeswax candles on silver spigots and small glowing braziers on golden wheels shed heat and light. Their fire sparkled on the many precious objects which stood on shelves or adorned the tops of tables and cupboards around the room.

'Are you going to stand there and gawp till Christmas?'

The shadowy figure behind the desk at the far end of the room stirred. As the bishop's chancellor coughed noisily and closed the door behind him, Nicholas hastily remembered protocol. He walked forward and made the most reverential obeisance towards the desk.

'Stand up! Stand up!' The voice was harsh and imperious.

Nicholas obeyed. He studied the frail, ascetic-faced figure who sat swathed in purple robes and sable furs in the high-backed chair behind the desk. Burghersh had the face of a holy, austere monk, but when he leaned forward Nicholas saw that his eyes were hard, black pebbles whose stare never faltered.

'You are here at the Crown's express command?' Burghersh's voice had lost some of its hardness. He waved a scrawny, beringed hand to a chair beside the desk. 'Sit down! Sit down!'

'My Lord,' Nicholas said, 'I carry letters and warrants from Sir Amyas Petrie, Sheriff of London.'

171

He passed them to the bishop, who studied them closely before handing them back.

'So, what do you want to know?' he asked.

Nicholas licked his lips.

'Well, come on, man!' the bishop barked.

'Her Grace the Dowager Queen Isabella of England is dead,' Nicholas began.

'God assoil her and give her rest.' Burghersh's words came out in a rush and Nicholas caught the flicker of fear in his voice.

'My lord, many years ago you were Queen Isabella's chancellor.'

Burghersh smiled. He picked up a stiletto from his desk and balanced it between his fingers.

'Oh, come, come, master lawyer! You can do better than that.' He tossed the knife down and glared at Nicholas. 'Why not tell the truth? In September 1326, thirty-two years ago, Isabella, God rest her, aided and abetted by her paramour, Roger Mortimer, deposed her husband King Edward II and thrust him into Berkeley Castle, where he died. Our present sovereign lord, God bless him, was only a youth. Mortimer ruled the roost like Chanticleer the cock, and Isabella was his Petronella.'

He must have caught the surprise on Nicholas's face. He waved a bony hand.

'I merely tell the truth, and what is wrong with that?' He jabbed the air with one long finger. 'Now, remember this, master lawyer, I was their chancellor but never their accomplice. So, why are you here?'

'Did the queen harbour any great secret?'

'None except that she hated her husband and loved Mortimer.' Nicholas moved restlessly. 'No, I mean some secret which, even now' – he chose his words carefully – 'might be dangerous if it fell into the wrong hands.'

Burghersh shook his head, but Nicholas was skilled enough in interrogation to sense that he was lying.

'My lord,' he reminded him, 'I am here on royal business. You were, I understand, present when Mortimer and Isabella fell from power?'

'Yes, I was at Nottingham Castle. A chancellor has to be present, always is present, close to those who wield power.'

'Precisely, my lord,' Nicholas replied. 'Power is like a wheel – there is a rim, there are the spokes and there is the hub. You stood at the hub, and that is why I am here. Why was it so important, so essential, once Mortimer was arrested, that he was gagged and not allowed to speak even during his own trial?'

Burghersh leaned forward, his tongue flickering like that of a snake, his face flushed with rage. Nicholas flinched at the venom in his voice.

'You stupid, stupid, little man!' the bishop hissed. He stared around the room as if expecting eavesdroppers. 'You tawdry, little mountebank! You landless jackanapes!'

Nicholas pushed his chair back. 'My lord, keep a civil tongue. Your language does not befit a gentleman, much less a man of the cloth, a bishop.'

Burghersh blinked as if he had forgotten who he was and where he was. Nicholas sensed the fear behind the rage. The bishop rubbed his face in his hands; he slouched back in the chair and drummed his fingers on the desk-top.

He jabbed a finger at Nicholas. 'I shall give you some advice, master lawyer. If this is what you hunt, then give it up. Go back to London and say your wits are befuddled.' He smiled mirthlessly. 'I doubt if that will be hard. Or, if you wish, hasten to the nearest port and take ship to foreign parts.'

'Why was Mortimer gagged?' Nicholas repeated, fighting hard to control his own anger.

The bishop raised his scrawny eyebrows. 'I don't know,' he said softly. 'I never knew. I don't want to know. I will never know.'

'Was Mortimer the real father of our present king?' Nicholas blurted out.

Burghersh looked at him in surprise then threw his head back and crowed with laughter, clapping his hands. He laughed until the tears rolled down his cheeks.

'No, no, no!' he gasped. 'Oh Lord save us, no!'

Nicholas waited until the bishop had composed himself.

'So, what was this great secret?'

Burghersh pulled a face. 'I don't know!'

Chirke had had enough of the bishop's 'games'.

'In that case,' he said, 'I'll continue my search. And if I do discover anything, I'll tell my masters in London it came from you.'

He gathered up his cloak and walked to the door. He had his hand on the latch when Burghersh called, 'Wait! Master lawyer, come back!'

Nicholas turned and walked back to his chair.

'Sit down! Sit down!' Burghersh forced a smile. 'Would you like some wine?'

Nicholas shook his head. He did not trust this arrogant, devious prelate squatting in the lap of luxury, playing with secrets that had cost other men their lives.

The bishop pointed to a huge bible, in a richly gold-embroidered cover, that was chained to a lectern beside him.

'I want your oath, master lawyer,' he said solemnly, 'that

what I tell you will be revealed to no other person. Only then will I talk. Moreover, what I tell you will be delivered in such a way that it can never be attributed to me.'

Nicholas nodded his agreement and crossed to the lectern. He placed one hand on the bible and carefully repeated the oath Burghersh dictated to him. The bishop then waved him back to his seat. He leaned forward to whisper, as if the mice scrabbling behind the wood-panelled wainscoting, or the spiders weaving their webs in the corner of the room, could overhear his secret and pass it on.

'I was Isabella's chancellor,' he began. 'They were stirring times.' He sipped from his goblet. 'Mortimer and Isabella ruled the realm. As I have said, the present king was only a boy when they began. Now Isabella and Mortimer were constantly closeted together as lovers. I was party to their secrets – or perhaps I should say to some of them, for time and time again I would enter their chambers when they were discussing some matter and they would abruptly stop when once I arrived.'

'What was this secret matter?' Nicholas asked.

Burghersh shook his head. 'God knows! I know that Mortimer sent one of his henchmen, John Travis, to search through certain records at the University of Oxford. On another occasion Isabella herself went down to search the records at King's Bench. She and Mortimer went through them carefully. I don't know what they were looking for, but on the night Mortimer was arrested Isabella screamed something at her son.'

'What was it?'

'*La paume!*'

'What does that mean?' Nicholas asked.

'It's Norman French. I thought it meant "palm" – perhaps one of those dried palm leaves pilgrims bring back from Outremer.'

175

'And how did her son react?'

'He immediately had Mortimer gagged. Travis as well. They were both despatched to Westminster to stand trial. The following morning the queen mother asked to see her son. Young Edward, a man of eighteen then, agreed to this. They met in the queen mother's chamber. She was tearful and distraught after Mortimer's capture and insisted on speaking to her son alone.' Burghersh smiled mirthlessly. 'I was in disgrace. True, I had been in Mortimer's faction but, thankfully, the Crown does not kill those who serve the wrong masters. Anyway, the room was cleared. I stood outside with the rest. I expected to hear wailing, screams and cries for pity, but it was silent, quiet as the grave. One of the young king's retainers went to the door and listened, but all he could hear was a murmur of voices.' Burghersh slumped in his chair, rolling the wine cup in his hands. 'The chamber door was then flung open. The young king stormed out. I have never seen him, either before or since, look so angry, so frightened. He was pallid, with a sheen of sweat on his brow and cheeks. I was sent back to my diocese. Mortimer died at Tyburn and Isabella was banished to Castle Rising in Norfolk.'

'Did she ever leave there?' Nicholas asked.

'She was trotted out now and again on state occasions, but the king kept a careful watch on her. His most trusted henchmen were placed in her household – childhood friends such as Gervase Talbot, commander of the castle. For the twenty-eight years, between 1330 and her death in August this year, Isabella was carefully watched. Did you know that a company of archers, the best in the kingdom, constantly camped in the woods around Castle Rising?'

'What is happening there now?' Nicholas asked.

Burghersh shrugged. 'It's all gone. Isabella's household has been dispersed and the archers withdrawn. The king's spies in Bishop's Lynn and Great Yarmouth, who reported what ships arrived and what departed, are no longer needed.' Burghersh smirked. 'So, master lawyer, you with your cunning, dark face and shrewd eyes, what was the secret, eh?'

'Is that all you can tell me, my lord?' Nicholas asked icily.

Burghersh extended one scrawny hand for Nicholas to kiss. 'Yes, that's all. Now, you may go!'

Nicholas left the bishop's palace, collected his horse from the stables and rejoined his companions at the tavern.

Crabtree and Scathelocke were in the taproom, toasting themselves before the fire. Nicholas joined them, after ordering a bowl of meat and vegetables. Once a scullion had served it – it was heavily spiced to hide its rancidness – Nicholas told his companions about his meeting with Burghersh.

'We have to go to Castle Rising,' Scathelocke said when Nicholas finished. 'If we've discovered one truth, master, it is that the old bitch held a great secret which terrified her son, the—'

'Why do you call her a bitch?' Crabtree interrupted.

Nicholas looked quizzically at Scathelocke. Crabtree's question was a good one. Scathelocke's eyes glittered with anger.

'She came of bad blood,' he said. 'Her father, Philip IV of France, sprang from hell. He probably went back there.'

Crabtree looked at Nicholas and raised his eyebrows.

'But what shall we be able to learn at Castle Rising?' Nicholas asked, between mouthfuls of hot food.

'We can listen to any gossip.'

Nicholas leaned against the side of the fireplace and sipped from the tankard of yeasty ale the potboy had brought.

'We'll go,' he decided. 'And then back to London.' He

gazed anxiously around the tavern.

'No, master,' Scathelocke murmured, 'before you ask, there's no one following us. At least not here, perhaps beyond the city walls.'

Scathelocke's words proved prophetic. They left Norwich early the following morning after breaking their fast on slices of fatty bacon and tankards of ale. The weather soon made them forget the interest caused by Burghersh's revelations. A severe hoar frost had hardened the ground and a thick sea mist had swirled in, blanketing the countryside and hiding the road which stretched east to Bishop's Lynn and Castle Rising. A few miles out of Norwich they found themselves on a small track which, Nicholas confidently claimed, would lead them down to a crossroads and the more direct road to Bishop's Lynn. Dense forests ran along either side of it and, although the misty silence depressed them, Nicholas and his companions only became alarmed when the silence was abruptly broken by the clink of chain mail. Nicholas and Scathelocke loosened the swords in their scabbards. Crabtree, no brawling boy, quietly moaned in fear until Scathelocke told him to shut up.

Nicholas rode on, believing the sound was a phantasm of his imagination, when a file of hooded figures rose out of the mist to block his way. They slipped like black ghosts across the road. Armed with swords and spears, they waited for Nicholas and his companions to stop and dismount. Nicholas's heart leapt with terror and it was his panic that saved him. He forced his horse from a trot into a gallop and bore down on his would-be assailants, yelling and waving his sword as if he was a veteran of a hundred successful charges. Scathelocke did likewise, whilst Crabtree yelled until his lungs were fit to burst. Their assailants, surprised, stood disconcerted, then Nicholas was amongst them,

178

lashing out blindly with his sword. He saw one of his attackers scream in agony and lurch away clutching at his arm, from which blood was gushing. Another reeled away, his face a bloody mass. Then Nicholas and his companions were through, riding like the wind.

Eventually they pulled off the track, stroking their horses and straining to hear any sounds of pursuit. Crabtree dropped from his horse and, between a litany of muttered curses, crouched on all fours and vomited up his breakfast. Nicholas dismounted, made sure that Crabtree was uninjured, and looked up at Scathelocke, who sat like a rock in his saddle.

'Who were they?' he whispered.

Scathelocke shook his head. 'We were followed. The bastards must have been waiting for us to leave Norwich.'

'Who sent them?' Nicholas asked. 'The Guardian of the Gates?'

'Oh, don't be stupid!' Crabtree got to his feet, wiping his mouth on the back of his hand. 'I rode through those bastards with my eyes closed but my ears open. One of the wounded moaned in French.'

Nicholas felt his heart lurch in deep despair. He grabbed the reins of his horse and leaned his flushed face against the cool of the leather saddle.

'God help us!' he muttered. 'We have Sir Amyas Petrie and the powers he represents hounding us. The Guardian of the Gates also hunts us. And now the French.'

He cursed so eloquently that Crabtree exclaimed in admiration at his stream of colourful oaths and curses. Finally, he got back into the saddle.

'Why did the French attack us?' Crabtree asked, following suit.

179

Nicholas pulled his hood back over his head. 'They didn't attack us,' he said thoughtfully. 'We escaped because they thought we'd dismount. They wanted to take us prisoner and find out what we knew. After that they might have killed us.'

'But why?' Crabtree wailed.

'You're supposed to be a cunning man,' Scathelocke told him, 'but you can't tell your elbow from your arse. Ten days ago, two Frenchmen followed us round the city. One is stabbed, the other is poisoned. The following day two of them meet Master Chirke in a show of friendship. They are later killed in an alleyway. The French probably hold us responsible for all their deaths.'

'Let's ride on,' Nicholas said.

They left the wood and went back on to the track. They stopped that night at a small priory where black-garbed Benedictines provided a friendly reception, simple but good fare and comfortable beds in white-washed cells. The following day they reached Bishop's Lynn, lodging at the Sea Barque, a bustling tavern where sailors and fishermen from the port of Hunstanton rubbed shoulders with merchants and farmers from the fertile Norfolk Broads. They rested on the first day. Nicholas kept to himself, thinking back over what Burghersh had told him and wondering what secret, if any, the word *paume* concealed. Why had Mortimer commissioned a special investigation at Oxford, he asked himself. And why had Mortimer and his paramour, Isabella, searched amongst the records of King's Bench?

After they had settled in they set about making themselves acceptable to the locals. Despite the constant flow of travellers, places like the Sea Barque were suspicious of strangers. Nicholas ordered Scathelocke and Crabtree not to approach the locals, who studied them suspiciously in the taproom, but to wait until the locals approached them. At last, one evening, they were drawn into a group of local farmers who were talking about Queen Isabella. After a while one of them slammed the table-top with his fist and delivered a vicious diatribe.

'I am glad the old bitch is dead!' he said hoarsely. 'She was greedy. Whatever she wanted, she took. When we presented our bills we were told to go to the Exchequer in London. And who amongst us has time for that, eh?' He looked round at his companions, who nodded in assent. 'There were other things too,' he added darkly. 'The king's men-at-arms and the archers who patrolled the roads. They were as awkward as only soldiers can be, stopping our carts and flirting with our women.'

'And the officials from the port.' One of the others spoke up. 'The harbour reeves, the bailiffs constantly scrutinizing everything from the bumboats to fishing smacks.'

'Then there were the French,' another muttered.

'The French?' Nicholas queried.

'One of the great secrets of Norfolk,' the farmer replied. 'Few people know about it.'

'Know about what?'

The man placed his tankard on the table and leaned closer. Nicholas tried not to flinch at the stale smell of onions, cheese and ale on the man's breath.

'Oh, about twenty years ago, just after our king's great sea victory at Sluys, a French galley came up the coast at night and put soldiers ashore. They launched an attack upon the castle. Terrible killings! The night sky was bright with flames and the fields were wet with blood. The French were driven off, but at great cost. There were so many corpses we had to dig a ditch six feet deep and twelve foot across and a good quarter of a

181

mile long to bury them in. You'll see it to the right of the castle road. The French corpses, and a few English, were thrown in like a pile of logs.'

'Why did the French attack the castle?' Nicholas asked.

'We don't know, but an archer later told my cousin that they came for the old queen. If I'd had my way, they'd have taken the old baggage, but they were driven off.'

'They were driven off?'

'Aye, and that was the end of the matter.'

'And the castle now?' Scathelocke asked.

'Empty as a graveyard, sir. Empty as a graveyard. You can go up there now. Only a few soldiers and men-at-arms remain.'

'And the old queen's household?'

'Oh, they have now dispersed. Once the old queen was buried, that was it.'

Nicholas thanked them and ordered fresh stoups of ale. Once he and his companions were back in their little garret, they made preparations to leave for Castle Rising the next morning.

'Why do you think the French came?' Crabtree sleepily asked as he lay on the cot bed, plucking at pieces of straw from the thin mattress.

'God knows!' Nicholas replied. 'But they knew the queen possessed some secret and were prepared to spill blood for it. By the way, what does the word *paume* mean?'

'I've been thinking about that,' Scathelocke replied. 'How could Isabella use that to threaten her son?' He grinned self-consciously. 'When I was in London, talking to my friends, they did tell me one strange thing. Isabella's husband, Edward II, lies buried in Gloucester Cathedral under a beautiful tomb of Purbeck marble. However, his son, the present king, never contributed a penny to the shrine of his murdered father. The monks at Gloucester built it. Moreover, most kings are buried at Westminster, but Isabella and Mortimer refused to allow the old king's corpse to be taken there.'

'A pity,' Crabtree said. 'Royal funerals are a source of merriment in the capital. Wine flows in the conduits and, if you are quick enough, you can go down to Westminster and collect scraps from the royal banquets.'

'So, why wasn't the old king's corpse brought to Westminster?' Nicholas asked.

Scathelocke shrugged. 'It's an old tale, but some say that Edward escaped from Berkeley Castle and went to a country of the Middle Sea.'

'Lord save us!' Crabtree breathed. 'You mean the old king's not dead?'

'It's possible,' Scathelocke murmured.

Nicholas grabbed his manservant's arm. 'Where did you hear that?'

Scathelocke tapped his nose. 'Come, come, master! You have your secrets and I have mine.'

Words between the pilgrims

The man of law paused in his tale and went across to refill his wine cup. The rest of his companions stared open-mouthed. Even the tactful, cheery-faced Chaucer was now studying him from under lowering brows.

'Is this true?' the pardoner screeched. 'I have been to Gloucester and prayed before Edward II's marble tomb.'

'I have heard these rumours,' the friar intervened. 'Apparently a member of our Dominican order, Thomas Dunheved, together with his brother Stephen, launched an attack upon Berkeley Castle late in the summer of 1327.'

'What happened?' the prioress whispered excitedly.

'According to the stories, or at least one of them, the Dunheveds managed to get into Berkeley castle and free the king.' He shrugged his corpulent shoulders. 'But that could be a legend.'

'What happened to the Dunheveds?' the manciple asked sharply.

The friar stretched. 'Now, there's a story. They disappeared into gaol, they and all their band.'

'And did they hang?' the reeve asked.

'Oh, no, they died of a fever.'

'All of them?' the Oxford clerk whispered.

'Oh yeth.' The friar's lisp became more pronounced. He moved, his figure round as a bell, pushing his cord further up his plump waist. 'Oh yeth.'

'That's strange,' the franklin said. 'All of them to die of gaol fever.'

'Aye, and I could tell you more.'

The friar was now in his element. He stared across at the man of law, but he sat lost in his own thoughts.

The friar lowered his voice. 'Thomas Dunheved, the Dominican, was the old king's confessor. He was out of the country when Isabella deposed her husband. Dunheved had been sent to Rome by the old king' – he lowered his voice still further – 'to obtain a divorce from Queen Isabella.'

'Nonsense!' the manciple intervened. 'Holy Mother Church does not agree with divorce.'

The friar waved his fingers angrily. 'Don't preach to me, good sir. I know canon law. The king wanted his marriage annulled. Now, why should he do that, eh?'

'But if the king did escape,' the pardoner asked, 'who lies buried in Gloucester Cathedral?'

'I went there.' The wife of Bath spoke up, her cheeks flushed, eyes gleaming from the mead she had drunk. 'I was a mere girl when my father took me. We'd heard the rumours about Edward II's murder. Don't forget Bath is just down the road.' She crossed her plump arms, relishing this gossip about her betters. 'We'd all heard how the old king had been forced face down on the floor and how two assassins thrust a red-hot iron poker up into his bowels so as to kill him without leaving any trace of violence to his body.'

'Fat good would that do,' the summoner interrupted. 'I wager you could tell by the expression on his face that he hadn't died in his sleep!'

The wife of Bath tried to hit him, but the summoner quickly dodged.

'Don't speak ill of the dead!' she snapped. 'They say you could hear the poor king's hideous shrieks a mile away. Now, as I was saying, the corpse was laid out before Gloucester cathedral in an open coffin with a wimple round its face. Now it's possible,' the wife of Bath continued, 'that people go and see what they expect to see and dismiss any changes as those wrought by death. Perhaps it wasn't Edward II. And that,' she concluded triumphantly, 'is why Jezebel Isabella wouldn't have the corpse taken across country to Westminster.'

'But if the old king escaped,' the pardoner insisted, 'why didn't he make himself known?'

'Ah, I can answer that,' the wife of Bath said confidently. 'They say he tried to and communicated with his half-brother Edmund of Kent. Mortimer found out and sent Kent to the block and that was the end of that.'

'Is that the secret?' Chaucer, or Sir Topaz as he liked to call himself, spoke up from where he sat in the inglenook opposite the knight. 'Master lawyer, is that the secret?'

The saturnine man of law shook his head and smiled.

'Well, what is it?' Chaucer asked.

The man of law winked and sipped from his cup. Now the knight turned, his face grave.

'What you are talking about, sir, is treason!'

'Treason!' the man of law scoffed. 'Come, come, sir! I do not plot against our noble lord the king or have commerce with his enemies. I merely tell a tale whilst what we discuss here is mere gossip.' He rose and stretched. 'If you wish, I can leave it there, because I cannot tell you all.'

A chorus of disappointed cries greeted his words.

'True, true,' the knight murmured. 'After all, this is only a tale, is it not?'

'Of course,' the man of law replied, looking steadily at the prioress.

She squirmed uncomfortably on her chair and began to caress the little lapdog.

'One question I must ask you,' she said softly.

'Ask it, madam.'

'Why did this laywer not go and visit the woman he loved?' The prioress shrugged elegantly. 'True, she married his brother.' She raised tearful eyes. 'But both of them would have been pleased to see him.'

The man of law gave a half-bow. 'Madam, a pertinent question and eloquently put, but there are some things best left hidden, some pools in our souls which ought not to be stirred.' He smiled thinly. 'Perhaps the hero in my tale was too hurt. After all, as you well know, madam, the heart can only take a certain burden of sorrows.'

The poet Chaucer, watching all this, narrowed his eyes and half-turned to the knight.

'Do you think this story is true?' he whispered out of the corner of his mouth.

The knight tapped the pommel of his dagger and looked up.

'Master Chaucer, haven't you realized there's no such thing as a lie, only the truth slightly twisted?'

Chaucer grinned, rose and walked over to the man of law.

'Sir, Harry the taverner will fill your cup once again. Continue, we beg you, your intriguing tale.'

PART V
Chapter 1

The next morning Nicholas and his companions made their way up to Castle Rising. The fortress stood on a hill surrounded by a high bank and a deep ditch. They crossed the lower drawbridge and entered the outer bailey. Before them reared the gatehouse and curtain wall of the inner bailey, protected by another deep ditch. The great square donjon within towered above them.

'Impregnable,' Scathelocke murmured. 'No wonder the French failed. We passed the burial mound,' he added. 'It's now overgrown.'

Nicholas stared around the outer bailey. It was deserted except for the occasional scavenging mongrel or scrawny, thin-legged chicken. The sheds and outhouses were empty and neglected. The smithies were silent, the stables open, the straw within them rotting and decayed. Once they crossed the second moat, however, and went through the great gatehouse into the inner bailey, Nicholas realized what had happened. Here it was more lively – soldiers lounged against the wall, children ran chasing geese and ducks whose squawking was dimmed by the iron clang of the blacksmith's hammer.

'The castle garrison's been reduced,' Nicholas said. 'They are living within one bailey.'

They dismounted and tossed their reins to a groom. A dirty, unshaven servant, knocking dogs and children aside, led them up the wide stone staircase of the forebuilding into the keep.

'Who's in charge here?' Chirke asked.

'Ralph Aston,' the servant replied, in an accent Nicholas found difficult to understand. 'Now the old queen's dead there's few left.'

He took them into the great hall on the first floor. The room was gaunt, stripped of furniture and wall hangings, chilly and depressing. The only source of warmth was a weak fire trying to catch the green, sap-filled logs in the hearth.

They found Aston in his counting-house beyond the great hall. A choleric beanpole of a man, his balding, wart-covered skull was covered by wisps of greasy hair. He hardly raised his head as they entered, but kept on writing, his quill scratching and creaking.

'Master Aston?'

The fellow looked up and wiped his dripping nose on a dirty cuff.

'What do you want?' he snapped.

'We want nothing,' Nicholas replied angrily. 'We are here on the king's business!' He introduced himself and his companions.

Aston's face visibly paled. He threw the quill down in a splatter of ink and sprang to his feet.

'I am sorry,' he muttered. 'But we have visitors who come to gawk at where the old queen lived. Do you wish some wine? The cooks have yet to fire the ovens in the kitchen but – '

Nicholas shook his head.

'Sit down! Sit down!' Aston murmured. He ran around the room pulling across stools. 'Why are you here?' he asked.

Nicholas wished the fellow would blow his nose. He tried

not to look at the catarrh gathering on the man's upper lip.

'To look at the old queen's things,' he said.

Aston spread his hands. 'Master,' he wailed, 'everything has gone. I could take you round the chambers and private apartments but there's nothing, nothing at all.' He drew in his breath. 'The old queen lived here in great state but, within a week of her death, the king sent carts, wagon after wagon from Norwich. All her possessions were loaded into them – tapestries, hangings, carpets, furniture, coffers and chests, books, every scrap of manuscript and document. They were gone within the day.'

'You were here with the old queen?' Nicholas asked.

'I was a steward in the castle,' Aston replied. 'I was one of many – Queen Isabella had a large retinue and household. Now they have all gone. Some went to Gascony, others to France, a few entered monastries and nunneries. The royal officials were given posts up and down the country in towns as far afield as Dover and Carlisle.'

'Tell me' – Nicholas forced himself to look at Aston – 'what was the old queen like?'

'I didn't see much of her. She was tall, severe-faced, dressed like a nun, though her garments were costly. The servants called her "the Empress". She was imperious and would not be brooked. She ruled Castle Rising as harshly as any baron would his fief. Everything had to be the best.'

'Were you here,' Scathelocke asked, 'when the French landed a force and attacked the castle?'

'Oh yes,' Aston snorted. 'But they were all killed before they reached the gatehouse. You don't realize how strong Castle Rising is until you are inside it.'

Nicholas drew his eyebrows together. 'So, why did they attack?'

191

Aston looked surprised. "A good question, master lawyer. Can you answer it?'

Nicholas smiled and shrugged.

'Inevitably there can only be one conclusion. The French must have known about the high walls and towers, the deep ditches, the fortified gatehouse and the large garrison.'

Aston leaned forward. 'So?'

'You can take a castle either by force or by stealth,' Nicholas said, pressing on with his argument. 'Does Castle Rising have postern gates?'

Aston nodded. 'One to the south-east, the other on the south-west.'

'In which case,' Chirke continued, 'the French must have expected help from within the castle. When that failed, they were beaten off.'

'You mean help from the old queen?'

'Either her or one of her retainers.'

'Lord save us!' Aston breathed. 'But, there again, she was eager to return to France.'

'Did you hear that yourself?' Crabtree asked, crossing his arms for the room was becoming chilly.

'Oh yes, that was the gossip below stairs. Ten years ago the French king was rumoured to have made a request for Isabella to be sent to France to work for peace between England and France.' Aston rubbed his hands. 'But our king was too wily. He never let his mother go.'

'Was it so apparent?' Scathelocke asked.

'Oh, of course. The king used to visit here: oh, he'd fuss his mother, throw largesse at her but Isabella never left Castle Rising.' Aston blew his lips out. 'Now and again she was allowed to go on a pilgrimage to Walsingham but always with

192

a military escort: archers, hobelars and mounted men-at-arms.'

Chirke half-listened, trying to ignore Aston's nose. He stared down at the piece of manuscript that lay beneath the scroll on which Aston had been scribbling. It stirred memories of Berisford's house and Mawsby's death. He felt a chill of fear. Berisford, a homosexual who kept his secrets well hidden, was a justice. Mawsby, whose sexual tastes may have been similar, was only a lawyer's clerk.

'Master Chirke?'

Nicholas looked up.

'Master Chirke,' Aston repeated. 'What do you wish to know?'

'How did the old queen die?' Chirke asked hastily.

'Of the pestilence. She lay alone in her chamber for days, then died speedily. Her corpse was dressed in the robes of the Poor Clare nuns. She was placed in a coffin and the funeral obsequies began.'

'And Vallence?'

Aston grinned sourly. 'Oh, the pretty boy! He was her favourite and insisted on preparing the old queen's corpse.' Aston sniffed. 'No one objected. The queen had died of the pestilence and the squire was her one and only favourite – "Vallence this and Vallence that", scurrying to and from London, Windsor, Sheen and Nottingham, always dressed like a popinjay.'

'And when did he leave?'

'Oh, with the funeral casket. He accompanied it into London. Why do you ask?'

Chirke just shook his head and stared down at the manuscript, ignoring Crabtree's and Scathelocke's curious looks.

'Did anything untoward,' Nicholas asked, 'happen during the queen's stay here?'

'Well, I was only here for some of the time. Castle routine was well established.' Aston looked longingly at the door as if he wished his visitors would disappear. 'No, nothing untoward happened. Nothing at all.' He drummed his fingers noisily on the desk to show his impatience. 'Is there anything you wish to see? Anything at all, gentlemen?' He gazed around at them. 'Oh!' Aston's fingers flew to his mouth. 'Master Chirke, you asked about the old queen. Yes, she used to play games.'

'What do you mean, games?'

'Well the castle was commanded by a succession of knights banneret, trusted men chosen by the king. These were changed quite regularly, once every three or four years, just in case any became too friendly with the old queen. After all, she had a persuasive tongue.'

'You talked about games?' Nicholas persisted.

'Oh yes, well, apparently the old queen hated these royal nominees and loved to bait them. Now and again she would hide.'

'Hide?' Nicholas exclaimed.

'Yes, she'd suddenly disappear from her apartments, quite regularly in the months preceding her death. The castle would buzz like an overturned beehive – soldiers and servants scurrying about, anxious-faced messengers despatched into the countryside. Then the old queen would re-appear. She'd be seen walking serenely along some gallery or passageway, quietly enjoying the chaos and confusion she'd caused.'

Thankfully, Aston stopped speaking to wipe his nose on the sleeve of his jerkin.

'Oh, "the Empress" knew what she was doing.'

'How long did these games last?' Crabtree asked.

'Oh, a morning or an afternoon. On one or two occasions

the old queen didn't appear till late in the evening after being missing since dawn. She just loved to taunt those officers.'

'But where could she hide?' Nicholas asked.

Aston spread his hands. 'Castle Rising is like a rabbit warren, Master Chirke, nooks and crannies everywhere. Believe me, if you wandered off, especially now the place is so deserted, it might take me a day and a half to find you.'

Nicholas nodded, rubbing his arms. 'Sweet Lord, Aston,' he murmured. 'The place is freezing.'

Aston rose and moved a charcoal brazier closer. Crabtree pulled his stool forward, almost knocking Nicholas aside, to stretch out his hands towards the warm glow.

'Oh yes, she was a real madam,' Aston continued, sitting down. 'And yet on other days you'd find her in the chapel, kneeling at her prie-dieu as piously as a nun. Ah well, it's all gone. Would you like me to show you the castle?'

Nicholas shook his head. 'No, no. Perhaps if my companions and I walked around and saw what we could?'

Aston nodded his head vigorously. Nicholas, relieved to be away from Aston and his filthy mannerisms, walked back into the depressing great hall.

'Well, what do you make of all that?' he murmured to his two companions.

Crabtree stared around the deserted room. He noticed the cobwebs and the places where the hangings and tapestries had been ripped from the walls.

'Lord save us, master! It must have been a veritable hell-hole to live in.'

'Let's see for ourselves,' Scathelocke murmured. 'Aston may snivel that everything's gone, but' – he shrugged philosophically, 'you never know.'

'And what happens if we find nothing?' Crabtree wailed. 'Master, I am cold, I am hungry and my arse is saddle-sore. I'm sick of the bloody countryside. It's cold and black and the people are like scarecrows. I want to be back in London.'

Nicholas grinned and clapped him on the shoulder.

'Virtue is its own reward, Master Crabtree, and this is your longest period of virtue since you left your mother's womb.'

'Did he have a mother?' Scathelocke asked sarcastically.

'And a father!' Crabtree snapped angrily. 'Which is more than I can say for some people!'

Both men indulged in good-natured banter until Nicholas told them to shut up and they began their tour of the fortress. Aston was right, Castle Rising was like a tomb. The chambers were empty and gaunt, the galleries and passageways gloomy and cold. Now and again, in the queen's private apartments, they would catch glimpses of former grandeur – there were cornices of gilded gold whilst some of the walls had breathtaking pictures depicting, in an array of colours, various scenes from the bible. Nevertheless, the place was empty, stripped clean by the royal purveyors.

'They wouldn't miss a needle in a haystack,' Nicholas murmured. 'If they could have lifted the walls and taken them, they would have done so.'

They went up and down stairs, into different rooms. Now and again they would meet the occasional servant or soldier but these were lack-lustre and, when asked for directions, replied slovenly.

'No wonder the old queen could play games,' Crabtree muttered, peering into one darkened recess. 'It would be like catching coneys in the hay. The place is full of trapdoors, nooks and crannies.'

Nicholas nodded. 'It's a bit like the old queen's great secret,' he said. He stopped outside what appeared to be the castle chapel. 'And I tell you this, dear companions all. My mind's made up. When we return to London, I shall seek out Sir Amyas Petrie. I'll tell him all I know, say the task is beyond my capabilities and, if he doesn't like it, let him go hang.'

Crabtree grinned from ear to ear, but Scathelocke looked uncomfortable. Nicholas ignored him. What was the use, he thought, pushing open the door of the chapel. Whichever way they turned they reached an impasse. He walked in and stared around the gloomy place. Its windows were all shuttered.

'Aston's apparently not a man of prayer,' he muttered, his words ringing hollow. 'Crabtree, light those torches.'

The cunning man obeyed and the chapel flared into life. Chirke gazed around.

'A large place,' he murmured.

He tried to remember their wanderings through the castle and realized the chapel must be on the ground floor, at the far side of the great keep. A simply carved rood screen divided the chancel from the nave. Through it Nicholas glimpsed steps and a raised altar. The window shutters clattered eerily in a cold breeze which made the torch flames dance and the shadows flicker against wall and floor. It was a bare, austere place, stripped of all furniture except for a tall, high-backed chair, with a bench on either side of it, that stood in front of the rood screen.

'She must have sat there,' Nicholas murmured. He smiled. He could hear Crabtree clattering from the chancel, probably looking for something valuable to steal.

Nicholas glanced quizzically at Scathelocke, who stood with his back to the closed door.

'What's the matter, man?'

'It's ghostly,' Scathelocke murmured, 'it's eerie. There's a malevolent presence here.'

Almost as if in response to Scathelocke's comment came a rap on the door. Nicholas's heart leapt. Scathelocke whirled round and pulled the door open. An old woman shuffled in. She was dressed in a dusty, grey gown; her yellow, seamed face was creased by a toothless grin which seemed to stretch from ear to ear; her grey hair hung lank and greasy. In the torchlight Nicholas glimpsed the frenetic look in her eyes. Saliva drooled from one corner of her mouth, which the woman's tongue, darting in and out, attempted to lick away.

'Well, well!' The woman's voice was sharp and cackling. She peered at Nicholas, who tried not to flinch at the rank odour from her body. 'Well, well!' the old crone repeated. 'King's men, eh? What are you doing here?' She scratched dirty fingernails against her cheek as she peered round. 'Ghosts!' she said, echoing Scathelocke's words. 'Ghosts walk here!'

'Ghosts, mother?' Nicholas asked.

The old hag glanced sideways at him, a sly smile on her face.

'Oh, yes, ghosts. You'll never catch any soldiers lurking here. At least, not since the old queen died. They claim to have seen her ghost here, walking up and down.'

The crone began to mimic the old queen, pacing to and fro, shoulders back, head turning to the left and right as she wrung her hands.

'That's what she used to do,' the old woman cackled, coming back to Nicholas. 'Up and down, up and down, either in the galleries outside her room or here in church.' She lowered her voice. 'She loved this place. God knows why! God knows why! Now she's gone, all the great ones have gone. Only poor Agnes is left, washing the clothes, scrubbing the scullery. Ah yes, all the great ones go.'

And, without further ado, the old woman spun on her heel and walked out of the door.

Crabtree, who had been watching the pantomime from where he was standing under the rood screen, came back and grinned at Scathelocke.

'One of your sweethearts?'

Scathelocke made a rude gesture with his fingers.

'Get the torches!' Nicholas snapped.

He grasped one himself, pulling it out from its rusting sconce. He walked into the chancel, empty except for a huge crucifix bearing a writhing figure of a suffering Christ. Then he went back into the shadowy nave. He realized then that the chapel was more decorated than he had first assumed. Some skilled artist, probably a court painter commissioned by the old queen, had covered the walls of the nave with colourful scenes from the bible and the lives of the saints. Many of the latter were French. The old queen, remembering her childhood days in France and the blood line of her family, had asked the painter to concentrate on her saintly ancestor, the Blessed Louis. Many of the scenes were from the life of that holy king. Now and again Nicholas would stop and study them. He recognized most of them as copies of paintings in Le Sainte Chapelles in Paris, which he had visited many years before. Crabtree joined him. They stopped before a painting of a decapitated man carrying his own head on a silver dish.

'Who's that, master?'

'John the Baptist,' Nicholas replied absentmindedly. 'Come, Scathelocke!' he called. 'There's nothing here for us.'

They left the chapel, collected their horses from the stables and rode back into the village.

Crabtree and Scathelocke were still quipping at each other

trying to secure an advantage. Crabtree kept insisting that the old crone they'd met would suit a man of Scathelocke's means and looks. Nicholas listened to their banter with half an ear as they sat in the taproom and ordered an evening meal of beef and vegetable pottage, boiled chicken stuffed with grapes and a flagon of wine. The taproom was warm, the log fire piled high, the flames roaring up the chimney. Travellers arrived. Crabtree became engrossed in flirting with a young prioress dressed in a costly grey woollen gown, her pretty face framed by a brilliant white starched wimple. Nicholas also studied the woman. The cowl and wimple hid most of her features but he glimpsed doe-like eyes, lips rich and red as a rose. He wondered why such a woman should enter a religious order. By the precious rings on her fingers and the delicate way she ate, he concluded that she was some noblewoman hiding from the world. The prioress sat talking quietly to her companion, a thin, austere woman dressed in the same garb, probably her protector or one of the officers from the priory she ruled. She seemed taken with Crabtree's merry smile and did not object when he crossed the taproom and edged his way first into her company and then into her conversation.

'Would you like some wine?' Crabtree asked her. 'A fresh napkin? How were the roads? Where are you travelling to?'

'The priory of St Austen outside Kenilworth.'

'Oh, yes,' Crabtree burbled. 'A beautiful place – its stone is honey-coloured and its mead the best in the shire.'

Nicholas watched with amusement. Scathelocke grunted his displeasure.

'He's a bloody fool, master,' he whispered. 'The prioress will probably make him pay for her meal and then dismiss him.'

Saying that, the manservant got up and stamped off,

grumbling about the horses and the need for a good night's sleep. Nicholas ordered a fresh goblet of wine, then left the warm taproom and returned to their own chamber. For a while he stood by the casement window, staring down into the stable yard, where a thick sea mist was beginning to boil, wafted inland by the cold night breeze. The mist muffled sound and turned the torches of the grooms and servitors into pinpricks of light.

Beyond lay the roads across the moors to Norwich. Should he go back? Nicholas asked himself. And go on to visit his parents' manor? Perhaps Robert and Beatrice would be pleased to see him? Perhaps his brother, astute and cunning, could give him sound advice in his present task? Or should he return to London? Seek out Sir Amyas Petrie and confess that the task was too great for him?

He sighed, placed the goblet on the table and lay down on the bed. He listened to the sounds from the taproom below – the clatter of dishes, the shouts of scullions, the murmurs of conversation, the occasional laugh. He let his mind drift back to that lonely, sombre castle, its gaunt, grey-stoned galleries and its empty soul-less chapel. What, he wondered, did the old queen know that had so terrified her son? Why was Vallence so intent on fleeing the kingdom and returning to France?

Nicholas rubbed his face. 'A Venetian galley,' he murmured. 'A Venetian galley was going to take him to a French port. Why a galley? Why a galley?'

'You are talking to yourself, master?'

Nicholas started. Scathelocke stood in the doorway.

'I have checked the horses. They are groomed and fed. Our saddles are locked away and that knave Crabtree is still flirting with the prioress.' Scathelocke pulled up a stool and sat beside his master on the bed. 'What's so important about a Venetian galley?'

201

'I was wondering why Vallence should flee the kingdom on a galley?'

Scathelocke shrugged. 'It's a fast vessel?'

'Yes, but one of the royal cogs could run a galley down, provided a good wind filled its sails.'

'What are you saying, master?'

Nicholas rubbed his eyes. 'I don't know,' he admitted. 'And there's another thing. I saw something in Aston's office that jogged my memory about the clerk Mawsby. The man drowned in the carp pond: he had been writing something. We thought it was Patricius, now we know it was Patroclus. The person who killed him was probably the woman Nightshade but Mawsby had perhaps already sent the letter. Maybe Mawsby had written to the very person who sent Nightshade to kill him? Now who could that be, eh?'

Scathelocke shook his head and began to loosen the laces on his brown leather jerkin. Nicholas stared at the crude crucifix fixed to the far wall of the chamber. He recalled the painting he had seen in the chapel at Castle Rising.

'Strange,' he murmured. 'I have seen pictures of John the Baptist, or rather of his head in a dish carried by Salome, but never one with the headless saint carrying his own head.' His jaw sagged. 'Oh, my Lord!' he murmured. 'Oh, Scathelocke!' He swung his legs off the bed.

'Master, what's wrong?'

'That wasn't John the Baptist,' Nicholas said. 'That was St Denis. Do you know the legend? Well,' he continued, not waiting for an answer, 'he's the patron saint of Paris, an early martyr who, after he had been beheaded by the pagans, picked up his own head and walked to Montmartre, where the great abbey dedicated to him now stands.' Nicholas got to his feet.

'Scathelocke, St Denis is the patron saint of the French monarchy. Vallence said that St Denis held a great secret. Can't you see?' he continued excitedly whilst Scathelocke stared woodenly back. 'We thought Vallence was escaping to France in a Venetian galley, carrying the secret on him. No, he was not! The secret's still at Castle Rising. Somewhere in that chapel, and the painting of St Denis holds the key!'

Scathelocke scratched his beard. 'Yes, that's why he needed a galley,' he said thoughtfully. 'Of course, only a galley could enter the small inlets on the Norfolk coastline.'

'Exactly!' Nicholas cried. 'That was Vallence's plan. He wasn't going to France, he was coming back here to Castle Rising to collect the secret hidden in that chapel!'

'But why say what he did to Berisford?' Scathelocke asked.

Nicholas scratched his head. 'I don't know but tomorrow morning go into the village and buy spades and pickaxes and a leather sack to carry them in. We are going back to Castle Rising!'

He was beside himself with excitement.

'No one will bother us,' he said, looking through the window. 'That keep's nothing but an empty mausoleum. The stories about the old queen's ghost keep everyone away.'

He went back to his bed and stared up at the rafters, reflecting on what he had discovered and vowing to himself that, if tomorrow's search proved fruitless, he would give the matter up. His eyes grew heavy and he drifted into sleep. When he woke a few hours later, Scathelocke was on the cot bed muttering in his dreams. Crabtree, apparently drunk as a lord, lay sprawled in the chamber's one and only chair, head back, mouth open, snoring like a pig. Nicholas rose and carried the protesting man out of the chair and on to the pallet bed. Crabtree half-opened his eyes.

'Beautiful!' he murmured, 'beautiful as the dawn!'

Nicholas grinned as he pulled the blanket over him.

'You should leave prioresses alone. Get a good night's sleep. Tomorrow we return to Castle Rising. Scathelocke will tell you what to do.'

Chirke walked back to the window and stared down at the mist-filled stable yard. The sounds of horses stirring made him think of Mawsby writing a letter, the letter that might have prompted his murder. A short note, waxed and sealed. The clerk would have hired some boy but where would he send it. He must have hired a messenger, Chirke reasoned, then waited for a reply. And he got it! Nightshade, the beautiful courtesan, tapping on his door. Mawsby would open it and allow Murder in. But who could the ckerk have written to? Chirke suddenly went cold.

'Impossible!' he murmured. 'Oh no, that's impossible!' He sat down on the bed. 'Oh Lord!' he breathed. 'Whatever happens, may God protect me!'

Further down the gallery in their own spacious chamber, the prioress and her companions, their gowns removed, their wimples off, sat on chairs warming their fingers over a dish of burning coal.

'Quite the courtier,' the elder one murmured.

The prioress, better known to her masters as the courtesan Nightshade, flexed her fingers and smiled.

'And he babbles,' her companion continued.

Nightshade chewed the corner of her mouth.

'Most men do,' she murmured. 'Tomorrow, when we find out where they are going, then we'll decide.'

Chapter 2

They returned to Castle Rising the following morning, long before the mist lifted or the cocks, hungry for daylight, began to crow. No one paid them any heed. The castle had been stripped of all possessions and the bitter memories left by the old queen's long residence had dulled any curiosity. Aston greeted them brusquely. He didn't even bother to pass comment on the leather sack Crabtree carried containing spades and picks hired from the landlord of the Sea Barque.

All three made their way to the chapel. Crabtree dropped the sack, scraping and clattering, to the floor.

'Be careful!' Nicholas warned. 'They are not ours.'

'We should have bought our own in the village as you said,' Crabtree retorted.

'That would have meant wasting hours,' Nicholas replied. 'And the sooner we make our search, the better.'

They entered the bleak chapel, closing the door firmly behind them. Scathelocke produced a flint and lit the torches and the nave, in particular the area in front of the picture of St Denis, glowed with life. Nicholas examined the wall, but the brickwork was firm and secure. Then they turned their attention to the floor; covered in dust and dirt, it looked as if it hadn't been swept for years. At first they found nothing, not a crack, not a crevice. Nicholas cursed in frustration. Crabtree sanctimoniously reminded him that they were in church. 'We are committing blasphemy already,' Nicholas said.

He crouched, looking down the length of the nave. He began to examine the floor methodically, moving on all fours. After a few minutes he stopped and, pulling out his dagger, began to scrape at the mortar between two paving stones. It held rock-hard and he gave up. Scathelocke and Crabtree joined him.

'Look, master!' Scathelocke exclaimed.

He took a torch and moved a little further down the nave. Nicholas followed. What Scathelocke had found was a small grating in the corner of one paving stone.

'And there's another over here!' Crabtree exclaimed.

Chirke stared round at the pool of light thrown by the torches.

'There's a cavern or cellar beneath here,' Nicholas muttered. 'But how do we get in?'

All three crept across the paving stones, holding the torch up. Nicholas stopped where a seam of mortar seemed fresher than the others. He began to scrape away.

'This is the entrance!' he exclaimed. 'Look!'

He pushed the spluttering pitch torch down to reveal that one of the paving stones was different from the rest. Although it seemed tight against its neighbours the mortar surrounding it was loose and sandy and it could, despite its weight, be raised like a trapdoor. Beneath yawned a black, cavernous hole. Nicholas lowered his torch. In the uncertain light, he saw stone steps leading down.

'Scathelocke, follow me!' he ordered. 'Crabtree, stay here!'

He went down the steps. Scathelocke gingerly followed him. At the bottom Nicholas held the torch up – and stifled a scream.

He was never to forget what he saw in the flickering torchlight. There was a table, a chair, a prie-dieu, a small coffer, a wicker basket – and a bed. On it, dressed in costly robes, sprawled the decaying skeleton of a woman. The flesh had shrivelled, the nose decayed, the scalp going back so the hair hung lank. The gaping, toothless mouth seemed to be grinning at them. Scathelocke dropped his torch, crossed his arms over his belly and crouched against the wall.

'Oh, master, what is that?' he gasped.

Nicholas walked towards the bed, pinching his nostrils against the fetid, sour smell. He studied the skeleton carefully. Jewels winked on bony fingers, one arm lay across the chest, the other hung beside the bed. Nicholas crouched down. He picked up the cup and the small pitcher lying beside the bed and sniffed them gingerly.

'Is everything all right?' Crabtree called down.

'Yes,' Nicholas shouted back. Staring around, he quickly noted what was there. On the prie-dieu was a Book of Hours. The wicker basket probably contained food and wine. He opened the small coffer but it contained nothing except trinkets – a brooch and a rather ornate necklace. In the far corner beneath one of the gratings was a small garderobe which probably drained into the moat. He went back to stare down at the skeleton on the bed.

'Come on, Scathelocke!' he urged. 'We don't have much time.'

Scathelocke was now standing, his face covered by a fine sheen of sweat.

'Master, I can't, it's forbidden!'

Nicholas looked at him curiously. 'What's forbidden?'

Scathelocke shook his head. Nicholas shrugged, closed his

eyes and scooped up the decaying skeleton from the bed. He felt as if he was embracing death itself. The clothes on the corpse were dusty and slightly damp, the meagre limbs seemed to have a life of their own. He lay the ghastly remains on the floor and began to feel around on the bed. Under the bolster he felt a leather pouch and quickly pulled this out. It was tied by a cord at the neck and sealed with purple wax. He scooped this up and put it inside his doublet. Above him he heard a sound as if Crabtree, tired of waiting, had sat down. He looked around the cellar once more.

'Come on!' he urged Scathelocke. 'Enough is enough. We can always come back.'

Scathelocke needed no second bidding. Nicholas once more scrutinized the eerie death chamber then, satisfied, climbed the steps. Still only half-way out of the secret entrance, at first he failed to understand why Crabtree was lying near the hole, his eyes fluttering, his face white as snow, a trickle of blood seeping out of the corner of his mouth.

'Master!' he gasped.

Chirke, half-way out of the secret entrance, whirled round. Scathelocke, who had preceded him up the steps, was standing, arms crossed, staring at two grey cowled figures standing just within the chapel door.

'Come, come, Master Chirke! Quickly now! Quickly!'

The voice was low and throaty and had an edge of laughter. Nicholas peered through the gloom of the nave as the two figures walked forward. The first pushed back its hood. Nicholas closed his eyes in despair. He had last seen that pretty face in the tavern outside Newgate. He cursed his stupidity. The prioress of the night before was no nun but the murderous courtesan and professional assassin, Nightshade. She stood, elegant as any court lady, golden curls framing her ivory, heart-shaped face. Her eyes danced with amusement as if she had enjoyed the game and was now looking forward to a swift conclusion. Nicholas's hand fell to his dagger, but the grey cowled figure beside Nightshade raised a small crossbow and the bolt flew above Nicholas's head, smashing into the pillar behind him. Scathelocke stepped forward, but Nightshade held up her own crossbow whilst her companion slipped another bolt into the groove.

'Master Chirke, quickly now, out of there! Beside your companion!'

Nicholas looked despairingly at Crabtree and at the crossbow bolt buried deep in Crabtree's stomach.

'For sweet pity's sake!' he murmured.

'He's dying,' Nightshade said softly. 'So, say your farewells.' She gestured with her hand. 'Don't fret, you'll follow him soon.'

Nicholas walked over to where Crabtree now crouched like a baby, knees up, no merriment on his white, slack face, his eyes like those of a frightened child. Nicholas gently rolled him over. Crabtree coughed, blood bubbling between his lips.

'I am sorry, master,' he gasped. 'What an end for a cunning man. You won't tell them in London will you? They were in the door before I knew it. Tell, Scathelocke . . .'

Crabtree's eyes fluttered. For a few seconds his entire body went rigid then his eyes clouded over, a spurt of blood came out of his mouth and his head fell sideways. Nicholas felt for the life beat in his neck but it was gone. He looked over his shoulder.

'You murdering whore!' he spat.

'Stand up, Chirke. Go beside your dull-eyed friend.'

Nicholas watched the crossbow with its jagged bolt waiting to fly from its groove.

209

'I suppose your master sent you?'

'Yes he did. You are not too hard to follow – Norwich then Castle Rising. And now you have found the secret, haven't you?' Nightshade smiled. 'In a thousand years I would never have guessed what a clever old bitch·Isabella was.' She nodded to the cellar entrance. 'She must have found the old crypt, or at least that part of it, before the builders of this sombre pile gave up. And what a brilliant plot! To die of the plague or some pestilence. No one would dare to go near her corpse. The coffin was sealed, placed in a leaden casket and taken to London to be mourned by the king and all the great ones of the land. What did it contain, I wonder – a statue, stones?' Nightshade sniffed, wrinkling her nose at the dust which was beginning to rise from the cellar. 'Then a swift burial in London whilst Vallence hires a Venetian galley to bring him into one of the inlets on the coast here, then back into a now-deserted Castle Rising, to take his mistress from her hiding hole.' Nightshade cocked her head. Beside her, her silent companion hardly moved.

'Who told you all this?' Nicholas stammered.

Nightshade shrugged prettily but her eyes never left Chirke's.

'Once I came in here I knew what you had found. It stands to reason. Only a woman would think of a plan like that. And only some stupid man like Vallence could ruin it. He had to hasten from Greyfriars. It he had stayed in the city another day he might have escaped. I suppose the old queen had supplies to last her for weeks. She could have been free within seven days of her supposed death.'

'Why didn't she get out?' Scathelocke asked.

'The stone can only be raised from the outside. In any case, with no Vallence or galley, what was the use?'

210

'How would she have died?' Nightshade asked, genuinely curious.

'Eventually she would have starved,' Nicholas replied. 'Perhaps she would have weakened, slipped into a faint. But in fact she chose the Roman way.'

'You mean suicide?'

'Yes, why don't you see for yourself.'

Nightshade smiled bitterly. 'Oh, come, come, Master Chirke. I am not as stupid as you look. I know what you've found. I saw the smile of triumph on your ugly face as you left the cavern. Now, why can't you hand it over?'

'What are you talking about?'

Nightshade held her hand out. 'Come, come, toss it on the floor.' She pointed to a spot near her. 'Close enough for me to take but far enough to prevent any stupidity.'

Nicholas looked at Scathelocke who just stared, glassy-eyed, back. Nicholas put his hand into his doublet – and the chapel door abruptly crashed open.

'What's this? What's this, eh?' The old crone who had troubled them yesterday shuffled into the church.

Nightshade and her companion whirled round. The old lady fell back as a crossbow bolt took her full in the throat and sent her spinning like a rag doll against the half-open door. Scathelocke sped forwards, even as Nicholas launched himself against Nightshade. He felt the crossbow bolt whizz by his face, then he smashed into her and they both went sprawling to the floor. Nightshade felt warm and supple, squirming like a cat beneath him. Nicholas panicked, trying to grab her hands beneath the voluminous robes. He kicked her away, fearful that she had already drawn her dagger. She rolled, nimble as a dancer, dropping the crossbow, and rose to a half-crouch, an

Italian stiletto in her hand. Nicholas made to rise but his foot caught in his robe and he staggered, crashing back to the floor again. Nightshade was near him, swooping down like some avenging angel, both hands clasped round the dagger hilt. Then Nicholas heard the whirr of a crossbow bolt and the courtesan's beautiful face erupted into a bloody pulp as the bolt hit her between mouth and nose. He rolled away even as Nightshade crashed to the hard pavement. Scathelocke stood above the body of her companion who lay sprawled, cowl pulled back, her throat one bloody gash from ear to ear. Scathelocke threw the crossbow bolt on to the floor and crouched, clutching his stomach, as if he was going to be sick. For a while Nicholas could only stand and watch him as he tried to control the trembling in his own body. His stomach heaved and his legs turned to jelly, twitching as if the muscles flickered with a life of their own. He tried to talk but his throat was dry, his tongue seemed swollen. He wanted to move but couldn't. He would never escape from this accursed place. At last he sprang forward and almost ran to the chapel door. He slammed it shut and walked briskly back to Scathelocke.

'It's finished,' he murmured, gripping his manservant's shoulder.

Scathelocke stared speechlessly at the corpses which littered the chapel floor.

'I know,' Nicholas snapped. 'We must remove them. Come on, Scathelocke, the sooner it's done, the sooner we go.'

He looked around the chapel and glimpsed the wineskin poor Crabtree had placed beneath the pillar. He hastened towards it and picked it up. The wine splashed into his mouth staining face and jaw, dripping down his jerkin. He handed it to Scathelocke.

'For God's sake, man, drink! If others come we'll never leave here!'

Scathelocke obeyed, after which they took the corpses down into the cavern. First Crabtree. Then the old crone, who had died instantly – the crossbow bolt had gone through one side of her neck and out of the other, turning it to a jagged, pulpy mess. Finally the two assassins. Sweating and cursing they replaced the stone and, with their boots, tried to scuff away the small pools of blood on the floor. They left the chapel, collected their horses, including Crabtree's, and thundered out over the drawbridge. Once outside the castle, Nicholas reined in and gazed at his white-faced companion.

'God save us, Scathelocke, and bless poor Crabtree's soul!'

'Amen!' Scathelocke muttered. He scratched his face and pulled his cowl close against the cold, biting wind.

'Master, we should flee.'

'Where to?' Nicholas asked. 'To France to be questioned? Scathelocke, you may not have a family but I do – remember Catherine, John and the twins, and my brother Robert in Norwich.' He shook his head. 'We have to return to London, but not by road. We'll go to Yarmouth, leave the horses there and buy a passage on some vessel bound for the Thames.'

'They'll be waiting for us,' Scathelocke said quietly, tapping the reins in his hands.

'Oh, I know they will,' Nicholas touched his doublet. 'But I have the queen's secret. It's a source of danger, but it could also be our protection. Now come on, the sooner we get out of here the better.'

They rode all day, entering Yarmouth late in the afternoon. They secured a passage on a small cog taking supplies to East Watergate. The burly red-faced captain charged them a high price and all they received was a bed of old sacking on deck. Nevertheless, the food was surprisingly hot and tasty and the captain's prediction about the weather proved correct – the ship fairly sped along under a brisk, northerly wind. Both Nicholas and Scathelocke were still shocked after the murderous attack at Castle Rising. Nicholas felt guilty about Crabtree and found his death harder to take than he would have expected.

'God save me!' he murmured as they stood on the deck of the cog staring out at the mist-shrouded Essex coast. 'All my life, Scathelocke, I have begged for tasks, walked up and down St Paul's pleading for business. Now look at me. I am patronized and trusted by the great ones of the land.' He laughed sourly. 'Really I have been handed a poisoned chalice which is stuck fast to my hand. God knows what will happen in London!'

'I am leaving,' Scathelocke announced flatly. He smiled thinly at Nicholas's look of surprise. 'No, don't misunderstand me. I am not frightened. You have been a good master. Catherine and John have been brother and sister to me. I shall miss the twins.' Scathelocke leaned against a halyard and stared out through the sea mist. 'But I am dangerous. When everything is finished and ready for the grinding, the truth always comes out.'

'What is the truth?'

'I believe Pilate asked the same question and didn't get an answer. So, why should I try? I'll return to your house because I have left things there, but after that I will leave.'

Scathelocke refused to be drawn any further. Chirke went below deck where, begging the use of a tallow candle, he loosened the pouch he had seized in that macabre chamber and pulled out a thin roll of parchment. He scrutinized it carefully, not surprised at the cryptic signs, the secret cipher of some clerk, possibly the old queen herself. The letters were bold but cramped together. Nicholas realized that it might take months to decipher it fully. He studied each line carefully. Now and again he recognized certain words – 'Palmer', 'University', 'Oxford'. There was a strange sign in the narrow margin. He rolled the parchment up and put it back in his pouch, which he tied to a string slung round his neck. For a while he sat listening to the ship creak and groan. He watched a brown, furry, long-tailed rat scurry along one of the timbers, a piece of ship's biscuit in its mouth.

'We are like that,' he murmured to himself. 'Creatures of the dark, scurrying about for any juicy morsel that might bring us comfort.'

He leaned back against the tarred timbers and drifted into sleep. Scathelocke came down and made him comfortable. The next morning both were woken by the patter of feet on the decks above them and the shouts of the captain. Nicholas struggled awake and stretched to ease the cramp in his body. He heard the captain shout again and gave a sleepy Scathelocke another shake.

'They have sighted the Thames!'

They went on deck. The mist had lifted and a weak sun was beginning to struggle through, lighting up the muddy, sluggish waters of the estuary. Nicholas caught the eye of the captain and called him over. Scathelocke watched him argue vigorously with the seaman who, at first, made to refuse. Money was handed over, the captain agreed and Nicholas walked back.

'Well, master?'

'They'll take us upriver to Westminster and allow us to land at King's Steps. It will be safer. There may be port officials watching for us at East Watergate. I'd like to renew an old acquaintance without any interference.'

215

The captain was true to his word and, two hours later, Nicholas and Scathelocke put ashore at the quayside of Westminster. Already the place was coming to life – eel-sellers, coal boys, water-sellers and the usual swarm of sharp-eyed beggars milled about. In the streets outside the palace the wooden fronts of the small shops were already down, their owners, tradesmen muffled against the cold, shouting for business. Nicholas and Scathelocke ignored them all as they followed the cobbled trackways which led them through the guard gate into the great, gabled palace next to the majestic gardens, halls and buildings of the abbey. Nicholas knew the place well but, as always, the awesome abbey church, with its intricately carved stone which seemed to hang fairy-like in the misty air, made him catch his breath. He felt a pang of nostalgia, recalling the days he'd spent there touting for business, then he glimpsed a soldier dressed in the royal livery watching him sharply, so he walked on, leading Scathelocke through the crowds and into the vaulted hall of the palace. Here, in various corners and alcoves, sat the different royal courts already busy despite the early hour. Each court was cordoned off. The red-robed judges presided in high-backed chairs and before them, around long, oval tables, sat the soberly dressed clerks and black-robed lawyers.

Nicholas crossed the hall. He went down a passageway and out through a rear entrance which led into a grey-stone courtyard.

'Master,' pleaded Scathelocke, 'where are we going?'

'To the Memory of the Crown,' Nicholas enigmatically replied.

He went across and knocked on a door. An ageing, bald-headed monk opened it. He was dressed in a long, black robe,

216

tied round the waist by a yellowing cord. The monk's rheumy eyes glared at Nicholas.

'What do you want?'

'Don't you recognize an old friend, Elias?'

The monk stepped forward, eyes narrowing.

'God bless my soul! It's Nicholas Chirke!' The man's head came back like a bird's, lips pursed under a sharp, razor-like nose. 'What do you want?'

'A little of your time.'

The old monk smiled and waved them into his chamber. Scathelocke stared around in astonishment. Apart from a long table down the centre and the stools around it, the rest of the room was taken up by stacks of shelves stretching from floor to ceiling. On these lay rolls of parchment, some yellowing with age, others white and smooth as the winter snow. The air was fragrant with the smell of ink, wax and freshly cured parchment.

'What is this place?' he murmured.

'The Memory of the Crown,' Nicholas repeated, smiling at the old monk. 'Here, apart from secret matters, are all the cases from King's Bench and the royal Justices of Assize.'

Elias came back with a tray of cups.

'None of your milk and water stuff,' he said. 'This is good claret. I stole it from the abbey kitchens.'

Nicholas and Scathelocke each took a cup as the old archivist beckoned them to the stools round the table. Scathelocke unhitched his cloak.

'It's warm,' he said. 'Yet there's no fire or charcoal braziers.'

'Ah!' Elias held up a bony finger. 'We can't have a fire in here.' He pointed to the metal-capped candles which stood like a column of sentries along the table. 'Even those have metal hoods and can only be lighted when I am in the room.' He pointed to the far wall. 'In the next room is the palace bakery and, at the far end, the royal kitchens. They provide heat enough. Now, what is it, you want?'

'Is it possible,' Nicholas asked, 'to have a look at the Assize Rolls from the City of Oxford for the ninth year of King Edward II's reign?'

'Of course! Of course!'

Brother Elias moved amongst the shelves, fingers to his lips. For a while he walked up and down talking to himself. He stopped, exclaimed aloud and set a battered ladder against the far wall and carefully climbed up. For a while he moved rolls of parchment about, clicking his tongue, turning now and again to apologize to Nicholas.

'It's here, it's here,' he murmured. 'Every roll is tagged. Ah yes, here we are, Oxford, 9 Edward II, 1316.' Elias peered at the tag carefully. 'The Justices arrived in Oxford on Midsummer's Day. Anyway, see for yourself.'

He came back down the ladder and handed the leathery roll of parchment to Nicholas, who placed it on the table and unrolled it. Scathelocke groaned when he saw how long it was.

'It's at least sixteen membranes,' Nicholas said, pointing to the stitching along the roll. 'The clerk would write out the record, the decision of the court, the membranes would be sewn together and lodged here when the royal justices returned to Westminster.'

'What are you looking for?' Scathelocke asked.

Nicholas ran his finger along the left-hand column, which gave an index of the names of the plaintiffs involved in each case.

'Palmer,' he said, 'I am looking for Simon Palmer.'

As Brother Elias went back to his duties, Scathelocke looked on, fretting at how the flame of the hour candle was busily eating away the time. Nicholas went through all the cases that had been brought before the King's Justice at the University of Oxford in that far-off summer of 1316. He quickly read through cases of murder, rape, arson, robbery on the royal highway, sacrilege and perjury – a sad catalogue of human misery. After each case the clerk would enter the punishment, a fine or *susp per coll*, 'hanged by the neck'. Ignoring Scathelocke's grumbling and Brother Elias pattering about, Nicholas continued his searching until—

'Oh sweet Lord!' he whispered. 'Brother Elias?'

'Yes, Nicholas?'

'Please search the records of King's Bench. Look for a case involving one Simon Palmer, some time in 1316 or 1317. And I need the list of executions at Smithfield or elsewhere in the capital. You will find them in the gaol delivery list.'

Elias, only too willing to help, hurried off. Nicholas, ignoring Scathelocke's pleas for enlightenment, continued reading.

'What is it?' Scathelocke seized his wrist. 'Master, what have you found?'

Nicholas glanced up and nodded at Elias who, although searching the records, was also trying to eavesdrop on what was being said.

'What I have found, Scathelocke,' he whispered, 'is the story of Simon Palmer, Christchurch Meadows and a sow.'

Scathelocke gazed at him.

'Master, have you lost your wits?'

'No, Scathelocke, but I think I have found the truth.'

He rolled up the scroll and watched Elias sift amongst the records, creating small puffs of dust. At last Elias stopped. He scratched his head and came back with two scrolls of parchment in his hands. Each was roughly cut along the edge.

'I can't understand this,' he said. 'This is the record of the court of King's Bench for the years 1316 to 1318 but it has been cut in two. Someone's taken a membrane out. Now, who would do that, eh?'

The old archivist pursed his lips and drew himself up, eyes flashing.

'That's not only theft, it's treason. Who ever did it should answer for such destruction before the king's court!'

'I doubt if you'll find the malefactor – or malefactors,' Nicholas said. 'They are probably long dead.' He ignored Elias's puzzled look. 'And the list of hangings?'

Elias went to another part of his treasure house. This time he came back crowing with triumph.

'Yes, yes, I've found it. You say Palmer, Simon Palmer? A student of Oxford?'

Nicholas nodded.

'He was hanged, but it doesn't say why. At Smithfield in November 1316.' He looked down at the manuscript. 'But it doesn't say why,' he repeated. 'And I can't understand why my records have been ruined.' He looked up, then gazed round in surprise – the room was empty.

Nicholas, pulling Scathelocke by the sleeve, was already racing across the courtyard through the palace of Westminster and down King's Steps to the riverside. Scathelocke protested, but Nicholas refused to answer his stream of persistent questions until they had hired a barge and were being rowed up river to Queenshithe.

'Master, you're never rude,' Scathelocke complained, 'but you didn't even bother to say farewell.'

'Elias will understand,' Nicholas replied, pulling his cowl

firmly round his head against the clinging river mist. 'I now know what this is all about or, at least, I think I do.'

'So why the hurry?'

'I am worried about Catherine and John. I am sure Nightshade will soon be missed, and the lords of this game will take hostages if they can't find us.'

'Do you want to be arrested, master?'

Nicholas peered across at the far river bank. 'Yes, I do. If they hold me, they'll leave the others alone and, when they take me, I'll learn the full truth.'

Chapter 3

Nicholas was not disappointed. They left the barge at Queenshithe and made their way through the milling throng around the market stalls up to his sister's house. He scarcely had his hand on the latch when a knight banneret, wearing the royal livery, came out of the alleyway accompanied by a group of king's archers. The archers stood silently by as the knight marched up to Nicholas and placed his hand on his shoulder.

'Nicholas Chirke, I am Sir Godfrey Evesden. I arrest you in the name of the king!'

Two archers immediately seized Nicholas. They would have bound his hands, but the knight rapped out that this would not be necessary. He then clapped a hand on Scathelocke's shoulders.

'I also arrest you, sir, in the name of the king!'

Nicholas would have liked to have hammered on the door and made sure Catherine was well, but the youthful knight shook his head.

'I wouldn't do that, sir, if I were you. It's best if we let such matters be. I can have your wrists and ankles fettered.' He pointed to a master bowman standing behind the rest. 'But there again, if you tried to run, this man has orders to place a yard shaft between your shoulder blades.'

'Why are we arrested?' Scathelocke spoke up. 'What crime have we committed?'

'Crime?' The knight turned, his face grim. 'Crime? Why, sir, the greatest crime of all, treason. Like charity it covers a multitude of things. Now, sirs, let us walk down to the riverside.'

Nicholas looked at Scathelocke and shrugged; it would be foolish to resist. These captains were not city bailiffs or apprentices wearing the livery of some guard, but professional soldiers, master bowmen who would kill them if they tried to escape.

'Where are we going?' he asked.

'On a river journey, to the Tower.'

The knight clicked his fingers. Nicholas and Scathelocke, surrounded by their escort, went back down the alleyways to the quayside. A royal barge took them upstream to the Tower. They shot under London Bridge, where the river frothed and boiled. Nicholas averted his eyes – he had no wish to see the decaying heads of traitors spiked above the gateway. Instead he tried to control the heaving of his stomach and the panic which made his legs tremble and his lips and throat dry.

A thick bank of mist obscured his view. Chirke had always regarded the Tower as a bleak, lonely place but, when they disembarked, with the fog swirling round, he found it even more sombre. The soaring great walls, crennellations, forbidding gatehouse and the raucous cawing of the yellow-beaked ravens who feasted on the severed limbs and heads of traitors spiked above the walls or on the gallows along the riverside. At the Lion Gate, an officer wearing the royal livery, questioned their escort. Only then was the portcullis raised and they were allowed through the sombre gateway which controlled the entrances to the concentric ring of towers. In the swirling mist Chirke could distinguish little. He heard the cries of sentries high on the walls above him and the rattle and clatter from the stable yards. The knight led them across the great green expanse before the White Tower but, instead of going there, they turned left and entered the royal apartments. The knight took them up into a shadowy, high-vaulted room. Clean rushes had been strewn on the floor. Blood-red drapes hung against the walls, but the light was poor for the windows were shuttered. The figure at the great desk sat with his back to the fire. Candles placed in black-iron candelabra on either side of the desk provided light but kept the recesses behind the desk hidden in the shadows. The man seated there raised his head as they entered and Nicholas's heart skipped a beat as he recognized the saturnine features of Sir Amyas Petrie.

'Come in, Nicholas.' Sir Amyas waved him to the chair placed before the desk. 'Welcome home.'

He nodded a dismissal at the knight, who pushed Nicholas forward then left, closing the door silently behind him. Sir Amyas made no attempt to acknowledge Scathelocke's presence except for a quick look, a flicker of the eyes. To Nicholas, however, he was most solicitous.

'Are you comfortable?'

Nicholas leaned back in his chair and nodded.

'Some wine?'

'Please, yes?'

Sir Amyas filled a goblet to its brim and pushed it across the table. Nicholas glanced over his shoulder. Scathelocke stood a little way behind him, arms crossed, staring into the fire. Sir Amyas sat down. Nicholas tried to see what was in the dark recesses behind the desk. He was certain there was someone else there and thought he caught a glimpse of blond hair and a

225

silken gown. Sir Amyas sat opposite him, studying him intently. He watched Nicholas's eyes straining into the darkness.

'No, we are not alone,' he said. 'But that doesn't concern you, does it? You had a task to perform, did you not?'

Nicholas smiled to himself. Sir Amyas raised his eyebrows.

'You found the task amusing?'

Nicholas looked at this powerful man, with his neat black hair and hooded eyes.

'Well, kinsman?' Sir Amyas rested his elbows on the desk, playing with the amethyst ring on his left hand. 'Your task may have been amusing but have you completed it?'

'Better than you think, kinsman,' he replied.

The smile on Sir Amyas's face died. 'Well,' he snapped. 'First Berisford. What happened to him?'

'He was killed by a professional assassin called Wormwood, who tried to beat information out of him. When he died, Wormwood made a clumsy attempt to make it look like suicide. He wrapped Berisford's corpse in a canvas sheet and took the corpse out to Primrose Hill. Late in the afternoon, on the day it was discovered, he unwrapped the corpse, leaving it in a ditch as if it had just been placed there.'

'And why did Wormwood do all this?'

'Because he was hired by the Guardian of the Gates.'

'And what did the Guardian want?'

Nicholas smiled. 'Kinsman, you should know that. He thought that Berisford knew the great secret that Vallence, the dead queen's squire, had brought with him to London.'

'And did he?'

Nicholas gazed over Sir Amyas's shoulder into the darkness behind him. He could hear the rapid breathing of the man hiding there.

'No, Berisford knew nothing. All he was told was that the secret was with St Denis. Unfortunately for him, the Guardian of the Gates knew he was a sodomite and he was blackmailed into visiting Wormwood's house. The rumours about him being seen round the city at different times were, like everything else, just a ploy to spread confusion and doubt.'

'Sir Amyas moved in his chair, steepling his fingers.

'And Fromlich?'

'Fromlich was a dupe. He had no more to do with Berisford's murder than the great Cham of Tartary. When he had served his purpose, he was killed by a courtesan, a professional assassin known as Nightshade, who also, I suspect, despatched Wormwood to his Maker.'

Nicholas didn't know whether it was the warm room or the full-bodied claret, but he felt relaxed and confident – or perhaps he was just tired of this devious game.

'I see.' Sir Amyas turned in his chair as if listening to the sounds of the sentries outside. Somewhere deep in the Tower a bell began to chime.

'And all this was the work of the Guardian of the Gates?'

'Yes. He had heard about the great secret, so he used Berisford, Wormwood, Fromlich and Nightshade for his own devious ends. But that is not why I am here, surely?' Nicholas continued. 'The knight said I was under arrest for treason.'

Sir Amyas gave a lop-sided grin. 'You were seen talking to French agents in a tavern.'

'Aye and they were murdered, as were their colleagues, but not by me!' Nicholas grasped his cup and drank again. 'Moreover, if I was a traitor, why should the French attack me outside Castle Rising? I am their foe, not their collaborator. There's no proof or evidence of any treachery on my part.'

227

Sir Amyas leaned forward and filled Nicholas's cup.

'Treason's a strange flower,' he murmured. 'It takes many forms.'

'As does murder,' Nicholas snapped. 'But why play games, Sir Amyas? Why not ask me about the secret?'

Sir Amyas looked directly at him. 'And do you have it?'

'Yes, I do.'

'Then hand it over.'

'I will to the Guardian of the Gates.'

Sir Amyas's face grew dark. He looked nervously over his shoulder. 'What do you mean?'

Nicholas dug into his doublet and threw the pouch on to the table.

'I said I would hand it to the Guardian of the Gates and I do. Sir Amyas Petrie, Sheriff of London, let's not play games – you are the Guardian of the Gates.'

Sir Amyas stared at him, mouth half-open.

'What stupidity!' he spluttered.

'Oh yes, you are the Guardian,' Nicholas insisted. 'And probably with the blessing of those you serve. What a marvellous way to control London's underworld! There must be thieves, housebreakers, felons and footpads so, if you can't wipe them out, why not control them. And you do so in your own devious way. In this matter you were both guardian and sheriff.' Chirke used his fingers to emphasize the points. 'You were present at Vallence's death in St Bartholomew's and heard his whispered comments. You arrested Fromlich on evidence which was a farrago of nonsense. You knew about Berisford's weakness. Above all, you knew about Patroclus. Mawsby sent you that name, didn't he? At first I thought he wouldn't, but he was the ever-faithful clerk, passing on information to his superiors.

228

However, Mawsby might chatter, so you sent Nightshade with her garrotte string and Mawsby is no more. You managed Nightshade, you knew where to send her, where Wormwood would be waiting. Above all, you protected her, allowing her to move round the city free of interference by any law officer.'

Nicholas shrugged. 'It stands to reason. You won't be the first Sheriff of London to control the outlaws and wolfsheads of St Paul's. You won't be the last. In doing so, you control crime. You can recover lost or stolen property and have an army of informers at your fingertips. If any felon gets above himself then, heigh ho, the law officers take him and he's into Newgate then hanging at Tyburn before he can even reflect on what has happened.'

Sir Amyas licked his lips. Nicholas paused, encouraged by the look of nervousness in the sheriff's eyes.

'It's true what I say,' Nicholas insisted. 'In Lincolnshire the Cotterell and the Ashby-Folville gang were led by the very sheriff who was supposed to be pursuing them. London's no different.' He spread his hands. 'And in the pursuit of this great secret you controlled the game. Berisford was your catspaw. So was I. And in the darkness you used your assassins to root out the truth.'

'So, what is the truth?' Sir Amyas asked.

'I shall tell you from the beginning,' Nicholas said soberly, 'so that you understand the full extent of my knowledge and of your evil.' He paused to collect his thoughts. 'You, Sir Amyas, are both Sheriff of London and Guardian of the Gates. I suspect other sheriffs before you have acted in the same duplicitous way.' He held up a hand to still Sir Amyas's interruption. 'After Vallence's death you tried, as sheriff as well as Guardian of the Gates, to learn his secret. You had little success, but you did

229

discover a scandal about Berisford – you were already vastly intrigued by Vallence's recognition of him and the squire's dying whispers. You therefore appointed him to investigate the matter. Berisford failed so, as Guardian of the Gates, you try other methods. Wormwood began to blackmail Berisford over his homosexuality and tortured and killed the poor bastard. Fromlich was arrested and charged with Berisford's murder and Blueskin the grave-robber disappeared. This distracted anyone from probing too closely into what Berisford had been doing, as either of these could be blamed for his murder. You then hired me. Fromlich, of course, had by then served his purpose so he was killed, as was his kinswoman.'

Nicholas paused.

'I don't know why she was murdered. A warning to me? Or had Nightshade already visited her? Did she know something? Anyway, she was sent out into the darkness. You continued your games. You allowed me to blunder around the city. Your agents, particularly Nightshade, kept an eye on events. Crabtree' – Nicholas fought to keep his voice level – 'was warned off me, to emphasize the great gap between the law and the criminal fraternity in this city. Nicholas smiled over his shoulder at Scathelocke. 'But Crabtree was no coward. He hated to be threatened, as you well knew, so he joined me and became a useful guide through the murky, twisting paths of London's underworld.' Nicholas shrugged. 'In the end, however, I was never meant to present a formal reply. Once we had stumbled on the truth, we would have gone the same way as Fromlich. Now and again you intervened. The French attempted to bribe me so they were despatched. Mawsby discovered a juicy little morsel of information and he was killed in case he became suspicious.' Nicholas again looked over his shoulder at

Scathelocke. 'We were your hunting dogs,' he mused. 'Perhaps we might startle something out into the open – something we wouldn't realize but you would appreciate. I am right, am I not, kinsman?'

Sir Amyas shrugged. 'I can make no comment on what you say,' he remarked drily.

Scathelocke coughed, as if trying to conceal laughter. Sir Amyas threw him a contemptuous glance, pointing a finger in warning.

'You, sir, will remain silent, for I know who you really are!' He turned back to Nicholas. 'Well, kinsman, the secret?'

'The secret,' Nicholas replied, 'is that Isabella of France, mother of the present king, knew of a festering scandal – a scandal that is recorded in the manuscript in that pouch. For years she tried to flee to France to tell her secret, but her son kept Castle Rising, and the area around it, under close guard.'

'Why didn't she just send a letter?' Sir Amyas interrupted.

'No. No.' Nicholas scratched his face. He suddenly realized how tired he was and vowed to take no more wine. 'Oh no, this was a secret which had to be declared in person, which needed to be guaranteed by solemn oath and public declaration. Now the years passed. Queen Isabella grew more desperate, until she conceived a plot on which she gambled everything, including her life. She pretended to fall sick of the pestilence then die, attended only by her faithful squire Vallence. What happened is that, in the death chamber, Vallence filled the coffin with a statue or stone and sealed it in its leaden container. Isabella then hid herself. She knew the secret tunnels and passageways of Castle Rising. It is a veritable rabbit warren and she had spent twenty-eight years searching out its every nook and cranny. She had discovered a secret cavern, an unfinished crypt beneath

231

the chapel floor. With Vallence's assistance, she hid there. Vallence then escorted the coffin into London to be buried with great pomp and ceremony at Greyfriars near Newgate. Meanwhile Vallence, probably with the connivance of French agents in England, hired a Venetian galley which could thread its way into the narrow coasts, inlets and bays of the Norfolk coast. He would return to Castle Rising, now deserted, as the old queen was supposedly dead, and take his mistress abroad.'

Nicholas stopped to stare at Sir Amyas. The sheriff looked pallid, his tongue constantly wetted his lips and he kept looking over his shoulder at the figure lurking in the shadows behind him.

'Isabella hid there?'

'Yes, but she made two mistakes: first, she under-estimated her son, who knew about Vallence's close relationship with her; secondly, Vallence moved too quickly and so alerted the king, who thought that his mother might have entrusted the scandalous secret to her trusted retainer.' Nicholas shrugged. 'The rest you know.'

'And so Isabella died of starvation?'

'I doubt it. She realized her mistake: Vallence wasn't returning. She might have been able to escape, but for what? So, she took poison.'

'And the proof for all this?'

'Send your most trusted men to Castle Rising. Let them rip up the floor of the chapel. They'll find the queen's corpse' – Nicholas's voice became hard – 'next to that of my good friend Crabtree. They'll also find the bodies of your assassins and that of an old woman whose aimless blundering saved my life.' Nicholas leaned across the desk. 'So, kinsman, that is my story. Now you have the secret, what will you do with it?'

232

Sir Amyas, his hands slightly trembling, undid the neck of the pouch. 'You have looked at this?'

Nicholas nodded. 'I didn't understand it,' he lied. 'But I have had it copied. The copy rests in a secret place, with my sworn affidavit.'

Sir Amyas laid the manuscript from the pouch on the desk. 'Wait outside.' he ordered. 'You and your' – he flicked a hand at Scathelocke – 'creature.'

Nicholas obeyed, Scathelocke following silently behind him. They stood in the gallery, conscious of the knight and his archers, who blocked the stairwells at either end. Scathelocke refused to meet Nicholas's eye. He realized that Petrie was now consulting with his master. But who was that – the king, golden-haired Edward, or his warlike son, the Black Prince? Nicholas knew that his life was now being decided, together with the lives of Scathelocke, Catherine and John and Beatrice and Robert.

'I don't think I'll see you again, master,' Scathelocke said unhappily.

Nicholas looked at him. 'Tell me now,' he urged, 'who you really are.'

Scathelocke smiled and shook his head. 'Why should I? We will both be told our fates in the next few minutes.'

The door of the chamber was flung open and Sir Amyas ordered them in. Nicholas peered into the shadows behind the desk – he was sure that whoever had been lurking there had now left by some secret door.

'Sit down, sit down!'

Sir Amyas was all smiles again, though he still ignored Scathelocke, who had to remain standing.

'Well, well, kinsman.' Sir Amyas settled in his chair, beaming

233

at Nicholas. 'You are to be given further preferment. I—'

Nicholas roughly interrupted him. 'But what about Berisford, cold and rotting in his grave, foully murdered. What about miserable Fromlich, his life and that of his kinswoman snuffed out like candlewicks? And the others? Mawsby, garrotted to death? That poor old woman in Castle Rising. And Crabtree? Who will reward them, eh? Or the Frenchmen, shot down, killed like vermin in an alleyway. No, kinsman,' Nicholas spat out the words, 'I refuse your offer. I prefer to walk the aisles of St Paul's, lean and hungry as a wolf. I have my sworn affidavit. I'll put my trust in God and whatever justice is left in this miserable city!'

Sir Amyas leaned forward across the desk. 'Then listen to this, Chirke,' he declared hoarsely. 'If you refuse you will not leave the Tower alive. And your companion here, Scathelocke, will be arrested.'

'For what?' Nicholas exclaimed.

Sir Amyas leaned back in his chair. 'For treason. But also because he is a Jew – and, as you know' – Sir Amyas smiled at the consternation on Nicholas's face – 'the Jews were expelled from England in 1290. They are not allowed to return except by special licence. Scathelocke, or Christopher Ratolier as he is more accurately called, has no such licence.'

Nicholas spun round and glared at Scathelocke.

'Is this true?' he asked.

Scathelocke nodded. 'Why, master? Don't you like Jews?'

Nicholas blinked and shook his head. 'Why couldn't you have told me?' he asked. 'It would have made no difference. I could have protected you.'

Scathelocke stared back and smiled. 'No one could protect me, master. I knew what I was doing. There are Jews here in

234

the city – quite legally, they have a licence to be here. I do not, but I am their agent and messenger. I travel unnoticed, or so I thought, between them and our people abroad.' He shrugged. 'It was only a matter of time before I was caught. Well, someone else will take my place.'

'I should have guessed,' Nicholas murmured. 'You never attended Mass; you said your own prayers in that little garret. And, although a man of great appetite you never touched forbidden foods. And, of course, Crabtree knew, didn't he?'

'Yes,' Scathelocke replied. 'But he held his peace, and I loved him for that. Men like our sheriff also knew, but they left me alone to be used as a weapon against you. I should have fled immediately,' Scathelocke added bitterly, 'but you needed help and you'd only have thought I'd deserted you!'

'Do you have family?' Nicholas asked.

'Killed in Bremen, by Christians.' Scathelocke pointed at Petrie. 'Ignore him, master. I have met his type a thousand times in a thousand cities – men of darkness, steeped in their own foulness.'

Sir Amyas would have leapt to his feet, but Nicholas banged the desk.

'No threats, Sir Amyas!'

Sir Amyas sank back in his chair, breathing heavily.

'I haven't finished,' he said viciously. 'The king's commissioners are mustering troops for the new war against the French. Your brother-in-law John Gawdy is able to bear arms. So is your brother Robert, who owns land outside Norwich. I am sure he could also be persuaded to render the king a loan on his lands.'

'You're a bastard!' Nicholas told him. 'You are a murderer, an assassin, a thief, a man steeped in foulness!'

'Am I?' Sir Amyas's voice rose to a shout. 'Am I, Chirke? You don't know what you dabble in. This kingdom needs strong rule and a good prince. Or, like, other lands, it will be riven by civil war. Isabella was a Jezebel. She and her mysterious secrets were a threat to the Crown and to the king's rightful claims to the throne of France.'

'What does it matter?' Nicholas said wearily.

'What does it matter!' Sir Amyas was almost screaming. 'Life will go on as before. But you will not go on. Scathelocke will burn at Smithfield and John will die in some French ditch – not because of me, but because of your swollen pride. Accept!'

'Accept, master,' Scathelocke murmured. 'Master Chirke, by all that is holy, accept his offer!'

Nicholas closed his eyes. Images flitted across his mind: Catherine pale and stricken; the twins screaming for their father; gentle John gasping his life-blood out in some rain-sodden ditch in Normandy; Scathelocke chained to a beam in the middle of Smithfield fires; Robert and Beatrice harassed and harried by the king's commissioners and tax-collectors. He opened his eyes.

'I accept, I swear, I accept. On condition. First, that Scathelocke is given safe warrants to leave England as well as silver for his pains. Agreed?'

'Agreed,' Sir Amyas snapped. 'But he must leave within twenty-four hours. If he returns, he dies. What else?'

A letter from the king assuring John Gawdy of the king's own favour, preferment in his trade, an exemption for life from any taxes, obligations to pay scutage, or perform military service for himself and his hiers.'

Sir Amyas shrugged. 'Agreed.'

'That is to be done within a week. The same letter is to be issued to my brother.'

'Agreed.'

Nicholas leaned back in the chair. 'I want Masses sung for the repose of the souls of Berisford, Mawsby and Crabtree. God knows what you do with your own creatures but Crabtree is to be given honourable burial in St Mary atte Bowe's graveyard.' He pushed his chair back, rose and walked to the door.

'Chirke!'

Nicholas turned.

'You must accept your own preferment,' Sir Amyas said softly. 'The king demands it!'

'Aye and I know why. As the king's lawyer, I have to take an oath on the Blessed Sacrament, the most solemn oath a man can take, never to reveal the king's secrets.'

Sir Amyas nodded. 'Then you may go, and Master Scathelocke with you. Once he leaves the Tower he will lodge at the Three Cranes tavern in the Vintry.' He held up a hand. 'Don't worry, he'll be safe. Tomorrow morning, at dawn, a sheriff's man will bring him letters of safe conduct and money and put him on board a cog bound for Dordrecht in Hainault. If Scathelocke leaves the tavern before that messenger comes, if he is found wandering the streets of London, if he refuses to leave, he will be killed as a wolfshead. Now, go!'

Scathelocke and Nicholas left the chamber. The knight escorted them back towards the riverside. Outside the river gate, when they were alone, Scathelocke turned.

'You had no choice, Nicholas. No man would have done any differently.'

Nicholas blinked to hide his tears and stared up at the overcast skies.

'Do you know,' he whispered, 'I have just received what I

always needed and now I don't want it.' Turning his back on Scathelocke, he walked down to the riverside. He stared into a bank of fog moving in from the river. 'You should have told me,' he said over his shoulder. 'It would have made no difference. Christopher Ratolier or Henry Scathelocke, whatever you call yourself, you were never my servant, always my friend.'

He heard the gravel behind him crunch. When he looked round Scathelocke had gone.

'Scathelocke!' he called. 'Scathelocke!'

Only the cawing of the crows answered him. The fog billowed about him.

'For the love of God!' he shouted.

'Goodbye, Nicholas,' a voice answered, ghost-like from the swirling fog. 'Goodbye, and may your God ever watch you. I shall never forget you. Do not look for me in the Three Cranes. You are safe, but I do not trust Sir Amyas Petrie. I'll be gone before nightfall!'

Nicholas stared around, but couldn't decide from which direction the voice was coming. He sighed and walked back towards a wherry waiting at the quayside steps. Cursing the icy tears that wetted his cheeks, he stared back at the Tower, its turrets soaring above the mist.

'God damn you all!' he muttered. 'God damn you and all your secrets!'

The Epilogue

The man of law stopped speaking. He brushed his eyes gently and dug his face into a blackjack of ale.

'Was it you?' the wife of Bath asked. 'Are you Nicholas Chirke?'

The man of law kept his face hidden in the tankard, though he watched his friend the manciple out of the corner of his eye.

'Well,' Harry the taverner spoke up. 'Are you Master Chirke?'

The man of law lowered the tankard and smiled thinly at the prioress. She was staring at him, tears welling in her pretty eyes. He shook his head imperceptibly and glanced at the summoner, who clumsily winked back.

'Oh come, come,' the friar trumpeted. 'Surely you can tell us?'

'I have told my tale,' the man of law replied.

'Yes, but what about the secret?' the friar asked.

'If I told you,' the man of law retorted, 'it wouldn't be a secret, would it?'

A chorus of dissent greeted his words.

'You can't do that!' Harry the taverner exclaimed.

'Yes, sir, I can and, yes sir, I will!'

The man of law pushed back his chair and walked across the taproom. The prioress made to rise but the lawyer shook his head at her and walked out into the garden. The rain had stopped. The air was heavy with the scent from the herb banks and wild flowers. He walked away from the tavern until he reached a bench concealed by a hedge from fellow pilgrims. He slumped down, put his face in his hands and began to sob.

'Scathelocke, Scathelocke,' he muttered. 'How I wish you were here. I went to the edge but not over.'

He looked up, startled at the sound of a footstep. At first, because he was looking into the sun, he couldn't make out who it was. Then he recognized the brown-garbed figure of the priest.

'I'll go if you want,' the priest murmured. 'But you looked so stricken, so much in pain, I had to come.'

The man of law smiled. 'Is it so obvious, Father?'

'Yes, it is.' The priest stretched out his legs and re-arranged his dusty cassock. 'You liked Scathelocke and, from what you told us, so did I. I thought he might be a Jew.'

'How?'

'His dislike of Isabella's father, Philip of France, a savage persecutor of his people.'

'Will you hear my confession?'

'If you wish.'

The man of law made the sign of the cross.

'Then bless me, Father, for I have sinned. It is many, many, many years since I was shriven. My name is Nicholas Chirke. I am a lawyer, a man of great counsel, well regarded at Westminster and the Inns of Court – a man who has everything but who may have lost his soul. I have whored. I have drunk. I have borne false witness against my neighbour. I have favoured the proud and despised the weak. But my greatest sin is cowardice. I hold a secret.'

The priest held up his hand. 'Do you wish to tell me this here?'

'It's why I came on pilgrimage to Canterbury,' the man of law replied hoarsely. 'To kneel at the tomb of the Blessed Martyr Thomas. I want to press my face against his marble tomb and tell him all my secrets and so find a cure for my soul.'

The priest nodded. 'Then tell me.'

Chirke beckoned with his head back towards the tavern.

'I told a lie in there. I knew the secret. I didn't keep a copy, that was a mere ploy to protect myself. You see, when I studied that manuscript taken from the dead queen mother, I noticed a reference to the records of King's Bench. Now, when I went there, as I told you in my tale, the record had been removed, but the manuscript I found in the crypt filled in the gaps.'

'What was it?' the priest asked.

'You must tell this to no one, Father.'

The poor priest smiled. 'I cannot break the seal of the confessional.'

Chirke stood up and looked round the garden. Only when he was sure it was deserted did he sit down and begin to whisper in the priest's ear.

'Father, listen to this: I have done my own studies in the matter. King Edward III was a puissant, noble king, yes?'

The priest nodded.

'He waged war against the Scots and captured their king and, because his mother was French, laid claim to the throne of France. His armies ravaged that country from Calais to the Pyrenees?'

'God forgive him!' the priest interrupted.

241

'Aye, but the war still goes on. Now his father,' Chirke continued hoarsely, 'was Edward II, married to Isabella, Princess of France. Their marriage was not a happy one. Edward was well known for his love of favourites and for his detestation of his royal duties. Instead, his pleasures were rustic: he liked thatching, ploughing and digging ditches, no wonder the nobles called him a peasant.'

The lawyer paused and watched a pale-coloured butterfly drift like a piece of gauze above the herb garden.

'Now, in 1316, a young student at the University of Oxford, one Simon Palmer, came forward and claimed he was the legitimate son of Edward I and that Edward of Carnarvon, the husband of Isabella, was an imposter. His allegations were investigated by a tribunal which sat in the refectory of New Hall College, the King's Justices of Oyer and Terminer being present. Palmer claimed that he was the king's first born son and that, years earlier, at King Edward I's palace at Woodstock, he had been playing in the courtyard when he had been attacked by a sow which had bitten off his left ear. The old nurse in charge of the child had been so frightened of the old king's furious temper that she had switched him for a peasant child.' The lawyer licked his lips. 'Palmer produced proof: even the commissioners said he bore a passing resemblance to the old king. He showed the tribunal the scar where his left ear had been torn off by the sow. His story, of course, explained why the king, in effect a peasant, was so interested in rustic pursuits.' The lawyer stared up at the clouds now breaking into white wisps. 'According to the memorandum I found at Castle Rising, Palmer produced certain documents, the hearing was suddenly brought to an end and the case referred to King's Bench.'

'But, when you went there, those records had disappeared?'

242

'Precisely,' the lawyer replied.

'What are you claiming?' the priest asked.

'I believe Palmer was correct. He was later hanged. Most of the documentation has disappeared, but he may have been the rightful King of England. That's why Mortimer ordered his investigation at the university and why he and Isabella paid a secret visit to the records of the King's Bench at Westminster.' The lawyer emphasized the points on his fingers. 'It also explains why the word "Palmer" was mentioned the night Mortimer was arrested and why Mortimer was hustled south to London and not allowed to speak throughout his trial.'

The lawyer paused as a door opened and closed. He stood up, but it was only the knight going out to check the horses in the stables. The man of law looked down at the priest's white face.

'That's why the old queen wanted to escape to France,' he continued. 'It was her revenge, not only against the Plantaganets of England but against her dead husband and the son who had killed her paramour and thrust her into a cold, grey castle.' The man of law laughed sourly. 'And if she had escaped, what a trumpeting there would have been! The great Edward III, the son of a peasant, busily claiming the thrones of France and Scotland, plunging all of Europe into a bloody war when he has no right even to wear his own crown.'

The priest put his face in his hands. 'God save us!' he whispered. 'And they let you live, even though you know that?'

'Oh, yes. They are frightened that I have hidden away some documents. Perhaps a copy of the one I took from the old queen's corpse. I wager not even Sir Amyas Petrie knew the full secret, but the old king did and so did his son, the Black Prince. They looked after me. I have a secure post, fat fees, property here

243

and property there.' He sat down beside the priest. 'But what does it profit a man, Father, if he gains the whole world and suffers the loss of his immortal soul? Crabtree died because of me and Scathelocke was banished.'

'And Catherine and John?'

'John died of the sweating sickness. Catherine took the veil at Sempringham.'

'And the twins?'

'One's a powerful merchant. The other is training to be a lawyer at the Inns of Court.'

Nicholas Chirke blinked to hide his tears.

'Brother Robert died before I could make my peace with him. Beatrice became a prioress so that she could have the power and wealth to which she had always been accustomed. But sometimes' – his voice fell to a whisper – 'when I'm in a tavern, I half-close my eyes and Scathelocke's beside me, laughing and joking with Crabtree.' He chewed his lip. 'I should have told the truth,' he declared softly. 'Oh, they still watch me even on this pilgrimage. I make it every year in atonement for Crabtree's death. I kneel by the tomb of the Blessed Martyr Thomas and pray for him, Scathelocke, Brother Robert, Catherine and John.'

'Who watches you?' the priest asked.

'Oh, my friend the manciple. He has a house next to mine near the Temple. Where I go he always seems to go. At first I thought he liked me, then I began to detect the pattern. 'He's a spy.'

'What happened afterwards?' the priest asked. 'I mean at Castle Rising?'

'I went back there. The assassin Nightshade, her accomplice, and the old lady were buried in the castle cemetery. A simple wooden cross placed above the three mounds but I brought Crabtree's body back to London.'

'And the old queen?'

'The crypt was filled in. I went back three years ago, just out of curiosity. I think they left the old queen's corpse there. On a stone someone has carved the words "Isabella Regina". And maybe now the secret is out. The old king did nothing to beautify his mother's tomb in Greyfriars. And why should he have? It houses nothing.' He rose. 'So, Father, you have heard my confession.'

The priest patted the seat beside him. 'Sit down.'

The man of law obeyed and the priest whispered the words of absolution.

'And my penance, Father?'

The priest's weary face broke into a smile. 'Forget the past,' he said. 'Be happy. Do good with the wealth you have. Pray for those who have gone before you.'

'Is that all, Father?'

'No, when you return to London, go back to St Paul's and walk the aisles, but look for the widow, the poor man, the orphan and the needy. Plead their case and, when you walk, the spirits of Scathelocke and Crabtree will walk with you, as will Christ and all his angels.'

The man of law smiled and the priest nudged him.

'Now, let's continue our journey. The wife of Bath, has, I hear, an excellent tale.'

Author's note

Many of the strands in the story reflect historical truth. Isabella's invasion did occur. Edward II was imprisoned at Berkeley Castle and Isabella and Mortimer were eventually overthrown by a sudden coup carried out at night in Nottingham. Mortimer was sent south, where he was gagged during his trial; he was one of the first men to be hanged at Tyburn. Isabella was banished to Castle Rising and, in the late 1340s, her son, Edward III, resolutely refused to allow his mother to travel to France. Isabella was hastily buried at Greyfriars (the ruins of which now lie opposite St Paul's underground station). Strangely enough, before the church's destruction, her tomb was ignored, whilst Mortimer's mangled remains were later exhumed and moved to Wales. The ruins at Castle Rising still stand starkly, supposedly haunted by the ghost of Isabella. In the castle lies a simple stone memorial to 'Isabella Regina'.